On the Turtle's Back

Ceres
RUTGERS
STUDIES
IN HISTORY

Ceres: Rutgers Studies in History

Lucia McMahon and Christopher T. Fisher, *Series Editors*

New Jersey holds a unique place in the American story. One of the thirteen colonies in British North America and the original states of the United States, New Jersey plays a central, yet underappreciated, place in America's economic, political, and social development. New Jersey's axial position as the nation's financial, intellectual, and political corridor has become something of a signature, evident in quips about the Turnpike and punchlines that end with its many exits. Yet, New Jersey is more than a crossroad or an interstitial "elsewhere." Far from being ancillary to the nation, New Jersey is an axis around which America's story has turned, and within its borders gather a rich collection of ideas, innovations, people, and politics. The region's historical development makes it a microcosm of the challenges and possibilities of the nation, and it also reflects the complexities of the modern, cosmopolitan world. Yet, far too little of the literature recognizes New Jersey's significance to the national story, and despite promising scholarship done at the local level, New Jersey history often remains hidden in plain sight.

Ceres books represent new, rigorously peer-reviewed scholarship on New Jersey and the surrounding region. Named for the Roman goddess of prosperity portrayed on the New Jersey State Seal, Ceres provides a platform for cultivating and disseminating the next generation of scholarship. It features the work of both established historians and a new generation of scholars across disciplines. Ceres aims to be field-shaping, providing a home for the newest and best empirical, archival, and theoretical work on the region's past. We are also dedicated to fostering diverse and inclusive scholarship and hope to feature works addressing issues of social justice and activism.

James M. Carter, *Rockin' in the Ivory Tower: Rock Music on Campus in the Sixties*
Jordan P. Howell, *Garbage in the Garden State*
Maxine N. Lurie, *Taking Sides in Revolutionary New Jersey: Caught in the Crossfire*
Jean R. Soderlund, *Separate Paths: Lenapes and Colonists in West New Jersey*
Camilla Townsend and Nicky Kay Michael, eds., *On the Turtle's Back: Stories the Lenape Told Their Grandchildren*

On the Turtle's Back

Stories the Lenape Told Their Grandchildren

CAMILLA TOWNSEND
NICKY KAY MICHAEL

RUTGERS UNIVERSITY PRESS
NEW BRUNSWICK, CAMDEN, AND NEWARK, NEW JERSEY
LONDON AND OXFORD

Rutgers University Press is a department of Rutgers, The State University of New Jersey, one of the leading public research universities in the nation. By publishing worldwide, it furthers the University's mission of dedication to excellence in teaching, scholarship, research, and clinical care.

Library of Congress Cataloging-in-Publication Data

Names: Townsend, Camilla, 1965– editor. | Michael, Nicky Kay, editor.
Title: On the turtle's back : stories the Lenape told their grandchildren / edited by Camilla Townsend and Nicky Kay Michael.
Other titles: Stories the Lenape told their grandchildren
Description: New Brunswick, New Jersey : Rutgers University Press, 2023. | Series: Ceres: Rutgers studies in history | Includes bibliographical references and index. | Text in English, with some text in the Delaware language.
Identifiers: LCCN 2023004145 | ISBN 9781978819146 (paperback) | ISBN 9781978819153 (hardcover) | ISBN 9781978819160 (epub) | ISBN 9781978819184 (pdf)
Subjects: LCSH: Delaware Indians—Folklore. | Indians of North America—Oklahoma—Folklore. | Delaware language—Texts. | Delaware Indians—Biography. | Delaware Indians—Oklahoma—Social life and customs. | Indians of North America—Oklahoma—Social life and customs.
Classification: LCC E99.D2 O55 2023 | DDC 398.089/97345—dc23/eng/20230223
LC record available at https://lccn.loc.gov/2023004145

A British Cataloging-in-Publication record for this book is available from the British Library.

References to internet websites (URLs) were accurate at the time of writing. Neither the author nor Rutgers University Press is responsible for URLs that may have expired or changed since the manuscript was prepared.

♾ The paper used in this publication meets the requirements of the American National Standard for Information Sciences—Permanence of Paper for Printed Library Materials, ANSI Z39.48-1992.

rutgersuniversitypress.org

This book is dedicated to the living members
of the Delaware Tribe of Indians.

All royalties from its sale shall go to the Tribal Council.

Contents

Illustrations

Appendix C

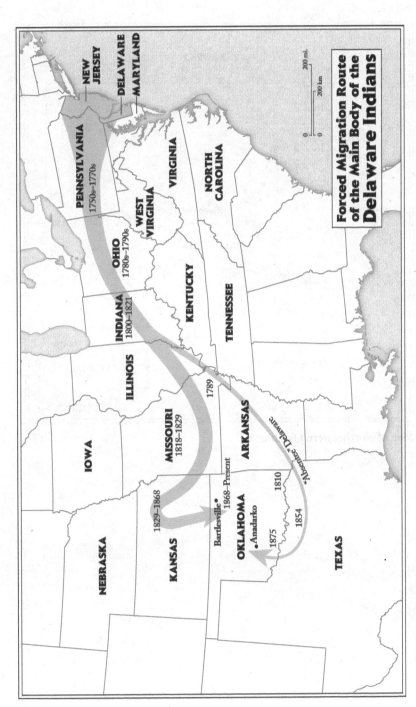

Map of Lenape Migration

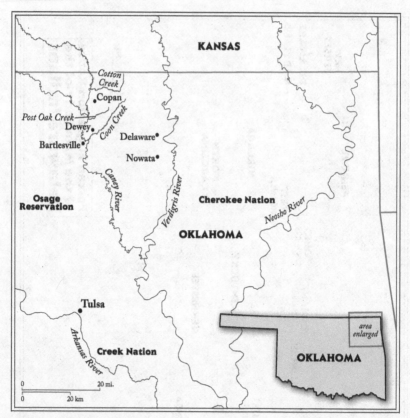

Map of Northeastern Oklahoma

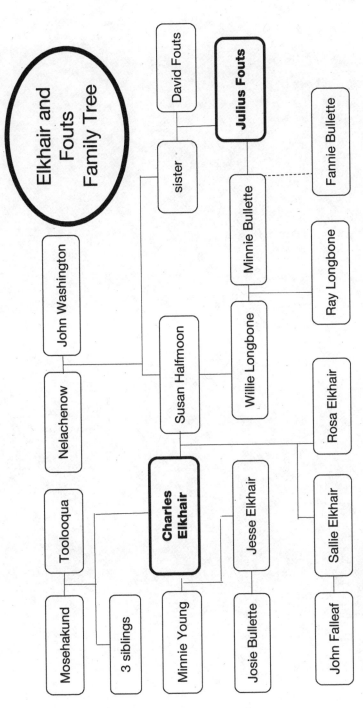

Elkhair and Fouts Family Tree

On the Turtle's Back

Introduction

THE STORYTELLERS' HISTORY

On a cold afternoon in 1820, a Lenape man came home to his wife's hearth from several days' travel. Though their people had originally come from the East Coast, they were then living near Muncie, Indiana, on the White River. "I have returned," he announced in a pleased tone from the doorway. The woman looked up and smiled calmly. "Wanishi," she said ("I am thankful"). Then she returned to her work.[1]

A stranger to their world might have thought the woman did not care about her husband's foray into the wider world. But nothing could have been further from the truth. The Lenape culture did not encourage effusiveness; people showed their affection and interest in each other—and their dedication to a future together—in other ways. That evening, the entire extended family gathered to hear the news that the man and his traveling companions brought concerning the tribe's affairs. They were to depart soon to the lands beyond the great Mississippi River, leaving the Eastern Woodlands behind forever, and so they were riveted by any information they could glean. After the tidings had been discussed, hours of storytelling began. One listener called for "a fabulous tale of times gone by," another for "an ingenious story of a wolf or a raccoon or of some great hunter." The narrators took turns, speaking one after the other, with no interruptions.[2]

In the succeeding weeks, the women packed what belongings they could and answered the children's questions. One of the youngest travelers was a boy named Mo-se-ha-kund ("hair of an elk.")[3] Many years later, he would teach his son Ko-ku-lu-po-we ("He walks backwards"[4] the stories he had grown up with; and that son, under his English name, Charles Elkhair, would one day ensure they were recorded on paper. Another young girl who made the trek across country would soon have a daughter named Ne-la-che-now ("She Appears to Have Her Own Way")[5] who grew up hoping that her children and grandchildren would survive to call themselves Lenape and cherish their past.[6] One of the grandsons, a stalwart boy named Pe-ta-ni-hing ("Throw Him Over Here"),[7] christened Julius Fouts, did take to heart the task of recording his people's culture. Today we can be grateful to Charles Elkhair and Julius Fouts for rendering permanent the stories that once were shared on starlit evenings.

WHO WERE THE LENAPE?

In calling themselves the "Lenape," the people were referring to themselves in their own language as the "common people," the ordinary mortals of the land. Others tended to refer to them by terms that meant "people of the East," for they lived mostly in today's New Jersey, the land between the Delaware River and the sea, but also stretching upward into the area around present-day New York City, westward into Pennsylvania, and southward into Delaware. For many years, they were nomads who pursued game, shellfish, berries, and other gifts of the earth. Then, a few hundred years before contact, seeds of "the three sisters" (corn, beans, and squash) made their way to them through long-distance canoe trade and they gradually became farmers for part of every year—though they still left their agricultural villages each fall to pursue the hunt.

After the Europeans arrived—first the Dutch at Manhattan and then others (the Swedes, Finns, and English) throughout the region—the Lenape traded and sometimes fought with them, depending on how they were treated. European diseases devastated their population, and they gradually began to retreat westward. Soon they were spoken of as the "Delaware" in honor of the river on whose banks they now clustered. They retained that name even as they were pushed farther and farther west; the name is still theirs today, though they are also known as the Lenape.[8] Despite their gradually dwindling numbers, the Delaware played a large role in America's unfolding national consciousness. They still have a secure place in the dominant culture's historical imagination. There, they sell Manhattan to the Dutch for a pittance. They befriend William Penn but still suffer the Walking Purchase. They promise George Washington their support and enter stories of the Revolution. They appear as the last of their kind in dramatic poems and novels of the emerging young country.

Yet all along the Lenape, or Delaware, were much more than props in someone else's national narrative. They had their own expressive lives. Their young people shouted in mirth; their children made youthful mistakes; their parents showed them the way; their old folks exhorted. They prayed, debated, and told stories. Today, however, very little is known of the people's deepest thoughts, poetic expressions, or greatest joys and fears in this early era. Archaeology can reveal a great deal about a people and the choices they make: we can map out their villages and admire their discarded gadgets. But the field can tell us relatively little about people's interior lives. Historical records left by Europeans can also be illuminating: we can study diplomatic exchanges in which the speech of Indigenous participants is recorded as well as the treaties signed and the battles fought. But from such sources we learn a great deal more about the thoughts of the European than those of the Indians; we can sometimes deduce what the Indigenous people of the era were thinking, but certainly not on the deepest level.

Some Native Americans managed to write their own books while memory of the old ways was still fresh and sharp. We have such writings, for instance, by Paiute, Ojibwe, Dakota, Lakota, Sauk, and Apache authors,[9] not to mention the Uto-Aztecans and Mayans of what is now Mexico, who had a long precolonial tradition of writing.[10] The Lenape, however, were pushed out of their homeland long before writing a book to record their perspectives was a realistic possibility. So in some ways, or on some levels, we are left wondering who they once were. Fortunately, as this book makes clear, some highly relevant Lenape sources do survive, thanks to the efforts of Charles Elkhair, Julius Fouts, and their families at the start of the twentieth century.

Remarkably, at that time the Lenape, or Delaware, had managed to maintain a great deal of cultural continuity over the course of the two hundred years during which they were regularly pressured to move westward. Indeed, it was this very desire to hold together as a people, to maintain their tribal structure, governance, language, and cultural traditions, that caused so many of them to choose to endure the extraordinary hardship of repeated removals. At various points, the U.S. government made it clear that they could remain where they were as individuals, if they surrendered that tribal identity. Some individuals did choose to stay where they were, marry white or Black settlers, and gradually blend in with the surrounding population.[11] In the 1970s and 1980s, in the context of great shifts in the nation's consciousness, some of their descendants or possible descendants began to claim their Indigenous heritage, eventually leading to the formation of a plethora of groups branding themselves as "Lenape." While it is all to the good that they are proud of their partial Indigenous ancestry, their enthusiasm does not give them the right to claim the Lenape tribal identity, which belongs to those who continuously worked as a community, over multiple centuries, to defend it.[12]

The main body of the Delaware chose to preserve their tribal identity—its structure, governance, and cultural traditions—even though this choice meant they repeatedly had to move on. Gradually, their numbers dwindled, in a process of "death by a thousand cuts."[13] Yet they were able to retain aspects of the world they once knew. Today, they live in northeastern Oklahoma and constitute the Delaware Tribe of Indians. In the late eighteenth century, while they were still living in Ohio Territory, one large group splintered from the main body and went south into Spanish territory, becoming known as the "Absentee Delaware," but they remained in touch with the main body and eventually settled in Anadarko, Oklahoma. They are now called the Delaware Nation. One small group of Lenape held on as a tribal entity in their original East Coast location a little longer than the others: the very last group who still maintained their tribal structure and governance in New Jersey were those who allied with Presbyterian missionaries in order to protect themselves. They left after the Revolution and joined the Stockbridge-Munsee separatist community in Oneida, New York. They later removed to Wisconsin, where they still live as the Stockbridge-Munsee Band of Mohican Indians.[14] These three groups remain in constant contact today, just as they have over the years.

It was in the process of making lives for themselves in northeastern Oklahoma that Charles Elkhair and Julius Fouts, the son and grandson of the generation forced to leave the Eastern Woodlands and cross the Mississippi, decided that some of their people's ancient stories needed to be written down. This book demonstrates what a labor of love it was for the Lenape people who elected to do whatever was necessary to preserve their communal life and tribal traditions, generation after generation. Elements of the world that existed before Europeans set foot in the Americas are to be found in the stories recorded at the end of two centuries of removals; and elements of the storytellers' late nineteenth-century world are to be found in the memories of elders recorded in interviews at the end of the twentieth, as will be seen. Even today, young people dance almost exactly as their forebears danced at tribal gatherings; they gather in numbers in Oklahoma classrooms and online to retain their language.[15] In short, the Lenape have worked together tirelessly as a community to keep their tribal traditions continuously alive over hundreds of years.

A Two-Hundred-Year Odyssey

Because of their central location in the mid-Atlantic, the Lenape played a major role in colonial politics, first in the greater New Amsterdam / New York area and then, after the 1680s, in Pennsylvania and the Ohio Valley.

In the earliest years after contact, there weren't enough Dutch or Swedish
settlers to displace them. European diseases did kill thousands of their
people, but their polities survived. In 1664 the English ousted the Dutch,
and in the wake of the takeover, Dutch settlers who had been living in the
city of New Amsterdam poured into New Jersey so as to maintain some
cultural sovereignty. Shortly thereafter, large numbers of English settlers
began to follow. It wasn't long before the Lenape were pressed against the
Delaware River and then crossed it, soon making new homes for themselves in Pennsylvania along the Susquehanna River, and eventually traveling as far as western Pennsylvania and then the Ohio Territory. They
played a key role in the French and Indian War.[16] During the years of the
American Revolution, George Washington saw immediately that the colonists were unlikely to emerge victorious if the Delaware sided with the
British in large numbers. His envoys worked night and day to keep those
living near white settlers neutral. In one of the best-kept secrets of American history, the Continental Congress signed the nation's first treaty
with Indians in 1778: they promised the leading Delaware chief, White
Eyes, that if he remained neutral and the patriots won, his people would
be given their own state in the new nation. There, they could welcome
as many other Native Americans as they wished. The Congress had no
intention of keeping their word. When White Eyes was later killed by
other Indians, one American colonel said it had been arranged on purpose, to silence him.[17]

After the war, the Indians attempted to defend their homelands, but
they soon realized that they had lost their ability to maneuver between
warring factions of European or Euro-descended peoples. Up to that time
they had always been able to buy arms and other goods from one party or
another. But the ground had shifted over the years. First the Dutch had
been removed from the geographical game board, and then the French
after the French and Indian War; now the British had been removed from
the immediate area. Only the Americans were left, and they were in no
mood to sell guns or ammunition to Indians. On August 3, 1795, twelve

Indian nations signed the Treaty of Greenville in Ohio. The Delaware, with a contingent of almost four hundred representatives, constituted the largest group present. By the terms of the treaty, they surrendered their people's claims to the Pennsylvania and Ohio lands they had now inhabited for a century and agreed to contain themselves—with several other tribal groups—to the western half of the Ohio Valley. The Indians were instructed to work it out among themselves who was to live where. By 1801, most of the Delaware people had moved to the west fork of the White River, between Muncie and Indianapolis, in the territory of Indiana.[18]

Within only a few years, white settlers were pouring in there as well. The settlers fenced the land to farm it, making hunting increasingly difficult. The Delaware had long had a relationship with Moravian missionaries and had worked closely with them in Ohio, but since a whole settlement of converted Delaware at Gnaddenhutten had been massacred by enraged anti-Indian settlers in 1782, during the Revolution, the Lenape no longer trusted these purported allies, who had proven utterly unable to protect them.[19] Now, when Tecumseh's brother, the Shawnee prophet Tenskwatawa, came to preach among them, they listened.[20] Many longed to follow his advice and return wholeheartedly to Native ways. But it proved increasingly difficult to follow a "traditionalist" path where they were. Not only were settlers arriving in droves, but other, less experienced tribes were electing to fight the Americans, creating tensions for everyone in the region. In 1818, the Delaware were pressured into signing a treaty ceding their lands in Indiana, in exchange for acreage west of the Mississippi. ("It was with the utmost difficulty that the Delaware could be induced to relinquish their claim. They were pressed repeatedly and for years on the subject," wrote one of the chief negotiators a few years later.)[21]

It was at this point that Charles Elkhair's father and Julius Fouts's grandmother or great-grandmother, as young children, were bundled up and perched behind horse riders or atop the baggage piled on wagons. In the summer of 1820, 1,346 Delaware Indians and their 1,499 horses left Indiana—and several smaller groups left a scattering of other communities—and made their way to the ferry at Kakaskia, Illinois.[22] There they crossed the Mississippi. The ferry had to make dozens of trips, requiring many days. In the commotion, at least thirteen horses were stolen by white settlers. But the people successfully traversed the Big River and were able to take up life in the West; they had hope.

The years they spent in Missouri were nothing short of a disaster. Traveling together had bred an outbreak of disease (probably measles and pneumonia), which weakened the people before they even started to establish their new lives. They had been sent to the James River at the foot of the Ozarks, and conditions there were not good for farming or hunting. In early 1824, their chief dictated a letter to the War Department (which had charge of all Indian affairs):

> We did not think That Big Man [the white official with whom they treated] would tell us things that were not true. We have found a poor hilly stony country, and of the worst of all, no game to be found on it to live on. Last summer our corn looked very well until a heavy rain come on for 3 or 4 days and raised the waters so high that we could just see the tops of our corn in some fields. . . . Last summer there was a few deer here, and we had a few hogs, but we was obliged to kill all of them and some that was not our own. . . . This summer my old people and children must suffer.[23]

Worst of all, perhaps, the neighboring Osage, fearing for their own future, made war on them, stealing their valuable horses. They killed the chief's young son and several others, including a son of White Eyes. On October 19, 1829, the chief and his counselors signed a treaty exchanging these now-hated lands for a place they could call their own in Kansas.[24]

This time, the move turned out relatively well. Their land in Kansas was good for farming and raising stock and still replete with game. By the 1840s, settlers passed through in large numbers, heading for the Santa Fe Trail and the West. In the long run this did not bode well, but in the short run it proved advantageous: Indians sold the travelers food and their services as guides. With the extra money that they earned, they purchased items they wanted, including beautiful calicos and brocades, with which they made lovely, colorful clothing. The young men sometimes participated in buffalo hunting, still a viable enterprise. This was not the life they had known in the East, but they were willing to make it their own. They were in active correspondence with small groups of Lenape people who had ended up living elsewhere (Wisconsin and Canada), and some of these now migrated to Kansas to join them.[25]

But the good years proved ephemeral. Today's schoolchildren still learn about "bleeding Kansas" when they study the years leading up to the Civil War. In the words of one historian, "One could scarcely conceive a worse place for Indians to be living [than the Delaware lands] during the chaotic period after 1854, when Kansas became a territory."[26] Settlers poured in; five railroads were chartered. Even the usually blasé Indian agent in Kansas felt that something had to be done. "Hundreds of whites have simultaneously invaded the Delaware Reservation and are engaged in surveying the Country, marking lines, making claims, etc., preparatory, I presume, to a permanent settlement." He spoke of a "flagrant violation of the laws of the country" and asked his superiors in Washington what to do.[27] The council of Delaware chiefs wrote to the government, "Whites come in upon us, steal our houses, and commit various crimes and we are without remedy."[28] Orders to cease and desist were posted, but little was done to enforce them. And then the new population of whites began to make war on each other. When the crisis came, the Delaware did their part, even though no one considered them citizens of the nation. Of the 201 men in their community who were between the ages of eighteen and forty-five, 170 enlisted to fight for the Union.[29]

During this time of drastic change, some Delaware had embraced what was called "the modern world," while others mourned the partial passing of their traditional ways and promised themselves they would try to protect them. Besides the Moravians, there were Methodists and Baptists active in their territory, and the missionaries now met with a more positive reception than they had in Indiana. The Baptists opened a school, receiving payment from the U.S. government in accordance with terms specified in the 1829 treaty. Many of the leading families sent their children. Generally, however, the traditionalists avoided such things, preferring to follow the ancient religion in the temple they called the Big House.[30]

But separate realities were hard to maintain. In real life, people did not maintain a true dichotomy between those who preferred traditional ways and those who wished to embrace modern times. Mo-se-ha-kund, "Hair of an Elk," who had traveled all the way from Indiana as a small child, was from a family of traditionalists, himself a practicing healer. In 1858, when he stood in a line with the other heads of household of his tribe to receive the payment owed to him by the terms of the last treaty, he gave his name as Mo-se ("Elk"), though nearly a quarter gave their name in English. At the time he was married to Too-loo-qua, who had also come all the way from Indiana as a girl, and they had four children.[31] Not long after his wife died in the 1860s, surprisingly perhaps, he sent his approximately fourteen-year-old son, now sometimes called Charles Elkhair,[32] to the Baptist boarding school and even occasionally allowed himself to be called James instead of Mo-se.[33] Perhaps Mosehakund felt comfortable sending his son to the school because for the first time it was being run by an Indian, Nancy (Nannie) Journeycake, the daughter of a longtime chief, who had married Lucius, the son of John Pratt, the Baptist minister who had recently (in 1864) also been named Indian agent; she had taken over the management of the school when her husband died.[34] In any event, young Charles didn't like school, stayed only one term, and later claimed not to have learned much. As an adult, he did not feel comfortable speaking English. But some lessons may have gone deep. Charley was a talented singer, and the missionaries, besides offering the reading, writing and arithmetic, apparently taught the children to sing hymns in their own language, handing out books that showed the Delaware words spelled out in Roman letters.[35] The young Charles would have seen immediately that alphabetic writing, transcribing sound so effectively, might turn out to have its uses.

Julius Fouts, born about 1862, was too young to go to school with Charley while they lived in Kansas. His family, too, was learning to negotiate
a changing world. They were good friends with some of the modernizing
tribal leaders,[36] yet the child was also warmly embraced by the traditionalists. Julius's father, David Fouts,[37] died when he was very young, so everyone had a soft spot for Julius and his mother.[38] It isn't entirely clear where
his father came from: he does not seem to have been listed on the 1858
roster in Kansas, though he was still alive then. It is possible that he was
from another tribe, but equally possible that he was the mixed-heritage
son of a white man, there being a substantial clan of white settlers named
Fouts in Indiana.[39] Julius's mother sometimes called her son by a traditional Lenape name of Pe-ta-ni-hing ("Throw Him Over Here"), but someone in her world, either a missionary or one of her more modern friends,
suggested the classical name of the famous Roman emperor (Julius) for his
Christian moniker. She pronounced it as "Jo-Lus" when asked to give his
name to a white official in 1866 and again in 1867.[40]

Whatever the people's disagreements about the old religion, or about
the most practical strategy for coping with the future, everyone, modernist and traditional, agreed that they wanted to preserve the tribe's identity—
its language, customs, and political structures. In 1862 they had asked
permission to send a delegate to Washington at government expense and
had been rejected. But toward the end of the Civil War the railroad com-
panies had come to want the Delawares' land enough that they became
involved. In 1864, with the war's end on the horizon, John Pratt, the Delaware Indian agent, received a telegram ordering him to bring a delegation
to Washington to negotiate the release of Delaware land. They were lodged
for twenty-nine days at the elegant Kirkwood House Hotel.[41] Everywhere
in Kansas, they learned, Indians were to be removed to make way for white
settlers. They could stay on as individual American citizens, giving up
their tribal identity and tribally held lands, and some families chose that
option. But most elected to hold together as a tribe; they would be allowed
to do just that, they were informed, in the portion of Oklahoma that had

been legally designated as Indian Territory. Many tribal members protested vociferously, but after further negotiations, on July 4, 1866, the leading chiefs—who were Baptists tightly aligned with John Pratt—signed a treaty exchanging their land for a new home in Oklahoma.[42]

Nevertheless, even then matters dragged on, as the federal government was slow to settle affairs and some members of the tribe continued to say they would not move. In September 1866, the Indian agent wrote that people were loath to plant crops, as they expected to be leaving any day. Despite this, he said, "There has been little suffering [from hunger] as the influx of colored men has enabled them by renting their fields to live with comparative ease."[43] It seems that African Americans fleeing the South in the wake of the Civil War were finding that they could initially rent lands to till from the Delaware. Soon, in the spring of 1868, some Delawares were authorized to travel to Kansas ahead of the rest of the group to ready things for the others. Young Charley Elkhair must have been among them, as he disappears from the rolls at this time.[44] By the end of 1868 most of the Delaware—about a thousand people—had traveled the two hundred miles south. The Delaware Tribe of Indians had been on the move for two hundred years, but this place—at last—was to become their permanent home.[45]

In Oklahoma

The Delaware had been invited to choose land in Indian Territory that had been relinquished by some other tribe. An advance party selected an area in the northeast corner of the state in a part of Cherokee country that was scheduled to be relinquished shortly and could thus serve as a distinct Delaware reservation. The Delaware signed a legal agreement that they believed would allow them to live at first under the auspices of the Cherokee and yet maintain themselves as an independent entity in perpetuity. Sadly, the promises were not kept; the resulting legal problems persist even today.[46]

The Delaware transplants established three communities of like-minded people along the Caney and Verdigris rivers, focused around the towns of

Nowata, Bartlesville, and Dewey. Those nearest to Dewey, on the upper reaches of the Caney, tended to be traditionalists, actively practicing the ancient Big House religion, while the other two communities were more deeply connected to missionaries and other non-Lenape neighbors. Indeed, Bartlesville was named for the trade post established by Jacob Bartles, a white man who was successfully integrated into the community precisely because he was married to Nannie Journeycake, the daughter of chief Charles Journeycake. She was the widow of Lucian Pratt, the son of Indian agent John Pratt, who had managed the Baptist school while they were still in Kansas. It seems that she was once again doing her duty to her people by serving as an intermediary with a key white family.[47]

It was the traditionalists who were most interested in seeing their cultural past preserved, despite criticism that they often received, living in an era that saw little good in such things. The specifics of their lives demonstrate how they remained dedicated to maintaining aspects of tradition even as they moved forward into the future. Charles Elkhair and Julius Fouts lived near each other, in the vicinity of Dewey.[48] At the end of the 1870s, when they had been there about ten years and Charley was in his twenties, he was married to a young woman, Minnie Young (sixteen in 1880), and they soon had a son, Jesse.[49] Ten years later, in the early 1890s, his life was quite different. Charles and Minnie had separated and Jesse was away, first at the Baptist mission school nearby on Post Oak Creek, then off at Haskell Institute in Kansas. Charley was now married to Quil-lup-pona-shkwa, ten years his junior, with whom he had two little daughters, Rosa and Sallie, born about 1886 and 1888; but by the mid-1890s, Quil-lup-pona-shkwa had died.[50] Now Charley married a woman almost exactly his age, Susan Half Moon, or Ke-she-lung-o-ne-shkwa ("Finished-Wings Woman").[51] Like him, she had been born in Kansas. Her mother had also been born in the Ohio Valley, but her father had apparently been born to members of the splinter group (the Absentee Delaware) who had left Indiana and gone south into Texas, then Mexican territory.[52] She, too, had been married before. Together, Susan and Charles raised the two girls,

Rosa and Sallie, who later went to Chilocco Indian School.[53] They became English speakers and readers. Indeed, this was the beginning of a serious assault on their culture that would have a demonstrable effect in later decades.[54] Yet in their home, everyone still spoke Lenape, and over the years their father became an increasingly central figure in the Big House ceremonies, known far and wide for his wonderful singing voice and his lyrics and stories. He officiated at community members' funerals in the Delaware language.[55] The Big House was everything to him. Charles and Susan were even married in the traditional religion, not the Christian one: in 1903, when they were both about fifty years old, right before the official Delaware per capita roll count of 1904, they had to take a quick trip up to a courthouse in Kansas to obtain a marriage license, presumably to get the legal documentation they thought they might soon need.[56]

Susan Half Moon Elkhair was remembered by her granddaughter as a "fine lady" conscious of being descended of an ancient and "very fine family."[57] Her clan was indeed extensive and related to several chiefly families.[58] She had had children in a prior marriage and in those years had also generously raised her sister's son: this was little "Jo-Lus," or Julius Fouts, whose father had died before the family left Kansas and whose mother passed away within a few years of arriving in Oklahoma, leaving him entirely orphaned.[59] As he grew up, he too briefly went to a local mission school and developed a smooth signature and easy conversational ability in English, but he wasn't interested in the white man's learning, and later in life he sometimes let census takers think he couldn't read or write at all.[60]

The orphaned Julius set himself up as a farmer very young. He had less than most of his peers—only two horses, when most others had horses, hogs, fruit trees, and other resources.[61] In 1893, at age thirty, he was living with a woman named Nannie, but there were no children.[62] In 1895, he took up housekeeping again, this time with Minnie Bullette, We-me-eh-el-e-shkwa, or "Reverberates Everywhere Woman." Minnie was the great-granddaughter of a French trader named Georges Bullette who had married a Lenape woman from a chiefly family back in the Ohio country and with her founded an extensive family line. Though Minnie's own father was named Boston, her grandfather and her brother carried the name of George Bullette and were active tribal leaders.[63] In about 1890, she married Willie Longbone, a son of Susan Elkhair by her first marriage. Their first baby died, but the second, Ray, survived. The marriage did not work out, however, and Minnie found herself drawn to Julius. He happily helped her raise Ray, and later they took in her infant niece, Fannie, her brother George's daughter, when the child's mother died three months after giving birth. They called the new arrival Willis-ta-quah, "Something Like a Whirlwind."[64] It was a good partnership: with Minnie at Julius's side, the farm thrived. By 1910 they had a poor white man (Honor John) working for them and had also taken in a Delaware bachelor (Charles Whitefeather) as a boarder.[65]

Minnie Bullette Fouts was clearly something special. "Bless her dear heart, she was so sweet and kind—everybody loved her!" remembered a young friend many years later.[66] Indeed, in later years everyone seemed to remember her clearly. She, too, could sing and tell stories with the best of them and deeply valued efforts to keep the old ways alive, even if they couldn't preserve them perfectly. She would insist that "much was accomplished when we prayed and did the best we could with what we had." She was regularly one of the three female *ashkashak* (singular: *ashkas*) or attendants of the Big House annual ceremony, working hard to gather everything that was needed ahead of time and to clean the Big House, both literally and spiritually. Julius also sometimes participated as one of the three male attendants, seeming to love it all every bit as much as she did.[67]

After Chief Charles Journeycake died in 1894, and it was no longer evident who the next chief would be, the governance of the tribe came to be conducted by a collective known as the Delaware Tribal Business Committee. George Bullette, Minnie's brother, was elected the first chairman in February 1895. He remained part of the tribe's power structure, in one position or another, through 1921. After Bullette resigned as

chair, Joseph Bartles, the son of white trader Jacob Bartles and his Delaware wife, Nannie Journeycake, took over. Meanwhile, however, an
entirely separate leadership committee of nine people, often called the
Big House Committee, actually continued to govern internal tribal affairs.
Three members represented each of three ancient clan groupings—Turtle,
Wolf, and Turkey. Charles Elkhair was the chief or leader of the Turkey
clan. Years later, in 1932, the traditionalists became so disgruntled at the
high-handed behavior of the modernist Business Committee that they
petitioned to have it dissolved. Yet in all the intervening time, Minnie
Fouts, married to an active supporter of the Big House Committee and
sister to a leader of the Business Committee, does not appear to have
suffered any noticeable heartache on the issue—at least none that the
surviving records reveal. The divisions were real, but they were also regularly traversed, as everyone's real life was complicated, whatever their
theoretical views.[68]

However, despite their flexibility and resilience, by 1907—when Indian
Territory joined with Oklahoma Territory to become a state and the tribal
members became U.S. citizens—the traditionalists definitely recognized
that what they wanted to protect was in danger of slipping away. At that
point, there were only 870 Delaware people living in northeastern Oklahoma. (Another thousand were scattered in even smaller communities in
Oklahoma, Wisconsin, and Canada.) The 1907 census of Indian Territory
shows that even in the vicinity of Dewey, Indians were vastly outnum-
bered: there were 1,759 whites, 60 Blacks, and 240 Indians. In the vicinity
of Copan, where the Elkhairs lived, the ratio was only slightly better: 887
whites to 131 Indians.[69] Many of the youth were away at Chilocco or other
distant boarding schools. It seemed that each year fewer people were able
to attend the annual Big House ceremony in October. Worse, fewer and
fewer of the surviving tribal members had been sent out into the wilderness as boys to seek their visions, which formed the backbone of the Big
House ritual connections to their ancestors.[70]

Then, in 1908, an opportunity presented itself.

CONTEMPLATING PRESERVATION

The Delaware had always been adept at forming and maintaining alliances; partnerships formed a key element of their survival over the course of their odyssey.[71] Now, in the era of the rise of professional anthropology in the early twentieth century, Julius Fouts decided to pursue a useful relationship with an anthropologist.

The backstory was lengthy: The tribe had worked with a famous anthropologist before. In the 1850s, Louis Henry Morgan (who later became famous for writing about the Iroquois) visited the Delaware in Kansas. The Baptists took him under their wing, and William Adams, a Delaware man who had become a devout Christian and helped to found the Baptist mission in Kansas, was his chief informant.[72] As a young man Fouts was on friendly terms with Richard Adams, the son of William. In the 1890s and early 1900s, Richard worked actively with the tribal Business Committee and even went to live in Washington, D.C., at tribal expense in order to attempt to solidify the Delaware Tribe's legal separation from the Cherokee Nation. There, although he was ultimately unsuccessful, he worked with extraordinary energy, gathering major collections of documents relating to his people's history and lodging important lawsuits.[73] Given their friendship and Richard's outgoing, self-confident nature, it seems virtually certain that Julius Fouts knew about the family's relationship with Lewis Henry Morgan.

Thus, Fouts was apparently aware of the potential good that could come of a relationship with an interested scholar. Events certainly indicate that he was keenly attuned to it. In 1908, he discovered that his brother-in-law, George Bullette, had sold a spiritually valuable, heirloom wooden mask to a representative of a museum in New York City.[74] He was disappointed, as the mask had long been in his own possession (having come to him because the Turkey-clan family who had had it was becoming more inclined to Christianity). Fouts, fearing that he (a member of the Turtle grouping) would not care for the mask properly, had turned it over to

George, who was also of the Turkey clan. Now George had sold it—possibly to help pay the ongoing expenses of Richard Adams in D.C. Still, despite his frustration, when Fouts learned that the visitor from the East was asking to meet people who knew more of the tribe's traditional lore and yet also spoke fluent English, he agreed to talk to him.

The anthropologist whom Fouts and his friends would come to know well was Mark Raymond Harrington. Twenty years younger than Fouts, he was born in 1882 in Ann Arbor, Michigan. His people were among those who had largely replaced the Indigenous people of the West only one or two generations before—yet he displayed not arrogance but diffidence. The young man suffered from a speech impediment so severe that at first people had difficulty understanding him.[75] He was his parents' second child—but the first one to survive. Harrington's grandfather had been a professor at the then-new University of Michigan, and at first his father worked there too, as a curator in the museum, often traveling. In 1891, Harrington's father was named the first chief of the newly created U.S. Weather Bureau in Washington, D.C., and the whole family moved. By 1895 his father had taken a position at the University of Washington on the West Coast, and when that did not work out, he found employment in New York, then in Puerto Rico, but he shortly returned to New York. In 1899, when Harrington was in high school, his father, who by now was visibly mentally ill, simply disappeared and apparently lived on the streets; the family did not locate him for another six years, when he surfaced in a sanatorium in New Jersey.[76]

Meanwhile, Harrington had found an alternate father figure in a kindly academic named Frederic Putnam, who worked at the American Museum of Natural History. He began to pay Harrington to work summers on archaeological digs, the first one being the excavation of a Lenape village near Trenton.[77] Beneath the village they found an archaic settlement. Through this work Harrington found that he was able to put his own troubles in perspective. He wrote in his first published article, "When our finest locomotive is no longer a heap of red dust, the rude tools of ice age man will still be found in glacial gravels."[78] He shortly assisted other local digs at Croton and Throggs Neck and at various sites on Long Island. Eventually he was sent to Cattaraugus Reservation in Haudenosaunee or Iroquois country. By then Putnam had introduced him to another young friend of his, Arthur Parker, a Seneca, and they soon became partners. Parker really liked Harrington. He was then still a student and years later remembered his delight when Harrington invited him to join his labors: "A young man of remarkable talents whom I had learned to admire immensely called me into conference. 'Would I forget Greek and Hebrew and the origin of the Decalogue for a few weeks and undertake an expedition with him?'"[79]

Harrington soon became close friends with other Indians as well. A number of Abenaki, among them Beulah Tahamont Dark Cloud, came down from Maine to work on the sites on Long Island. Harrington briefly dated her, but she apparently preferred Arthur Parker, marrying him in April 1904. In June of that year Harrington married Alma Cocks, the daughter of the landowner at one of the Long Island sites.[80] Harrington and Parker remained close. Years later, in 1927, after the death of his wife Alma, Harrington would marry Arthur Parker's sister Edna and stay with her until she died in 1948.

When Harrington had been sent to work on these archaeological digs, he still had no college degree. He had been taking courses when he could back where he grew up, at the University of Michigan; eventually he transferred to Columbia and became a full-time student, majoring in anthropology, with Franz Boas—generally considered the founder of modern anthropology—as his adviser. By 1908 Harrington had obtained his bachelor's and his master's degrees from Columbia, but he did not wish to pursue a doctorate. He had hoped that when he finished school the American Museum of Natural History would hire him, but that did not materialize. So he took a job at Covert's Indian Store on Fifth Avenue. Their letterhead read, "Collections illustrating American Indian life for schools, colleges and museums, supplied with authentic material." Harrington thus came close to selling his soul, for his job was to convince Native Americans to part with their family heirlooms in order that Frank Covert might profit and schools enrolling white students might fill their supply closets. Fortunately, millionaire George Gustav Heye walked into the store one day, and before long Harrington was working full-time for him, collecting materials that Heye intended to be part of a great and permanent collection of Indigenous materials. (The following year Heye allied with the Museum of the University of Pennsylvania and then later endowed his own museum, the Heye Foundation, which ultimately formed the backbone of the collection of the National Museum of the American Indian.)[81]

Almost immediately Harrington was sent on buying trips to Oneida Town in Canada, to Seminole villages in Florida, to Eastern Band of Cherokee settlements in North Carolina, and to Oklahoma.[82] Over the next two years he would make repeated trips to that state, eventually setting up temporary headquarters in the town of Shawnee, complete with a Peoria Indian assistant and guide (Bill Skye) and an African American cook (Robert Moore). In his rental house he could receive visitors and purchase what they wished to sell. Shawnee's newspaper hastened to assure skeptical citizens who saw people coming and going that "there is nothing doing in the blind tiger or monte line, for the house is occupied as headquarters by the George G. Heye expedition of the University of Pennsylvania Museum, whose business it is to study and record the native customs and beliefs of the Indian tribes of Oklahoma." By then Harrington had already been, as he put it, "working among the Delaware near Bartlesville" for over a year.[83]

Harrington really was at least somewhat sensitive to the personal and cultural pain caused by selling ancient artifacts and realized that people usually relinquished their belongings because they felt they had no choice. In a short story he later wrote, an Indigenous character suffers acutely in this regard: "I returned home one night," explains the narrator, "tired out from my fifteenth successive fruitless day's hunting, and found my Whispering Leaves crying bitterly. Although I begged her to tell me what the trouble was, she refused, but at last she broke down. 'My dear mate,' she

sobbed, 'there is nothing to eat in this house, and there is no hope for anything, unless I sell that robe your mother made for you. All my pretty
things are gone long ago, and all yours except that.'"[84] Harrington must
have known of this pain because people told him about it; some also voiced
their suspicions. In 1910, he requested and received from the Museum
of the University of Pennsylvania an official-looking letter with a gold seal
declaring solemnly that neither Harrington nor the museum would profit
from the resale of any of the goods he bought; they were to be preserved
for the world's posterity, both Indian and white.[85]

Importantly, Harrington was not looking just to siphon valuable Indigenous works of art out of Oklahoma. He truly wanted to hear and preserve the people's words, stories, and beliefs. He rued the fact that he did
not speak any Lenape. Arthur Parker and his friends had taught him
enough of at least one Iroquoian language for him to manage basic conversation, but he had no knowledge of any Algonkian tongues.[86] With the
help of a Delaware man named William Brown, he sought people who
were willing to tell him stories, either in English or through friends and
relatives who could serve as translators from the Delaware. Then, if they
were willing, he would sit for hours, writing down everything they had to
say in notebooks that he ran out to buy at a local Oklahoma store. Sometimes he worked with a speaker one-on-one, and sometimes a storyteller
spoke to a group—he would note when the audience laughed. Today, many
dozens of pages of his notes in his own cramped handwriting sit in the
archives of the National Museum of the American Indian. Julius Fouts,
he later said, gave him more information than any other source, but he
was also deeply grateful to Julius's wife, Minnie, and to Charles Elkhair
and his wife.[87]

In what he later published, Harrington would come to emphasize
Charles Elkhair, spiritual chief of the Turkey clan, over all his other
sources, apparently having become convinced that such a source lent more
dignity and authenticity to his work. Probably Charley's own family and
friends accorded him special status, given that he was the eldest male in

the group and had a distinct talent as a storyteller. But it is also possible that Harrington wished to downplay the role of the women, as it would be many years before anthropology as a field recognized the importance of hearing their perspectives. We are left to read between the lines, as only a few stories are explicitly said to be the work of the women, though a number of them show their influence, as will be seen. Given the relatively egalitarian nature of Lenape society in general, it is safe to assume that the women played an active role in the process.[88]

Julius Fouts clearly liked Harrington and decided to trust him, which probably would not have been the case had the others in his milieu not felt similarly. We know what his feelings were because he actively cultivated the connection. After the first visit, Fouts wrote to Harrington. He had dictated another long story to his stepson, Ray, and was now sending it on. In March 1909 he wrote, "My Dear Friend: I thought I would send you a few lines of this story. My boy got back from school and I told him to put it down for me. From your Friend, Julius Fouts."[89] Fouts himself, Minnie, and Charley Elkhair ultimately sent on at least ten stories or ceremonial speeches dictated to their children. At the end of one, Elkhair's daughter (or perhaps another young friend) signed his name for him, but beneath that he somewhat laboriously signed himself. This was no occasion to deceive a white man by pretending he could only leave his mark, as he did on legal documents; this was a moment of import and dignity, when it behooved him to show that he knew perfectly well how to sign.

In the summer of 1910 Harrington was back in Oklahoma, trying to obtain a phonograph recording device, though that plan does not seem to have come to fruition.[90] He stayed for a few months and then returned to the East. In early 1912, Fouts wrote to him, showing eagerness to hear about the progress of Harrington's writings on the Delaware. Harrington responded,

Dear Friend: I received your letter some time ago but have not had time to answer it till now. I have been so very busy on other things since

I came back East that I have had not time as yet to copy the Delaware
stories and of course the book has not yet been printed. When it comes
out I shall surely remember you. I expect to come to Oklahoma again
in the last part of the summer, or early in the fall, and shall see you
then. . . . Did the people worship in the Big House last fall? Hoping that
you and your family are well.[91]

Fouts wrote again soon, and in June Harrington was able to answer, "Yes!
I am coming back!"[92] Sadly, though, his wife became so ill that he never
made it until the Christmas holidays. Harrington found that coming at
that time was a mistake, as with their children home from boarding school
most of the people went to visit other family members. "During the holidays, very few of the Indians are at home."[93] Still, Harrington must have
seen Fouts—indeed, may even have stayed with him—for that visit trig-
gered an active correspondence between the two men beginning in the
early spring of 1913 and lasting for the rest of the year, concerning whether
or not the museum would be interested in purchasing the Big House for
its collections and taking responsibility for paying for the erection of a new
building.[94] That project never came to anything—the museum ultimately
decided it would be too expensive a venture—but the men continued to
write to each other. Near Christmas, Harrington explained his situation:
"I do not know how soon I can get back to Oklahoma. My wife is sick all
the time now, and I am afraid to leave her. . . . You have never told me as
yet whether you got the little book I sent you. I am working on the big book
now, and may send you some parts of it later to look over, to see if it is all
right."[95] Long before it became a normal part of anthropological work,
Harrington assumed he should ask the Delaware people he knew if he had
recorded things correctly.

In the summer of 1914, Harrington finally judged his ailing wife was well
enough for him to leave her, and he returned to Oklahoma. It turned out he
had made an error of judgment. After only a few weeks he received a telegram sending word of her death; he returned immediately to the East Coast.[96]

We learn something about where he drew comfort from what happened next: in September he came back to Oklahoma to take a canoe trip in the rivers and creeks of the northeastern part of the state. After that Harrington chose to leave the museum's employ and work only for Heye, so there are no more of his carefully preserved letters in the institution's files.[97]

The correspondence from the period 1908 to 1914 certainly indicates that Fouts was at least as invested as Harrington was in the work they did together. It is possible that Harrington and Fouts between them more or less stumbled on the possibility of Harrington using his work for the museum as a way to record the Delaware stories, without either of them having had any such preconceived plan. In all likelihood the exchange started with Harrington asking if Fouts had ever seen any material objects that recorded stories in glyphic writing. Such a thing would have been the holy grail for a collector, as "experts" on the Lenape had long wished to believe in the authenticity of a document they called the "Walam Olum." In the early nineteenth century, a European immigrant named C. F. Rafinesque, hoping to gain some fame for himself, claimed that he had stumbled across a glyphic text that came from a Delaware Indian in the Ohio Valley and recounted the Lenape origin story. The document, including both the supposed pictorial glyphs and their purported translation, was by Harrington's day in the possession of the University of Pennsylvania and had been studied by scholars who were eager to believe in it. The anthropologists whom Harrington had met at Columbia certainly were.[98]

Today, scholars recognize that all the images had been copied from readily available published sources showing other cultures' glyphic writings, that the purported translation was a direct English-to-Lenape production based on published Lenape word lists, and that the arc of the narrative bears no resemblance to any Indigenous tale.[99] Yet we should not judge these late nineteenth- and early twentieth-century scholars too harshly. Their hearts were in the right place: what they wished to believe, at root, was not that Rafinesque was an honest man but rather that the Delaware Indians had their own literature.

Moreover, there is evidence that the Lenape did originally have their own glyphic writing. Two Moravian missionaries who wrote prolifically about their experiences living among the Delaware in the late eighteenth century both wrote in detail about the fact that they participated in the same custom common to other northeastern tribes, that of leaving a record of major events carved into tree trunks. Others passing by could read about a war party's successes or where a hunting party had gone or how many had died on a certain venture. Furthermore, they asserted, a famous Delaware medicine man in the 1760s used a glyphic map on a deerskin as a key visual aid in his preaching, and he apparently allowed others to make copies, to serve as mnemonic devices.[100]

In speaking with Harrington, Fouts and Elkhair answered both questions implicit in the Walam Olum debate in no uncertain terms: No, they had never seen any carved, written, or painted text containing glyphs and intended to be read in some way. They did not believe such a thing had ever been an integral or essential part of their culture.[101] But yes, the Lenape certainly had their own literary culture—songs, sermons, and stories that had come down to them in a rich oral tradition. Which did Harrington want to hear?

LENAPE STORIES

Lenape stories, like all other Native American stories, were meant to be shared. They did not entirely belong to one person or even, one might say, to one ethnic group. The circles of listeners were always mixed: they might contain a young wife who had been taken as a prisoner of war, a child who had been adopted, a returnee from time spent with another tribe. When these in turn told their versions of a certain story in later years, they might incorporate elements of different traditions. After the Europeans came, the early missionaries joined the circles in the evening and sometimes were invited to tell their own stories. In the seventeenth century, the Swedish, Dutch, and English ministers often carried with them a copy of the *Aeneid*, the story of a Trojan who flees his vanquished city and travels far afield before eventually founding Rome. (The tale appealed mightily to the young settlers from Europe.) When Aeneas landed in Carthage, on the north shore of Africa, and thought to settle there, his people asked the queen, Dido, if his men might take only as much land as an ox hide covered, and she agreed. But the clever Trojans cut the hide into a very long rope, starting at the edge and working their way inward in a spiral, and so were able to mark out a large swath of territory. The Lenape liked that element of the tale, for it reverberated with their experience of settlers taking more land than they had originally indicated. So they used the plot device in stories they told; they were already quite adept at incorporating the new without violating the old.[102]

How then, in a world without writing that was also a world of shifting terrain, can we have any idea what constituted a Lenape story in the early centuries? The answer is that numerous outsiders, and eventually one Delaware man, wrote down the stories they were told over the years before the project undertaken by Charles Elkhair and Julius Fouts. We have some skeletal tales written down by a handful of confused Swedes and Dutchmen in the seventeenth century, while the Lenape still lived in today's New Jersey and the surrounding area.[103] We find some more detailed stories in the late eighteenth-century accounts of the Moravian missionaries, especially David Zeisberger and John Heckewelder, when the Lenape lived in Pennsylvania and Ohio. Both Zeisberger and Heckewelder spent years learning the language and living among the people, and so their testimony, despite some obvious limitations, has real value. In the early nineteenth century, when the Delaware were living in Indiana, the territorial governor Lewis Cass distributed a cultural questionnaire to the various Indian agents under his authority, and later he sent a young scholar, Charles Trowbridge, to follow up with the Delaware. An American settler named William Connor had married a Delaware woman and lived with her for many years, and he helped Trowbridge write up a summary of his findings.[104] Last, at the turn of the twentieth century, Richard Adams, living in

Washington, D.C., as he went about his political errands, dedicated a great deal of time to writing down whatever stories he had access to. Many of them came from Zeisberger or Heckewelder or other published books, but some were clearly his memory of stories he had once been told.[105] Still, Adams, though he was a Delaware himself, was also the son of a Baptist pastor, and he was unable to offer a rich and detailed version of the stories in the Lenape language that had come down through the generations. This is why the work that Julius Fouts, Charles Elkhair, and their families did with Mark Harrington in the early twentieth century is of inestimable importance.

In what they said and wrote, we can catch a glimpse of the enormous complexity of the Delaware story tradition both as it existed in earlier centuries and as it had come to exist at the start of the twentieth century. Some elements of the oral tradition of the deep past are, in fact, lost to us today. For instance, in the seventeenth and eighteenth centuries, the Lenape, like other Native Americans, recounted intricate versions of their own history, complete with migrations, wars, peacemaking marriages, and natural disasters. Through the Moravians, for instance, we hear of an exciting sneak attack made on the dancers at a great feast.[106] But we cannot know more than that. As the past receded, the people let those histories pass from their knowledge. Other elements of the oral tradition are somewhat better known, if only in limited form. Elements of the sermons and songs—in short, the prayers—offered at Big House ceremonies were recorded at various points over the years, and eventually Charles Elkhair provided English versions of two different sermons. Almost every known instance of such writings has been collected and collated by Robert Grumet in a book providing ample proof of the continuity of the Big House religion from the seventeenth century through the twentieth.[107] However, it is the tradition of the story—spiritual and thought-inducing at root, but entertaining as well—that exists in fullest form. In the 1980s folklorist John Bierhorst listed every known telling of a Delaware story, from that of an early somewhat irate Swedish explorer all the way to the recordings of a

Delaware-speaking woman (Nora Thompson Dean) living in Oklahoma in the 1970s, and organized them both by order of production and by topic. His book proves that certain themes lasted throughout the centuries in an almost timeless sense; it is not concerned with the specifics of the stories' production or the realities of the authors' lives.[108]

Only now, for the first time, is the full set of all the stories told by Julius and Minnie Fouts and Charles and Susan Elkhair in the years 1908 to 1911 brought to print in order to create the book we like to think they would have wanted. We worked from the original notes that Harrington took or the letters that the informants sent, not from the edited and adjusted typescripts that Harrington's secretary later prepared (some of which Bierhorst published), for our goal has been to represent as closely as possible the story world in which the tellers had moved since childhood and which they were actively engaged in passing on. Only in doing this can we begin to get a sense of the depth and richness of the tradition in that moment, of how it had not only retained many elements of the past but also had been adapted to make sense of the real history experienced by the authors' people and themselves.

In the old tales Lenape people lived on the back of a metaphorical giant turtle, whose shell rose from the sea, sometimes bringing them closer and sometimes moving them farther from the edge that met the ocean. The story of human origins varied from teller to teller and over time, sometimes sharing more with Iroquoian neighbors to the north, for instance, and sometimes less, but there were certain common elements. It usually began in the sky, where divine man-beings and woman-beings dwelt together in harmony, knowing nothing of death or sorrow. But at length they came to know death, and as tragic as the event was, it opened up the joys and struggles and meaningfulness of human life, compelling precisely because it was lived in the shadow of death, with the potential for loss. It happened at that time that a woman-being struggled with her man-being husband, and he uprooted a sacred tree whose roots extended down into another world below, and she fell through the hole and passed into another existence. As she fell, she looked about her and saw blue on all sides, and though she didn't know it yet, she was looking on an expanse of water. A bird—or perhaps a water animal—noticed her reflection and said a woman-being was coming up out of the depths, but another said that a better way to describe it was that she was falling down from the sky. (The condescending David Zeisberger said with irritation that the Lenape contradicted themselves and could not seem to agree on whether the woman fell from the sky or came up out of the earth or the water. He missed the philosophical point entirely.)[109] The animals held a council and decided to save her. They placed her gently on the back of a giant turtle, and then the water animals—the beaver, otter, and muskrat—each in turn attempted to bring up some mud to place on the back of the turtle. It was a difficult task, and in some renditions they died in their efforts. But at length the vegetation took root and the waters receded. There on the turtle island the woman soon gave birth. Or perhaps she gave birth to a daughter who in turn gave birth. Sometimes it was human twins who were born to her, and sometimes different animals. In either case, the new beings argued among themselves, giving rise to the trials and tribulations—and the stories—of life among humans.[110]

Julius Fouts, as we shall see, offered his own version of this story, one largely in keeping with the first recorded version, coming from a Dutchman writing in 1655, though it had changed in certain regards. Yet what is perhaps most noteworthy is the way in which the narrative's deeper themes permeate much of what he and Charles Elkhair and their wives said elsewhere, beyond the story of the woman falling from the sky or rising from the depths in order to live on turtle island. They describe a world full of death and sadness, and yet for that very reason also full of the possibility of struggle, hope, and humor. They recount the existence of parallel worlds, the one we know well, and another outside our daily mundane view, which we can sometimes enter through some sort of hole, or by virtue of a special tree, which by its nature connects the deepest subterranean cavities with the glorious sky, or the water with the land. They paint a scene in which humans owe much to animals and other beings and sometimes are not grateful enough. They bring to life a world in which humans, in their limited wisdom, struggle with each other as well as with the elements of nature, but in which they also often choose to do the right thing. The choice, at least, is always there for them to make.

The traditionalist Delaware people living on the beautiful Caney River in Oklahoma in the early 1900s did not want the world to forget what their Lenape ancestors had once thought about as they watched the sun come up over the sea in the East, nor what they had thought about as they camped near other bodies of water in the long overland trek. Taking the long view, as they often did, they did what was necessary to ensure that this book could be published someday. As the children and grandchildren of the generation that left the Eastern Woodlands behind, they were uniquely well positioned to do this work, to become, as it were, a bridge to the future epoch of the Delaware Tribe of Indians.

Notes on Language: Terms and Transcriptions

The people who once called themselves the Lenape gradually came to be known as the Delaware; the direct descendants of Charles Elkhair are enrolled members of the Delaware Tribe of Indians, based in Bartlesville, Oklahoma. They most often refer to their culture and language as "Delaware," but they do occasionally use the word "Lenape" to describe both. After all, that is the only correct term in their ancestral language. When Charles Elkhair was telling stories in his own language, he used the word "Lenape" to describe the subjects of his narrations, and the translator would then present the word to Mark Harrington as "Indians." Yet in his dealings with the wider world, Elkhair himself did use the tribal name "Delaware." In this book, we use both terms interchangeably. If we were to use "Lenape" only, we would be ignoring the recent history of the tribe and even the name they currently go by; but if we were to use "Delaware" only, we would be employing only the English-language name given to the people by white settlers. It is essential to be respectful of both names.

We are also taking a stand on the issue of transcription. Some readers may wonder why we do not choose to "smooth out" what we have found in the files from the early 1900s, editing and correcting as we go along. That would indeed make for an easier read. But we think a great deal can be learned from grappling with exactly what is there. When Mark Harrington crossed out something he had heard and replaced it with what his informant said next, we include the words he struck out and the words he wrote next; we believe doing so brings readers closer to the moment when Charles Elkhair or Minnie Fouts spoke their piece, sometimes changing their mind about what they wished to say. Similarly, when, for instance, Julius Fouts took the time to struggle through writing a long piece in English, we retain the nonstandard spelling he used. In earlier days it was thought to be more respectful to "clean it up," as though there might be something embarrassing about the fact that Fouts did not write English fluently. Now we know there is nothing shameful about making errors when one writes in a language that is not one's own and in which one has had almost no formal education. On the contrary, we believe allowing readers to see the effort such a writer was making to preserve his culture for posterity is the most respectful choice we can make. We advise you to read the text aloud, and you will hear the voice or register he spoke in when he spoke English; you will hear the real man, not the edited or adjusted one—a man it would have been an honor to know.

OUTLINE OF THE BOOK

In the pages of this volume, readers will find seven chapters, reflecting the seven kinds of stories told by Charles Elkhair, Julius Fouts, and their families: "Creation Stories," "Big House Stories," "Culture Heroes," "Humans Learning Lessons," "Talking to the Dead," "The Coming of the Whites,"

and "Tales of Ordinary Life." Each chapter begins with reflections placing
the group of stories in context, in an effort to bring out elements that
audience members in the Delaware community of the early 1900s would
not have needed to have explained, but which may not be obvious to readers today. The stories are followed by what we call "An Afterword in Three
Parts": a summary of what happened to the storytellers after Mark Harrington went home; a set of four interviews with elders in the 1990s—people
who had been children when the storytellers were alive and who still
remembered what they had to teach; and a note on life in Delaware country today. The book constitutes a record of the imaginative mental world
of a cohesive tribe who stuck together through thick and thin, from
the time before any Europeans were present in this hemisphere through
to today. We are glad that you want to get to know that world. Nule-
lìntàmuhëna èli paèkw.[111]

CHAPTER 1

Creation Stories

Creation stories tell not just of the origin of the world as a whole but of the creation of all things in it: they explain how the elements of the world that we know came to be. What is perhaps most striking about the Lenape creation stories told in the early 1900s is how little they had changed from the versions told in the seventeenth century. In several cases readers will find that colonists described a very similar story between one and three hundred years earlier. In fact, on a deep level, the stories kept faith with what had been believed for millennia: we know this because they stem from a religion of hunters, even though the Lenape no longer lived by the chase. They had been part-time farmers for several hundred years before contact and had been even more dedicated to agriculture ever since the late eighteenth century, when they moved to the Ohio Valley. Moreover, during the hundred-year odyssey that took them from Indiana to Missouri to Kansas to Oklahoma, they had come into greater contact with the stories of the Indians of the Southwest, whose religion had long been that of agriculturalists.[1] Yet only one creation story told by the Lenape in the early 1900s was about corn and farming.

In some ways, the Lenape spiritual universe resembles that of most Native Americans. Humans are not beings set apart but rather share an affinity with animals, as all beings together constitute the natural world and are mutually interdependent. The whole world is not sacred—there are ordinary rocks and bedraggled flowers that are not inherently divine—but the whole world does have the potential to be lit with divinity, for the ordinary and metaphysical worlds are connected in various ways and may suddenly touch each other: humans can visit spiritual worlds, and spiritual beings may walk the earth. Like most ancient hunters, the Lenape believed in a supreme being or creator, but that being could fade in importance much of the time, for a collection of very active spirits represented the atmospheric powers that governed most of life, and a host of lesser spirits inhabited the earth, often in the forms of animals, interacting regularly with humans living their lives.[2]

Donald Fixico (Shawnee and Creek) has said that in the creation stories of Native Americans, "migrations are almost always involved."[3] He refers to figurative migration, and in this respect the Lenape are very much like their brethren. In each of the stories that follow, the beings involved move from one world to another, from the ordinary day-to-day world to the spiritual, or from water to land or from land to sky. The Lenape knew that it is in changing perspective that one gains wisdom.

These tales were written down by Mark Harrington, mostly without attribution, as he sat in the parlors of the Fouts and Elkhair families. Sometimes the speaker would begin a sentence one way, change his or her mind, and start again using quite different words. When that happened, Harrington would scratch out what he had written and record the new phrasing instead. We have chosen to show those deletions since they bring to life the hours that the group spent together, working hard to transcribe the old stories.

After Harrington went back east, Charley Elkhair, with his family's help, arranged to send him an additional creation story, as you will see.

The Turtle's Back[4]

A number of tribes of the Northeastern Woodlands—of both the Iroquoian language family and the Algonkian language family—share an
origin story of a woman falling from the sky toward the water and land-
ing on a turtle's back, on which the animals and birds place enough
soil that it gradually becomes the earth. (For a fuller summary, see the
introduction.) At first glance, it might be supposed that the two groups
share an important story mostly because, by the eighteenth century,
the Lenape had been pressured by colonists to move westward into
Pennsylvania, where they became the close neighbors of the Iroquois.
However, it seems that the story that the two groups held in common—
or at least certain elements of it—predated the influx of Europeans and
resultant migrations. We have Canadian Jesuit accounts of the Iroquoian story dating from the seventeenth century; and likewise we
have Swedish and Dutch accounts of the Lenape story as they heard it
in New Jersey in the 1650s and 1670s, before the Lenape had relocated.[5]
It seems—unsurprisingly—that the exchanges inherent to centuries of
long-distance trade, warfare, and intermarriage had yielded a common
vision of humanity's origins.

Toward the end of the nineteenth century, J. N. B. Hewitt, whose
mother was Tuscarora (the Sixth Nation of Iroquois), began the work
of transcribing the story as it was told by elders of different Iroquoian
confederacy tribes. The Iroquois, or Haudenosaunee, had not been
forced to migrate, and their languages were—and remain—fully
alive. Thus the versions of the story of the sky woman that he left us
are the richest in existence.[6] (For an example, see appendix A.) His
work reminds us, sadly, of how much of the Lenape rendition was
undoubtedly lost because no full record was made in the original language while it was still possible.

What we have from the Lenape are several short summaries or
partial tellings recorded over the centuries.[7] In the early 1900s,

Harrington heard two related short stories, one traditional and one an entertaining spin-off. We present them both here.

The earth was created once (by *Gicelemu'kaong*),[8] and then covered with water afterward. There was trouble in getting dirt to start a new earth. Various animals were sent down to get dirt, but all came up drowned. The Muskrat finally got the dirt in his paw; but he was dead when he came up. Whoever was fixing the new earth—perhaps God—took this dirt, and after inquiring which creature was able to hold it, put the dirt on the Turtle's back. At once it began to grow until it became the great Island we live on today.

*

When Someone created the animals, he asked, "Who can carry the earth on his back?" And the turtle (*da-gosh*)[9] said, "I can!" So the creator put the dirt on his back and made it grow, and it became the earth.

About the same time, he asked, "Who shall be the deer?" And the Rabbit said, "I will." "Well," said the creator, "just run by and we will see." So the Rabbit ran by and one of the Indians[10] was told to shoot it. So he did, and hit it with an arrow, and the rabbit squealed loud. When he was done squealing, the creator said, "Well, you cannot be the deer. You would make the Indians ashamed with your squealing whenever they hit you." So he appointed the deer to be "Deer"!

The Seven Stars[11]

Charles Elkhair and Julius Fouts often used the word *pilsit* or *pilsuw*, which they translated for Harrington as "clean." But they explained to him that it meant much more than the absence of dirt. It was not about chastity, as a Westerner might first imagine. A person was *pilsit* if they had kept to the old teachings, obeyed the elders, lived in harmony with the universe. Only one who was *pilsit* could hope to have visions, or enter the spiritual world and return from it. Some Lenape said that once, long ago, all humans could move from the sky world to the earth, or the reverse, much like the woman who fell from the sky originally. But most modern people had lost that ability.

This is a story about brothers, seven of whom were *pilsit*, but one of whom was not. With Indigenous stories' characteristic complexity, the eighth brother is not portrayed as truly evil. He is troublesome and at one point duplicitous, yet thanks to his tenacity he becomes a leader of men. Given the complexities of the world, there is need of him.

However, the most important element of the story would be the seven brothers who become the stars of the highly visible constellation Westerners call the Pleiades: we learn that long ago the brothers sought refuge in the sky when too many human beings persisted in their uncaring ways. For many years, the constellation's heliacal rising (the point at which it first appeared after months of being hidden behind the sun) had been in the fall,[12] so the stars' appearance constituted an announcement of winter. This same story was told to David Zeisberger in the late eighteenth century and to Lewis Cass in the early nineteenth; in the versions they heard, the seven brothers likewise chose to give up their ability to move between worlds and stay in the sky, from where they would still try to help people.

This story was handwritten in a notebook on three numbered pages and handed or sent to Harrington, but we don't know by whom, though

the handwriting looks very much like that of Julius Fouts's stepson, Ray Longbone.

There once were eight boys. Seven could go above in the air and down in the ground, while the other could not do anything, and their old man did not know what to do with him. So he took him to an Island and left him there. And the boy hallooed for his grandfather but received no reply. He staid there three days, and finally the animals of the water felt sorry for him, and they began to ask each other, who's to take him back to his grandfather? So finally the big round snake said he would. So the snake told the boy he would take him across [the water] if he would tell him when he seen a cloud come up anywhere.

So they started across and the boy got pretty near crossing, and he seen a cloud and he told the snake, and they hurried back and the snake got out of sight. And next day the snake came back, and the boy thought that he would not tell the snake this time. So they started, and he seen a cloud, but never said anything to the snake. And he reached the bank—and the snake was struck by lightning. So the boy made friends with the lightning, and they told him he would be a ruler some day and be a great man.

Those other seven boys got so they couldn't stay with their parents.[13] There was a hill just a little way from the house, and those boys went to the hill and turned to stone, all red. And they said, "If you want to see us you can come here. Only clean (*pilsit*) people can come and see us." And people went to see them often, and there was one fellow that didn't believe, and he dirtied the rocks. When this was done, they left from there and went to a better place, and turned into pines, 7 nice pine trees, and said, "This is the place [if] you want to come and see us."[14]

There were **lots** of people that came and see them, and lay under the shady trees. And so the seven found that they couldn't be trees, and went

up above and turned to be stars. And they said, "You people can always
see us up above. We will watch the frosts. In the spring, when you cannot
see us in the west, there won't be any more frosts. In the fall, you can see
us in the east. So you know that it is getting cold and frosts [will] appear.
We will always be in the skies and never change to another."

The Snow and Ice Boy[15]

Mä Xtcīkâk[c]

In the most complex surviving version of the "turtle's back" origin story, that of the Iroquois, or Haudenosaunee, a young woman becomes pregnant by an unknown father. That element appears here in the story of the Snow spirit. Some have wondered if this is an overlay of Christianity and the story of the virgin birth, but that is highly doubtful: the idea of an unknown father appears in numerous Indigenous tales recorded in Indigenous languages in the sixteenth century, stories that show no influence of Christianity.[16] It seems a profoundly human concern, not a peculiarly Western one.

The Snow spirit of this story is multifaceted, not "good" or "evil" as in Christian lore, but rather a being whose effects are both harmful and helpful, depending on the context. He causes frostbite, but he also makes it possible for hunters to track their game.

In the time when Charles Elkhair's father was a child, the Lenape were observed to make offerings to flows of ice,[17] just as this story describes was done "until recent years." Perhaps, indeed, it was still being done, or at least had been done in Elkhair's memory, for suddenly the storyteller shifts into present tense: "They tell [Snow Boy] they are glad to see him again." Or perhaps that was just the storyteller's way of bringing the moment to life: suddenly turning a past-tense story into a mini-play or skit had long been a common tactic in Indigenous storytelling.[18]

One time long ago, a young girl had a baby boy. No one knew who was his father. They say he had no father. as he grew When he was old enough to crawl around he would get angry at the other children sometimes, and when angry would take yo hold of their hands and suck their fingers. It was seen that their fingers turned black and stiff as if broken from cold when he had sucked them. When he got a little older he told the people that he could stay with ~~them~~ his mother no longer, that he did not belong there—he must go, he said. ~~he had been~~ "My name is Snow and Ice," he said. He sent by those above to show them how to track ~~animals~~ anything, ~~in the snow~~ people or animals, and told them how to do it. "When I come again," he said, "you can track anything. Remember when snow falls, that it is I, come to visit you." Then he told his mother to take him down and put him on a piece of ice to go down the river, for it was early spring. They took him down and put him on a cake of floating ice, and beside him a bark vessel full of sweetened pounded parched corn, [called] "Kâ ha mâ gu^{on}" ~~made of w~~ for they thought he might need food. Then he drifted away down the river.

Until recent years the Delaware would go down ~~if~~ to the river with a little bark vessel of "kâhâmagun" as an offering to the Snow Boy. When a large piece of ice appeared they would give two or three whoops and the ice would swing ~~into~~ in toward the shore. Then they put the ~~box~~ bark on the ice and talk to Snow Boy.

They tell him they are glad to see him again, and tell him to take this corn with him. Then they ask him to help them in tracking game.

When the hunters get back they make a new fire [on the ground],[19] carrying the old ash out the west door opened for this purpose, make a new drum and take four sticks, and paint wash the house anew.[20]

THE GIRL WHO SOUNDS THE THUNDERS[21]

This story contains elements common to many Native tales—a girl who does not want to marry but who at length does, a human who is tricked into marriage to an animal spirit but eventually escapes, and a person who finds themselves living under water. Conjugal relations were often fraught in Indigenous stories, probably because of the long history of warfare (frequently resulting in captive wives) and voluntary inter-marriage between groups (which was often a peacekeeping tactic, not always successful). Marriages, in short, often involved political and cul-tural negotiation, and that reality seems to have made its way into stories.

But this tale also involves a human living in a watery world, a mag-ical plane distinct from the human world, because it becomes the story of the Thunder spirits. These were mentioned to colonists in the eigh-teenth century as powerful bringers of storms.[22] Here we learn that a female spirit lives among them and can roll her skirt to create the thunder that warns human beings of coming storms. This figure, too, was an ancient Indigenous being: Uto-Aztecans spoke of her as "Jade-Green-Skirt."

One time there was a young woman, who was very good looking; but the years passed and she never married. But one time at last a handsome young man, a stranger, began to come around and talk to her; and at last she began to like him, and finally she went away with him. They travelled a long way and until they came to a big lake; here to her surprise the man went down into the water and she had to follow. But once beneath the water it did not bother her at all, it was just like air. Then they travelled on a long ways and finally came to a little house, where there was an old woman. She scolded the young man saying "I told you not to bring her here. She cannot live with us." But the young man insisted and they began to live there. Every morning the young man would start out, and came back in the evening with a deer. This kept on for a long time. But one ~~morning~~ time ~~or perhaps~~ the girl happened to wake up at night and thought she saw a great snake in the home. She got up and ran, but the young man followed her and caught her. "Why did you run away?" he asked. "I saw a big snake in there house," she replied. "No that was not a snake," he told her.—"that was just my clothes." The same thing happened several times and the girl made up her mind to escape. So on her trips after wood she would go as far as possible trying to learn the country, so as she would know how to get away.

One time ~~at last~~ she started soon after the young man had left, and went a long way before she was discovered; but at last she heard a hissing and a noise like a snake coming, and soon the young man appeared. She told him she was just going over to that hill to look around, then she went back.

Next time she tried it again, when she heard the hissing noise of the snake coming she thought of her vision helper, the weasel, and called on him to help her. He ran into the snake's mouth and down into his body and cut out his heart. So the girl got to the shore of the water: and when she came out the Thunders were waiting for her and carried her up into the air. She had never realized that she had been under the water until then. When they took her up they rubbed her, and at every rub little snakes dropped from her back into the water. By and by no more snakes dropped and she was clean and human again.

The Thunders took her back to her home, and she told the people there what had happened. But she said she could not stay with them, but must live with the Thunders. "I will tell you how you can know when I am coming." she said. "When a cloud comes up with a continual rumbling or rolling around, that is the noise made by my skirts."

A Snake Legend [Julius Fouts][23]

This tale contains numerous elements long part of Lenape lore. The number twelve, central in religious ceremonies, had been observed to be important even by William Penn in the seventeenth century.[24] The idea of a dwindling band of brave hunters or warriors appears not only here but in numerous other stories as well. The cottonwood tree was native to almost all the areas the Lenape had ever lived, from New Jersey to Oklahoma. Even the turtle with trees growing on its back makes a cameo appearance. The snake rising from the water might conceivably be an exception: such snakes fill Creek mythology, and in Oklahoma the Lenape lived (and live) in close proximity to the Creeks, but a fascination with serpents seems to be nearly universal, and various species were certainly present in the bog-filled original territories of New Jersey.

Importantly, when Harrington examined the old ceremonial woven bundle he bought from the Delaware—the purchase that later led to his meeting Julius Fouts (see the introduction), he found it contained numerous bits of glimmering mica.[25] He was told these represented the scales of a great serpent. Bringing them forth in ceremonies could help human beings make wishes successfully, as when they wanted to bring rain, for instance. Here Julius Fouts seems to have been telling the story that would explain this tradition.

Twelve men were out hunting in a party one time. Early one morning before sun-up one of them heard a turkey gobbling, and followed the sound toward a small lake near about which some large cottonwoods were growing. Bye and by the others killed a deer and waited for him. But he never came back to the camp. Next morning came they sent another man out to find him, but he heard the turkey gobbling and went that way, never to return. Now by this time the rest of the party felt sure that their comrades had been killed by something nearby. The Delawares had a medicine or power by which they could tell when their friends were dead, so their people knew that the two had perished. Now the brave man who was head of the party thought the turkey gobbling which they heard now and then had something to do with it. So he led the party down to the lake the next morning. They got there just in time to hear the last gobble of the turkey which seemed to be up in a great cottonwood They looked up and saw the head of an enormous snake up among the branches, the body of which ~~dropped~~ hung down the lakeward side of the tree into the water. As they waited it slipped down the side of the tree and into the ~~water~~ lake where it disappeared amongst a great frothing and bubbling of the water Evidently this was the thing that had killed their friends. That night they sang all night, and towards morning a great fish raised itself ~~for~~ in the water, and came toward them. "No, you are not the one we want" they cried and sent it back. So they sang for ~~several~~ a number of nights and "raised" many strange beings, one of which was a huge turtle with trees growing in its back. When the trees raised above the water they [roped?] some of the branches then told it "Go back! you are not the one we want." Finally they raised the great snake, and killed it. Then they ~~killed~~ burned its body, and hunted among the ashes for bits of bone to use as medicine.[26] As each one took a piece he made a wish as to what he was going to use it for.

THE DISAPPEARANCE OF CORN [CHARLES ELKHAIR][27]

On a February day in 1911, Charles Elkhair told this story to an amanuensis, likely one of his daughters, and had it sent to Harrington. It is
very different from all the other stories: indeed, it comes straight out
of southwestern religion, long bound up with corn farming. The Lenape
themselves had been farming corn for long enough to find the tale of
compelling interest. They had probably learned it long ago, during
their stay in Missouri, when they would have come across plenty of
people who were familiar with it and, by the early 1900s, recognized it
as one of their own. In fact, they had made it their own, bringing in
their divine Misingw (see chapter 2) and turning the most holy offering into mother-of-pearl beads made from shells found on the East
Coast, long valued by their culture.

It is probably no accident that this is the one place where Elkhair
recognizes the figure of the Mother as powerful: corn and agriculture
were tied to the female role in society, and in the Southwest goddesses
were central to religious stories. Was it perhaps a member of Elkhair's
female household who had suggested that he add it to Harrington's
collection? We will never know.

Scholars have long noted the resemblance of the Native American
story of the corn maiden to that of Demeter and Persephone in the
classical world; indeed, some of them used to believe that an Indian
had heard that story from a missionary and then adopted it, as happened with the story of Dido. (See the introduction.) But that seems
unlikely in this case. The stories probably developed quite separately.
It is profoundly different for the goddess of the grain to absent herself
from humanity because of grief for a kidnapped child than to absent
herself because humanity has so neglected her. That humans everywhere should want to explain why the earth's ability to grow crops
ceases for several months a year does not seem strange.

2/21, 1911

Corn was said to be a living spirrit. In days of old some young boys, making light of the idea of corn being human-like, said to one another, "Corn could not possibly leave the earth." Then the corn disappeared. Before them was the danger of great famine, staring them in the face, much to their regret. At this time, some person was blessed with a token[28] from the great spirrit, saying unless they could find someone who had the gift or power to communicate with the spirit of corn and coax or humor the corn that it might return, it would cause a continual famine. It was then that corn began to disappear. The heart of corn turned into living beings. It all began disappearing in flight with wings. A man who had communicated with the great spirrit was told by token the cause of the loss of corn and all other vegetables was because the boys or young men had made unnecessary remarks about the corn and its spirrit. Therefore the Misingw or "whole face," being the leading spirrit, was sent with the token to warn the people of the tribe the great wrong the young had committed in their estimation. One man is quoted saying that "corn could not get away from him" and so he filled a great skin bag, and always placed it under his head at night time, when he suddenly realized that his sack had disappeared— went to flight in form of a weavil.

It was a great mystery as to whom could restore Mother Corn They had learned that there was two boys, very poor and needy who lived with scant means to live. Being informed [of] the condition, they were at the great gathering of the people, where they offered their services to restore corn. They possessed the mystic power and spirrit.

At the gathering, the Indians were sitting in a ring, when the boys departed at night time, not leaving any clue as to how. But when the boys reached the great region above, there they made a burnt offering out of mussel shell,[29] sacrificing the shells for the return of corn. Mother Corn said she would return by request of the boys who were sent. They returned and brought the glad tidings, each bringing with them a hand full of corn, and the pledge that corn would never leave again. It is supposed that these boys took flight like the corn.

The corn famine had been in progress one year before the people found by what means they could induce the corn to return and did induce her by the influence of the two boys. Upon coming to the region above, the boys found the spirit of corn was in the image of an aged woman appearing to be a scabby person, indicating that it was because the people had misused her. She said, "When Corn was being oft times parched my children did me this great wrong. There are other ways to handle me, for instance, use tallow or other means to moisten me." It was then they made the burnt offering of the shells. Mother corn refusing to come back to earth at first, they went away in distress, but by the sacrifice with the shells, they brought mother corn. She wanted to partake of the offering, but was refused unless she would promise to return in the required time to earth, to which she finally consented. It was god's will that the spirit of corn abide in the far heavenly region, in image of an aged woman, with dominion over all vegetation. So this tradition comes from our forefathers, said to have happened before the discovery of this continent by the paleface, and centuries beyond, thereby we know that corn was here at the discovery of this continent.

The corn was divided until quantities were again raised, which is still mentioned [spoken of]. We are told that mystic power possessed by the two boys is the means of getting Mother Corn to stay, by the oath to never leave this earth and her children again. She being in image of a woman, it was the custom of the red man to have the woman to care for and culture the corn always, dressing neatly as [if] visiting when they were in the field to work and cultivate corn, [or] in husking the same, always planting [both] flour corn and hominy corn.

Very Respectfully, Charles Elkhair

CHAPTER 2

Big House Stories

For many generations, the Delaware people celebrated the *xingwikaon*[1] or "Big House" religious ceremony every October, with the ceremonies called the *gamwing*. It is not certain when it began, but elements of the ceremony were described by visitors as early as the seventeenth century. In the late eighteenth century, when the Delaware were living in Pennsylvania and Ohio and facing repeated crises, they began to build dedicated wooden meeting houses and to institutionalize a twelve-day rite. They carried the tradition with them wherever they went, and in Oklahoma in the early 1900s Charles Elkhair and Minnie Fouts were perennial leaders of the ceremonies.[2]

The Big House religion referenced a Creator, but ceremonial worship was focused on the Misingw, or Misingwe, the spirit of the game animals, a divine being who moved fleetingly through the woods on the back of a deer. On central posts in the meeting house were hung masks, also called *misingwe*, which were painted half black, half red.[3] Before these masks, the people gave thanks to Misingw for helping them to live, and they in turn promised good behavior themselves and exhorted future generations to keep to the rules and maintain balance in the cosmos. During the day the celebrants hunted and prepared food; in the evenings they sang and danced, telling each other of the visions they had once experienced, thus bringing the spiritual world near. Everyone was encouraged to attend, but only those who had been on vision quests could lead the singing rites. Eventually, there were not enough such people left, and the Oklahoma Delaware "put away" the Big House in 1924, rather than choosing to corrupt the tradition.

The Big House is the one element of Lenape religion that has been well studied by scholars, beginning with the early twentieth-century anthropologists of Mark Harrington's generation. In more recent times, Robert Grumet collected most of the existing accounts of the ceremony, ranging from the 1600s to the 1920s, and published them in one volume. To our knowledge, the only one that he missed is that of Julius Fouts, which is included here.

The Misingw^e [Charles Elkhair][4]

Mising'w'

Charles Elkhair explained the Misingw to Mark Harrington, who put
the story down in his own handwriting, referring to Elkhair in the
third person as "the chief" and amending his notes as Elkhair adjusted
what he wanted to say. Elkhair did not explain the origin of the deer-
riding god of the woodland animals as if he were telling a creation
story. Rather, he explained to Harrington how it was that humans knew
about the god and had a relationship with him. The concept was complex, and Harrington's notes would seem to indicate that he himself did
not fully understand what Elkhair was saying. The related word *mis-
ingholikan* means "manifestation of the misingw" and was generally
used to refer to a person wearing a striking bearskin outfit who made
appearances every year. Back in the eighteenth century, Presbyterian
missionary David Brainerd was horrified to see this figure, but Delaware children through the ages seemed to have been delighted by the
thrill of terror he inspired. What Charles Elkhair seems to have been
trying to say, however, is that adults could also see manifestations of
the Misingw—not just an impersonator—when they were out in the
woods on their own—but only if they were looking hard enough. He
had. Others, apparently, were not sensitive enough to see them.

In the story, Misingw teaches the people to respect the balance
between prayer, farming, and hunting. It is an ancient tale, with the
god of the hunt taking center stage, yet at the same time insisting on
the importance of all aspects of life.

The story of the misingw goes back many years. The chief does not know
how many years ago the M. came. It happened that when the Delawares
were down East there was an earthquake for twelve months' time. The
earthquake came to them because they had no gamwing ("church" worship)

for a long time. At those times they lived in towns. There was a chief [who] had a big bark house in one of the towns, and the people began to meet there at the time of the earthquake, and hold worship there.[5] While they were holding meetings there, they began to build a Big House *Xīng wī ka o*[n]. When it was built they began to pray in that house. They prayed all winter for relief until about May. They heard (The M. making) a noise ho[n] ho[n] ho[n] right east of them. When they heard this the chief said "I wish ~~three fellows~~ somebody would go over there and see what that is."[6]

~~Those~~ Three fellows offered to go because they said they knew what was making the noise and could find out what he wanted, ~~The M. asked~~ They went to him and asked him what he had come for. The misingw told them to tell the others to quit holding meetings and attend to their crops, and not hold another until autumn, and said, "If you quit this Big House now, I will come and live with you when you hold the next meeting in the fall and can help in that big house. You must make just one, and I will put my power in it so that it will [grant] what you ask it. When I come in this form, you must give me hominy[7] every year in the spring when I take care of the deer and other game; that is what I am here for. Whenever you ~~hold~~ make this meeting house I will help [bring] the deer close by, so that you can get them any time." He told them they must never drop this meeting house. "You must keep it forever. If you do not, there will be another trouble, another earthquake." That is how it comes that they keep their meeting house all the time.

When they had a meeting that fall, the misingw came up to the ~~Ind~~ people. They picked out men to go hunting and threw tobacco in the fire and asked the misingw for good luck so that they can kill lots of game. Then they started hunting and expected to have good luck. When they came back they had twelve deer. They were three days hunting their deer. And they found out ~~so~~ that the misingw was telling the truth. That is the reason they [used?][8] him there at that big house. And a certain ~~person~~ family kept the misingw from then on.[9]

Sometimes people ~~would~~ lose[10] their horses—strayed off or somebody gets them. When the owner of the horses misses them, he goes to the place where they keep the misingw and takes some tobacco along. And he tells the keeper of the m. what he came for—to ask the m. to look for my horses. The keeper tells the misingw: "He wants you to look for those horses." The loser-of-horses goes back home, and in two or three days he finds his horses right at home. When the horses are taken away as [they are] staked out or hobbled, the misingw comes and scares the horses so they break their ties.

And the misingw takes care of the children too. Sometimes you see weakly children, or children who do not mind their parents, and they send for the misingw and ask him to take care of the children. When the misingw comes, he scares the ~~weakness~~ laziness or sickness or weakness out of the children. And afterwards the children are well and stout and whatever they are told to do, they do it right now.

When the keeper of the misingw asks him for good luck hunting, it is that way every time. Sometimes when they are holding meeting he goes inside the meeting house, He goes there to find out who does not do right in the house. And if he finds someone who has not done right, the three men who guard the meeting house take that person out, whoever he may be. We know that sometimes people go into the meeting house who don't do it right. It is his business to help the Delawares that much when the meeting is going on. That is why they have him there, going all around the camp.[11]

While the meeting is going on, they eat their deer [right] there. Every night when they break up the meeting, they eat one of the deer and quit for that night. They have their meeting twelve nights. When they quit everybody goes home or in the [house] and the speaker says, "Tell the other people we will come again next year and have the meeting again if we live that long." So everybody knows they will have another next year. And when this misingw leaves us we don't know what we are going to do.

The Chief thinks we can't have no meeting any more. There is no one to help us now.[12] That is all.

———

The way they found there was a mising ha li ku [in pencil: mising^w ha li kan][13] above us was this: They was people at that time treated their children badly, did not take care of them, did not care whether they died or not.[14] Those children boys[15] saw this misingw at that time. Misingw gave them strength to be stout[16] so nothing would hurt them. Misingw told them one boy, "you go with me and I will show you where I am from." So misingw took this boy up and showed him where he is from. This is a place of rocky mountains above us, stuck out from the north and reaching toward the south. The boy came was brought back by the misingw and here was were was the one who knew there was such a thing. This place is quite nearby. But you cannot see it. (The dead do not go there.)[17]

The boy grew up to be a man. When he goes out hunting he can see the m. riding deer around, rounding them up. From that time on several knew that there was a mising hâ lī ga^n around because they saw him. Some people older than the chief never heard about the misingw—but he always knew [of] it.

———

Spring meeting of misingw.
Misingw haŭl'ikä

When the dance comes they give him [the misingw] hominy so they he will be glad spring comes, because the people around are glad that he is there to help, that is why they want to feed him. That is why.

Long ago the Indians did not know the name of the months, all they can say is there is another moon. They have the dance on the full moon.

The keeper[18] gets another man for one yard of wampum to ride around with the misingw [outfit] and tell them. All the Delawares know about the meeting, and another man behind him [the man wearing the regalia] goes to tell them [that it will be now]. They have the dance on a dance ground with log seats, the same ground where the doll dance[19] is held. When the people are gathered and all is ready, the speaker tells the misingw, "Take care of us while we are dancing so that everything goes off smooth." Then they commence dancing. The m. is outside of the ring. When this dance is over he dances by himself at last, 12 changes. It is daylight when they get done. Then everyone eats that hominy, and the misingw eats it, too. When they are done eating the speaker says, "We have eaten with our misingw. We will have this dance again next spring." Then everybody goes home, and they take the m. back home.

(The man puts on the mask out in the bush, and goes back there to take off the clothes. They pay the impersonator a yard of kekir.)[20]

Big House meeting
(posting done in day, meeting is held at night)

When the misingw rides around to the different houses to give notice of the dance, another man follows on another horse to take care of him. The misingw gets off at each house and says hoⁿhoⁿ and makes motions. They give him tobacco which he puts in his sack. They tell the bad, disobedient children they had better behave, or misingw will put them in a sack with a lot of snakes and cast them off!

Vision on the Kansas River [Charles Elkhair][21]

While Charles Elkhair sat and talked with Mark Harrington, he agreed to give a brief rendition of some of the prayers he led at the Big House. He offered a speech or song of thanksgiving, focusing largely on the Creator, which Harrington took notes on and later published.[22] Either Elkhair did not mention his own youthful vision, which was in fact the heart of each person's annual contribution, or else his references to it did not make it through the screens formed first by the interpreter and then by Harrington's own assumptions. Many years later, in the 1930s, when James War Eagle Webber visited Frank Speck at the University of Pennsylvania (see the afterword), he sang the song he had heard Charles Elkhair perform each day of the rites for twelve days, year after year, all through his childhood. He sang in Lenape, and Speck recorded him and transcribed the speech.[23] The two worked together to provide a stilted English translation; fortunately, in the 1970s, linguist R. H. I. Goddard was able to improve the translation while there were still numerous living fluent speakers.

War Eagle showed Speck how Elkhair and the other Big House celebrants not only sang but also danced around the floor, pausing to pray at the different carved masks as they moved. In this text the various elements are braided seamlessly together, just as they always were in life: Elkhair interspersed the story of his youthful vision with prayerful chants throughout the ceremony, at the same time as he led the dancers around the floor, pausing at each of the pillars that held the masks. The text tells us that the masks represented the spirit of the Hunt (Misingw) as well as such other elements as Fire and Water.

In the song, Elkhair never revealed exactly which spirit had appeared to him in his vision. War Eagle told Speck he always thought it was the Panther.[24] But that could easily have been his own imagination. One woman remembered hearing Elkhair's haunting song when she was a child; she recalled that Charley heard an unidentified voice in a great

Wind.[25] Given Elkhair's own comments to Harrington, and his name
and his father's name referencing the Elk, if could have been the Misingw himself.

I must now come to the point of relating my narrative about the Kansas
River when I was a child, when my now deceased father told me, "Now,
for your younger brother, life is ended." He caused me great sorrow, since
I really grieved for my younger brother. For I used to think that later on I
would play with him. Truly it bothered me very much. I did not know what
to do. That is why I began to wander away, and walked along there toward
the edge of the woods. I was unaware that night was beginning to overtake
me, and more and more my thoughts bothered me. I really did not know
what to do. Then, suddenly, I made up my mind to let whatever might
become of me happen. Under a tree I doubled up on the ground. In a short
time I began to feel that my grief had begun to flow out. It seemed as
though I were not asleep, for I thought, "I don't care if I die right here.
I don't have a younger brother now anyway." It was not long before I
heard something land on the ground nearby. I did not realize that I had
apparently gotten up halfway while looking over toward the north.[26]

Pitiful[27] me, I saw nothing although I could hear the Being well. From
right over the ridge I heard him say, "Do not think that you are not cared
for, my friend!" Then he was there walking about! The Being really star-
tled me when I looked over. I saw him stretched out; he seemed to me to
extend from the north[ern horizon]. He was kind of red looking. And he
said, "My friend, pay close attention! Look at me! This is what I do when
I walk about in this place!"[28] Every little while he would start running. The
sound he made was tammmmm, tammmmmm! [*The drums begin.*][29] That
being looked as odd as could be.

When I thought about him, when I looked at him, it was over the edge
of the southern land, where he apparently came to ground. And every
time that being started running, he sounded like, oooooooo oooooooo.

[*The drums pick up speed.*] And he said when he landed there, "This is what I do when I pass by here, bestowing my blessings." [*Here follows a chant.*][30] There in the direction of the north I had heard him. That Being every so often started running. More and more, I was concerned by what that being said. [2nd chant repetition]

Truly thank you, my kindred. I am glad that we have so far had good health and that I can bestow on you all kinds of spiritual blessings, even including all of those grandfathers of ours. And before long we shall shake hands with these drummers, who are lifting up the worship of the Delawares with song. [3rd chant]

More and more clearly could I see that Being. I took him to be over there in the north, where he originated, and he seemed, as I saw him going by, to be of red appearance. [4th chant]

Truly I am utterly inadequate to do it, my kindred, but I shall nevertheless do as well as I can and with all my heart, pitiful me! For that is what I thought when I heard that Being saying, "My friend, look at me carefully. I, too, bring blessings when I come here!" [5th chant]

My kindred, I am glad that I have reached this Fine White Path, our Father's Road. And now we have come here to where our grandfather[31] stands. We used to hear our now-deceased ancestors worship in the proper manner. They said, "This is how many times we dance around the place where our grandfather stands. So let us, too, say so: It will be four times. And then for a while we shall cease talking about that Being. But if only I have good health a little longer, we shall never cease for good talking about that Being. [6th chant]

Truly my kindred we are enjoying good fortune when we are given an abundance of pilsit[32] game animals as our spiritual meal, as a result of which all of us shall become glad when he our Father, the Great Manitou, comes to our aid. But still, we are pitiful people, that is why our pitiful utterances are heard here in our Father's House. [7th chant]

Now, my kindred, we have gone once around our Grandfather, the Misingw. Truly thank you for taking care of us until now and for our being in good health, including these our children. Now greet our grandfather. Twice we shall lift up our appeal, hoooo, hoooo! [8th chant]

And again, my brothers and sisters and also my children, we have danced up to where stands this grandfather of ours. All together there are twelve of our grandfathers, by whom every Manitou alike is represented: Here is our grandfather Fire, and here is our mother Water, and all the food that supports our life. It is enough, my kindred, to make us happy when we are given all the things that are growing. All of that which our Father, the Great Manitou, has provided, which is why it is possible for us to see it.

And that Being appeared to me right there in the south; he appeared to me and he seemed to possess power in all things. [9th chant]

Truly, my kindred, one more time we dance around where our grandfather stands. And this will be the last time when we shall go around. And then will everyone lift the prayer twelve times up to where his worship of the Delaware belongs, to the twelfth level of the sky, where dwells our Father, the Great Manitou. [10th chant]33

Truly thank you, my kindred. Now here we have come, here to where our grandfather stands. Now the time has come for us to offer up our adoration, to lift our prayer ten and two times to where dwells he who owns us, the Great Manitou, our Creator.

Truly thank you, that I shake hands with you, my brothers, my sisters, and these our children. I give thanks that I bless you with all and every kind of spiritual blessing. Truly it oppresses my heart when I see how we are orphans now. Many times we have heard how pitiful our deceased ancestors sounded when they recounted how pitiful were the conditions then. I make myself grieve very much, my kindred, when I see what happened in the past. But nevertheless, still try your utmost. Let us every one be helpful. Maybe if our pitiful plea were heard by the Great Manitou, we would sometime earn something good that he might do for us.

Truly my kindred, I feel utterly unable to give blessings from here where our grandfather stands. And I am truly thankful to greet all those

Manitous, all of them sitting round about and above. And when we remember how our now-deceased ancestors so thoroughly took care of the obligations of this worship, it is very good that we can still perform the ceremony as we used to see our now-deceased ancestors do it. This is enough for this occasion. Thank you.

The Future of the Big House
[Charles Elkhair and Julius Fouts][34]

Early in the nineteenth century in Indiana, shortly before Charles Elkhair's father was born there, a Lenape woman began to preach the Big House religion vehemently, as a prophet. The Moravians called her Beate ("Beatific"); we do not know her Lenape name. Wrote one Moravian, "[The Indians] say that their teaching came directly from the Great Spirit, who had recently appeared to a woman and told her that the Indians must live after their ancient manner, keep the sacrifices, and by no means believe anything else. This teaching makes a great impression on the Indians at the present time. They often resort to the heathen teachers in great numbers for the purpose of hearing the narration of the old woman's foolish fable, in which connection they spend eight days and nights in sacrificing and dancing and drinking. They live in constant fear, because the old woman told them that they would all perish, if they would not live up to the letter in everything that she had said."[35]

Despite constant dislocations and disruptions, some Lenape were able to maintain this sense of the importance of the old prayers and ceremonies performed at the Big House. By the time that Charles Elkhair and Julius Fouts met with Mark Harrington, they had become extremely concerned about the falling numbers of the faithful. Elkhair said he feared his people's death; whether he meant that in a literal or cultural sense it is impossible to say.

As always, when Harrington recorded the comments of Fouts, he seemed to be quoting someone directly, but when he recorded those of Elkhair, he seemed to be transcribing the words of a third party, probably an interpreter. Even so, there is a sense of immediacy when he records, for instance, that the group laughs at one of Charley's jokes.

[comments of Julius Fouts]

Did you ever hear that noise out in the timber in the fall of the year? Hooooo it says. What is it? It is the noise of the wind blowing in the trees. When the Delawares form up in the Big House they raise their hands and cry "Hoooo" to the mesingw. He understands this, for he is the same nature as a tree. They call him grandfather because the trees came into this world before the Indians.

The Big House is going out of use now because only the old people have visions of power to sing. The children of today are raised like the colonists. They are not pilsu (clean, sacred)—those above (O gwe yu^{n}k) do not speak to them anymore.

[comments of Charles Elkhair]

He thinks that the Delaware meeting helps everybody in the world. They pray for good crops and everything good. Even the wild fruit they pray for. Some time ago they quit having this church, about ten years ago. About that time they had high winds and big rains and everybody got scared. And grasshoppers came, but they came in the fall, a little too late to get all the crops (<u>laughter</u>). So they had a council and talked about a Big House again and thought they had better build another before any bad luck comes. So they built the house and commenced holding their ceremonies, and for years went every fall. Then it seemed as if all the troubles stopped. Last year we had no meeting, and he does not expect to have another soon. He thinks we are liable to get one of these storms, or something, maybe dry weather, to dry everything up.

He thinks this because the Delawares owned all of the land in the beginning but it is about all gone now, and Has no power to do anything. God in Heaven when he looks down, he does not see any more Delaware people. Reason he can tell that, is because the meeting house which was given to the Delaware—they cannot follow it now. When chief was a little boy he heard his folks tell that this thing will happen, just the way as is happening now. Because the young people who have been raised the past years do not believe in that. He said we are having good times yet, but we don't know when we will catch it.[36] Anything comes to us—and once begun, we can't stop it—it will be too late. He thinks that even if they have this meeting they cannot do right, even while it is going on. Because they must all pray for good times now, this year, and they can't do anything in the Big House, can't raise it up, because there are a lot of young folks who don't try to do what the speaker tells them. They don't believe in it. He knows that all the people could, if they followed the rules of the meeting house, they could get along fine, not only the Delawares but all the people around. Because when the Delaware prays, he prays for the children as well as himself, for the future time to come. But if anything come to destroy the world, they will be too late, if they think of their Big House then.

That is all.

Delaware Church [Julius Fouts][37]

After Harrington had returned to the East Coast, Julius Fouts decided to write a brief outline of everything that had to happen at the Big House in order for the Lenape to have their religious ("church") experience. We know he wrote the piece himself, for the writing is distinct from that of some of the stories he dictated to someone younger—probably his stepson, Ray Longbone, whom he explicitly mentioned once as taking his dictation—Harrington in his notes says it was from Fouts and implies it was in his hand. In the twenty-one small notebook pages Julius Fouts filled, we find his own style of writing (always a capital T) and his own spelling logic (the word "until" he assumed contained "till"). We can see that this was real labor for him, as he had had very little formal education. He sat down to the task because he wanted the ceremony preserved in his own words, not the words of an anthropologist, as all other accounts were. It is now in the Smithsonian; this is the first time it has been printed.[38]

   This text is a set of instructions more than a story; but toward the end it includes a story that offers an explanation of the Big House ceremony's complexity and length.

Nov 29/ [19]10   1

The First beginning[39] of the Delaware Church was to—is to daub up the holes between The boards in The church building with Mortar. Made of mud in old style way. The attendants[40] during The church was Three men and Three women. Those three men's work was to cut Two Forks to put in Ground, about one Foot in Ground, about ten feet apart Running east and west, a pole over The fork to hang about a 20 gallon kettle on. This pole's to make Hominy in for The people to eat after The meeting is over on each night—For Twelve nights. And They [are] all to cut up about one Cord of wood. This wood [is] Suposed to Do for the

Church, and only Done to make Hominy the First night. They make a
fire drill

2

or a mashine made of wood That has a wheel in the Outter [level] of, and
The main part That turns back and Forth, Which They use in making
Fire, The Fire They use in The church During Those 12 days, and They do not
use no other Fire in the meeting house During This Time of meeting, and
They all Dont allowe This Fire to be used on the outside. In the First beginning of the Church They Call one of The men and one of The women, The
attendants, to build up a fire in The church. That gives a light in The church,
and after, They get the Fire build up, which gives a good light in the church.

3

Then Each one of Those Two attendant, woman and man, Takes [a] Turkey
wing to sweep up The church, and after The church is swept up clean and
good, Fire light[ed], The chief gets up and makes a Speech Telling The people
The Regulation and The Rules of The meeting at The church. And after he
get Through making The Speech, The man That brings The church in, he gets
up and Tells about The gifts he has, while he holds a Turtle Shell[41] in one hand,
and shakes it while he Tells about his gift of Dream during his boyhood.
And sings [mean]while and dances around Those Two Fires in The church.

4

And These Two men That beats on a Deer Skin stuft with dry hay with [a]
flat Hickory stick tied on Top of The Deer Skin—They beat with flat hickory sticks, They beat on This Deer skin—and sing after The leader of The
church, after he sings while he dances. And This Turtle shell is dried and
has little stones in it, which makes a good Rattle when you shake it.

And after The leader gets Through Talking and singing and dancing, he Then passes The Turtle shell to The next person untill it Reaches The one That had a gift of dream During his boy hood. Then he does The same Thing. This gift of Dream They

5

get During Their boy hood, when They parents makes Them leave home and sleep in The woods or out on The prairie for about 3 or 4 days, without anything to Eat, and during This time Some wild animal or wild beast aproach Them and give Them a strong life, or helps Them so They will live Through untill Their parents finds Them To Take Them home. Great many days ago. The people use to abuse Their children,[42] make Them Sleep under the leaf or out of doors apurpose So They might get a Dream or gift or Some kind of Long life. And Those gifted people is The only people That Can Run This church. Of course other people

6

goes in The church to look on Only.[43] After one man get Through Singing and dancing There, They Smoke That wants to Smoke, until another man starts The Turtle Shell going. And when he quits Singing and dancing, Then They all Smoke again, all That wants to Smoke. This Same Thing goes on for .12. Nights and They keep This up untill This Turtle Shell goes around Those two fires and gets back where it starts frome. And Then They Call That one night's church. And 4. Days after The meeting Starts up, Then a gang of young men, Just as many as wants to go out hunting,

7

Goes out on a Deer hunt. And They Suposed to hunt deer for .3.days. At The End of 3 days, when They all come in Frome Their hunt, in [the] Case

[that] Some of The hunters Kill a Deer, just as They Come in Sight of The meeting house, They all Fire They guns. That gives Signal to The people at Meeting house, or The Campers, That The hunters had killed a Deer. And by [or at] the Signal of The guns, Then The drummers Hurry in[to] The Meeting house to Sing and beàt on The drum and Sing a Song That's only used in [the] Case [that] The hunters bring in a deer. Or if The hunters did not Kill no Deer, The hunters Suposed to Come in Quietly, not Firing They Guns.

8

After nine days of meeting, They Build a new Fire, which They use .3. More nights, and at The 12th night, The women has Their Church.[44] Each woman That Takes a hand in The women's church she get a share of the Vennison if They is any, The bigest buck The hunters kill. And They Cut it up, and The attendents of The meeting will cook it at The Fire where They cook Hominy. And next morning The men Takes up The church untill 12- O Clock and They discharge The attendents. [But] before They discharge The attendents, They all Form in a Roz—3. Men and 3. Women. They all hold Six yards

9

of beads where They all Stand in Roz. The first person holds one End of The Beads and The beads string on Their hands Frome one person to The other. The word Thats given Them is This, you attendents of This meeting, we Thank you For your Kindness That you done in Sweeping our Church For The .12. nights and The attention and The Care That you all have given during These Twelve nights of our meeting. [We] have heard our Older parents [say] That if you Sweep This meeting house For .12. Diferent times, That you will sweep up to where our great Father is in Heaven, as he is up in .12. Diferent skys. And

when The shadow of a person is shown near under him, That would be at
.12.o.Clock, Then The Speaker arises on his feet and Says all of us [are]
diferent Relations, and Relations shall now go out and End our meeting,
which is Seen going on For .12. Days. They all Form in a Roe, Running
north and South, and They all pray Six times Kneeling down, and Six
times Standing up, saying

   Hooohooo

and if the hunters Kill any Deer They Take Those Deer Skins with Them
when They go out to pray as above.

11

At The ninth day of the meeting at the begining of The meeting, They distribut 12. Sticks amongst The people in the church. Six of Those stick are
striped and Six [are] white ones not dotted. Those stick are distributed by
The attendents of The meeting, which Requires Two men to do This. One
man begins at Each End of The meeting house—inside—and The Speaker
There tells The singers to beat The drum, while They distribut Those Sticks
and [the] Rest of The people holds up Their hands while Those sticks are
distributed, and all Pray at The Same Time.

12

Those attendents distribut Those sticks in [?], not in Slow walk. During
This Time, in distribuson, if one white stick is not across The meeting or
church Room Frome The other white stick, They will have to pick Them up
again and do This Over. So, after They Distribut Those sticks, when They
pray, They Raze The Stick up Instead of They hand, like Before, and all
Those That has a Turtle Shell will be notyfied to bring Them in [the]

Church, and after They all bring in Those Turtle Shells, Then They put Those all in a Roz- in Front of The

13

head man of the church. And after They do This Then They notyfie The owner of These shells to come and get Them. [But] before They Take back The Turtle Shells, They measure all These Turtle Shells' backs with a String of beads, and They cut These beads off [at the] Length of The Turtle shells back. And when The owner comes and gets The Turtle Shell he Takes The beads and The Turtle Shell back, and he shakes The Turtle Shell as he picks it up, which has a little stone or Rocks in it, which when any one Shakes it, it Ratles. Then The big Laugh comes if The Shell don't Sound good!

14

After This is over, There They Call up 6 men That belongs to diferent bands, 2 of Each band, Turkey band and Turtle band and Wolf band. All of These men has to go out and pray by holding up They left hands Twelve times, and The first man They Call to go out and pray, after he goes back in The church again, he Then is called to Take one yard of The beads That's used in The meeting house in place of money.[45] He is Then Told to Cut Those beads off as many Times as Those men who went out doors to pray, so Each one of Those men can get Share of

15

Those beads for going out to pray. Each bead is valued at one cent. One hundred Beads is Considered one Dollar, and They Call up These men Every night untill The meeting is over, and in The 12th night, Then The women has their church. To begin, before The church starts up in The night, The Speaker First Orders The attendants to burn Cedar

in Those two Fires which all The people Suposed to Inhale. The Smoke of
The Cedar and Kinnickinnick[46] [comes to?] people with This burning
Cedar Smoke, and after This is Over, Then .2. Women is Ordered to get a
paint and Some Greasy Substance to

16

to use. One women holds The paint in a little plate made of bark off a tree,
and The Grease is fitted in Same way, and They Start Frome The door.
[They] Start on The Right hand Side of The Roz of The people in The
church. One women paints all The people in The Church on Their Left
Cheek and The woman That holds [the] grease, She Follows The one [with]
paints. She greases all The people in Church['s] hair on The head, while
The other woman paints The left Cheeks. And inside of This meeting
house, There are faces Cut on The main outer Post, on Each Side.

17

[They] Resemble a human face, which is ½ painted Red and The other ½
painted black, and The two men attendants, [right] Then after Those two
women gets Through painting The people in The church & Greasing Their
hair, They Take The paint and The grease and They paint and Grease Those
wooden faces in The Church, and also Those .12. Sticks are painted and
Greased and all. So The Turtle Shells are Greased and painted and all. So
The Deer Skin Drum is Greased and painted. All These Things are Greased
and Painted,

18

Same as Those people is painted, and Their hair is greased. In painting
and greasing, The painter use Just one finger, and The one using The grease

use Just one finger. And after The Delawares gets all of This Completed
Then They Claim That They have worship Every Thing on This Earth. God
gave to The High authorities above to go around and give all Tribes a
church, which was done, and They come to the Delaware Tribe The last.
So They give The Delawares a biger church Thats why

19

Note at top of page: The speech is that god had their things in a bundle,
and when he got to Dels. he had a lot left in it, so they got it

———

The Delawares have to do so many diferent Things when They all have
church. So They were given a big Church and They have This church Every
Fall of The year

And The attendents Continue Serving meals to The Head one That
Takes up The church, and The Speaker and The Drummers and all of his
near Relatives, [they] Serve The meals inSide The church building. And
The Runer of The church, after They all gets Through Eating Call in The
attendents to come

20

In and get Their dishes and pans. Each attendent has a cup which They
bring coffee in, and The Runer of The Church puts in 25. Beads in Each
cup For Their pay For Every meal. They do The Same Thing Over 3. times
a day for Eight days, and The Speaker gets one yard of These beads for his
Servis Every night untill 12 nights is over. And also The Drumer gets The
Same, one yard of beads Every night For 12. nights.

21

And The Speaker Takes Some Tobaco That grows wild and Throws it in fire
and Talks at The Same time as he Throws The tobaco in The Fire, Then asking
The misingwe to drive all The deer to The hunters, So They Can Kill Them

Truly yours

Julius Fouts

ON TRICKSTER'S BACK

CHAPTER 3

Culture Heroes

All societies tell stories of successful adventurers of their legendary past, and the Lenape were no different. Indeed, such stories were among the longest they told and could seemingly be stretched out to whatever extent the teller wished,[1] just by adding more steps before the resolution of the drama, so they clearly formed a central element of storytelling evenings.

What is remarkable about Native American tales of this type is that they did not favor just one kind of hero. Their protagonists were not all charismatic warriors or thoughtful leaders of men but could equally well be small boys or cussed individualists. They were not all admirable and generous but could be stubborn and demanding, or sometimes even a bit buffoonish. They were devout but could argue with a spirit or god. Sometimes it was just a matter of emphasis: the very same story could be used to evoke laughter or pound home an important lesson, depending on the narrator's emphasis.[2]

What Lenape culture heroes had in common was that they were all ordinary men who were bound and determined to be successful in their chosen goal and found a way to be so. They had to be brave, but they did not have to be buff or brilliant. This was a story world that made room for real people. The roving heroes were always masculine, but within the stories, women, back at the camp, could play important roles and have agency.

Little girls around the hearth would likely have been as riveted as their male companions. In a world in which women had always been powerful, both as deeply knowledgeable plant gatherers and agriculturalists and as the owners of homes, they would have noticed the key roles played by the stories' women.

Ball Player [Julius Fouts][3]

This is a dramatic story that stems from the quintessential ancient Indigenous war experience: a woman is stolen by a terrible enemy, and the people risk all to recover her and then defend themselves. It is the very youngest of a group of brothers who is successful and achieves victory, largely because he does not attempt to go it alone but rather enlists the help of the animal world. The man's other captive wives are also a big help: they have clearly been angry for a long time.

The hero's name is Ball Player. Because he plays ball with a bobcat's head, the story references all at once three major Native American motifs that appear in uncountable stories: a symbolic or sacred ball game that will determine someone's fate, a rolling head in search of something important from life, and a ferocious feline as an alter ego of a warrior. (These felines included not only bobcats but jaguars, panthers, and ocelots as well, depending on the region.)

Julius Fouts dictated this story to his stepson Ray Longbone and mailed the written text to Mark Harrington in 1909.

Once upon a time there was a family. Old Man and Old Lady told the boys, "We ought to go out and camp where there is plenty of game to kill."

So they went. When they came so far, they camped where there was plenty of game, and the boys soon went out to hunt. And the old lady made shelves to put the meat on. There were six of the boys and the youngest one never went hunting. He played with his ball whenever they went out hunting in the morning. The youngest boy would go out with his ball and play all day—sometimes he would go East! His ball was a skull of a bobcat. Whenever he would throw it, it would stick on a tree if it hit. The skull seemed to bite the tree and stick there.

They stayed there a long time and went hunting every day. They had lots of meat and the old lady told her boys, "Never go hunting very far

West." The oldest boy thought, "I will go hunting West." When he traveled far out west, he seen a lake and saw a young lady sitting on top of the water combing her hair. Her hair floated all around her. He just could see her—then she disappeared. He went straight home: he liked her looks very much, he never killed anything that day. When he came home, he thought, "I will try and get that girl tomorrow." But he never told his mother.

When daylight [came] he started off to the West, to where he seen this young girl. When he came close to the lake, he said "Whirlwind, my friend!" And he broke [off] a stem of grass and he went into it, and told Whirlwind, "My friend, I want you to help me get that girl." And when he done this, a wind started to whirl and the whirlwind took the stem of grass to right where the girl was sitting. And he couldn't get hold of but one hair from her head. And he took it home and when he got there, he put it on the back side of the bed.

When he came home his mother told him, "I guess you have seen that girl." The youngest boy kept playing ball. Every time he would hit a tree it would bite it. Next morning the girl came and brought lots of Bread—and he [the oldest son] married her. She was a pretty girl. Her hair was shining green and blue.[4]

She came to the bed and picked up her hair, and put it back on her head.

She told him that she couldn't get married,[5] for a[nother] fellow couldn't leave her alone. The fellow wanted her and [had] told her to watch for him. That man's name was Red-Feather-on-His-Head.

And the boys went hunting again, [with] their brother married. And this youngest boy grew to be bigger every day and would play with his ball and come late in the evenings! The oldest boy told the young boy to play around close to the house and watch his sister-in-law and see that nobody took her away. The youngest boy played with his ball close to the house, and finally he went off and stayed [away] all day. The youngest boy's name was Ball Player.

They got lots of meat and had a-plenty and never wanted anything. And one morning the old folks told the young people that they were tired of

living, and they went out where it was marshy and the old lady sat down
and said, "You can always think of me when you see this." And there stood
a weed instead of the old lady, and the old man sat beside her and he turned
[in]to a weed. And these young people lived there by themselves and
had a-plenty of meat of all kinds.

One morning when the boys went out hunting, the man came—which
is, Red-Feather-on-the-Head—came to the house, and the woman was
alone. The man took the woman, and took her home. The woman pulled
up trees on her way to Red-Feather-on-the-Head's house.

And when they came home from hunting—and it was a long time before
Ball Player came home—the next morning the oldest boy told his brothers,
"I am going to follow the woman." And [he] picked up his Flute and blowed
it and said, "If they kill me, in two days, blood will come out of my flute."

In two days the boys looked at the Flute and they saw blood on it. And
the other [next] older boy said, "I will follow where our brother went."
And he blowed the flute and hung it up and said, "If they kill me, blood
will come out of the flute." In two days they looked at the flute and saw
blood coming out of it.

But Ball Player kept on playing with his ball every day.

So the next older boy said, "I am going to follow our brothers," and
blowed the flute and said, "If they kill me, in two days blood will come
out of the flute."

In two days the boys looked at the flute and saw blood. And the next
older brother said, "I will follow my brothers," and picked up the flute and
blowed it and said, "If they kill me, in two days blood will come out of my
flute." In two days the other three remaining boys looked at the flute and
saw blood on it. But Ball Player kept on playing ball every day.

And [when] he wanted his brothers to let him go, he said, "I can bring
our sister-in-law back." But they told him that he was too little. Next morning, the next to smallest brother took the flute and blowed it and said, "If they
kill me, in two days you will see blood come out of the flute." When he came
to where Red-Feather-on-the-Head lived, Red Feather-on-the-Head

said, "What did you come for?" He said, "I am looking for my brothers
~~and~~ who came over this way, and my sister-in-law.

"Yes, Sir!" said Red-Feather-on-the-Head. He told the women to cook
for the man, who was very tired and hungry. "He must of come from a
long ways." The women went to work cooking. They broke up bear ribs
and cooked it and put it into a dish and gave it to Red-Feather-on-the-
Head. And he started to give it to Him, and he started to take it. Red-
Feather-on-the-Head jerked it back. "You think that I am going to give it to
you?? I am going to give it to my Yahquaha [naked bear].[6] He turned him
[the Yahquaha] loose and fed it to him and said, "Yahquaha, eat this, and
crush this man's skull in when you get through. He has been talking about
your sister-in-law." When he got through, he told the Yahquaha [again]
to kill the raskell, and he went to the man and soon killed him and took
him down to the ditch.

In two days . . . Ball Player looked at the flute and seen blood, and he
went out to a branch where they got water. He whooped and called all of
his friends around him, and he took his father's otter tobacco ~~bag~~ pouch.
When he whooped all of his friends were with him.

And he told the toad [at the water source]: "What can you do to help
me? The toad commenced to breathe, and whenever he would breathe, fire
would come out of his mouth.

Ball Player said, "That is good enough. You can be my pipe."

And then Ball Player took the snake and said, "You shall be my Pipe
Stem. And he took the otter tobacco pouch and shook it and said, "What
can you do to help me?" Then the Otter said, "I can eat on his spinal cord
and break him down." He said, "That is good enough."

Ball Player said to Saung queh [weasel], "What can you do to help me?"
"I can go down his throat and cut his heart off while he is fighting." Ball
Player said, "That is enough."

When he got enough to help him, he went on [up] the hill and made a
fire and made six arrows. And every time he made one, he would throw it
in the fire. And when it would burn to ashes, he would pick the ashes up

and rub them between his hands and throw a good arrow out on the ground. He done the arrows that way ten times each. And [he] took his ball, and when he had everything with him he took the same trail, for he could go by the trees which were pulled up along the road—[the trees] which the woman had pulled up.

When he came to where Red-Feather-on-the-Head lived he walked in, and Red-Feather-on-the-Head asked him "What did you come for?" Ball Player said, "I am looking for my brothers."

Red Feather said "I throwed some ornery little boys out here in the ditch. Maybe they are your brothers. My yahquaha killed them." He said, "Cook for him, women. Maybe he is hungry. He came from a long distance." The women went to work and cooked some bear ribs.

And Ball Player took his pipe out, and [his] tobacco pouch and started to smoke. Whenever he would draw the pipe, it would say, "We will kill him." Red-Feather-on-the-Head said, "Gee, your pipe sounds bad."

Ball Player said, "That is natural for my pipe to sound." And the Saung queh [weasel] come out of Ball Player's pocket and climbed all over him in a second. And Red-Feather-on-the-Head saw it, and he said, "You have a pretty little pet! We'll fight our pets. Mine can crush its head off in a little while."

Ball Player [said], "Alright. My pet never was whipped." And by this time the women had the ribs cooked. He wanted to give Ball Player the dish, but Ball Player said, "I don't want none to eat. I came to hunt my brothers."

So Red-Feather-on-the-Head gave it to the yahquaha and told him when he got through to crush Saung queh's head. "He is talking about your sister-in-law. The women all were glad—because they thought He would kill Red-Feather-on-the-Head.

Red-Feather-on-the-Head[7] was a fellow with one eye and had a red feather which he wore on his head. When Yahquaha got through eating, Red-Feather-on-the-Head told him to crush Saung queh's head. And they went to fighting.

When the yahquaha opened his mouth, the saung queh disappeared and the otter commenced to eat his hind legs off, and broke him down. Every time the otter got a mouthful he would go and puke it out and go after him again, and finally the yahquaha had to sit down to fight. And the little toad got in front of the yahquaha and commenced to throw fire out of his mouth so as to weaken him. And Red-Feather-on-the-Head said, "Take them off. They will kill my pet."

Ball Player said, "No, let them kill one another." In a minute Saung queh came out of his mouth and brought out the heart of Yahquaha, and then Yahquaha fell and [it] killed him. Ball Player told his pets to go after Red-Feather-on-the-Head, and Ball Player throwed his ball at Red-Feather-on-the-Head, and it bit him on the eye that he could see out of. And the ball stuck there, and Red-Feather-on-the-Head could not take it off. He couldn't fight because the ball was in his eye. They killed him in a few minutes.

They cut Red-Feather-on-the-Head's head off. The women were glad that he killed him, but they said, "You haven't killed him yet."

Ball Player went outdoors and built a fire. The women helped all they could—they went out and got wood to build the fire.

Ball Player throwed Red-Feather-on-the-Head and Yahquaha into the fire. They burnt a while, and then Red-Feather-on-the-Head's head popped up and went north, and Saung queh soon brought it back. It popped four times, and Saung queh got it every time. And next time it popped it fell about the edge of the grass. They throwed it back again, into the fire, and then it couldn't pop anymore. The women said, "You have killed him now."

The women all wanted to go with Ball Player, but he wouldn't go with them—only his sister-in-law. And from there they went to where his brothers were lying. He stretched his bow and took one arrow and shot the arrow up in the air and said, "Look out, it might hit you," And when the arrow hit the ground, the oldest one jumped up. And he done the rest the same way. And they all went back home to where they lived and took the sister-in-law with them.

This is the end of this story.

THE BIG FISH [CHARLES ELKHAIR][8]

This story has many classic elements from old Indigenous tales, but in a unique combination. A girl gives birth to an unwanted child by a mysterious father; the underwater spirit world impinges on the mundane earthly world; a pair of brothers resolve to take action; they are ordinary boys, except for their determination and cleverness; they are well rewarded for doing so much on behalf of their people.

One scholar who has studied Delaware politics for many years has analyzed the story as a parable of good governance.[9] At first, by putting the unwanted fish in a little pond, the elders try to distance the community from a problem; after all, it may be something avoidable, and there is no need to worry too soon. However, when it becomes essential that a problem be addressed, the chief calls everyone to a council (both male and female, only children are excluded) and honest deliberations take place, without false bravado. Anyone is welcome to try to resolve the community's issues, and so when two young boys tell their grandmother they think they can help, they are taken seriously. The only caveat is that once they have taken on the task, they must carry it through; the grandmother, who has bravely spoken publicly on their behalf, rather than asking a man to speak for them, is enraged when she thinks they have reneged. But the two do manage to complete the job, and the community rewards them as justice demands.

Charles Elkhair dictated this story to someone younger and gave Harrington the text. A few years later, in 1912, Harrington sent another anthropologist, Truman Michelson, to meet with Elkhair, and he took down another, slightly longer version of the story.[10] In essence, however, Elkhair's later narration was entirely consistent with this one.

There was one time an old lady that had a little grandchild, about 10 years old, and they lived right at the edge of the camp next to the crick [creek], and the little girl played on the crick. And finally the old lady noticed the girl was getting big, and she was surprised and didn't know what was the matter with her. In a certain length of time, the girl got sick, and the old lady watched her every day. And so the girl had[11] this little fish. The old lady picked up the little fish and wondered if this was her great grandchild. And [she] took it [to the] swamp and put it in a horse track which was full of water, and the little fish made lots of flops around there. And that evening she went back to see about the little fish, and she saw the little fish was getting big, and the horse track was larger, and it was still playing in it. And next morning she went back and seen nothing but a Great Lake, and when the lake got big, the little girl would play around its edge and wouldn't be bothered. And whenever any one would go that way, they won't be heard of anymore. And they decided that it was the fish that was killing all of the people. And the chief called a council and tried to find someone to kill the fish. There were lots of people [who] said that they couldn't kill the fish. The council went on for 2 or 3 days, but nobody would say that he could kill the fish.

There lived on the edge of the camp an old Indian woman with her two grandchildren, which were boys, for that is the way [of] the Indians' camps—The poor class of people camped at the edge of the camps. And the old lady attended the council every day, and finally the largest boy asked his grandmother where she was going every day, and she picked up the stick used for [a] poker and hit the boy on the head, and said, "What is the use of you boys to know where I go every day? You couldn't do anything. There is a big fish in the lake killing everybody, and you boys couldn't kill him." And the boy spoke up. "We *can* kill that fish. We know who he is."[12]

And next morning the old lady went back to the council and told the chief that her grandchildren would kill the fish. And the chief told [a] servant to go and get the boys, and he brought them to the chief, and the chief told the boys, "You boys said that you can kill the fish." The boys said "Yes, we can." And everybody gave wampum for a purse to kill the fish.

And the chief said, "If you boys kill that fish, I will give you all of this wampum." And the boys went home, and also the old lady. And that night the boys went to bed early and the old lady thought she seen them go to sleep. And she thought that they were in fun about killing the fish. The boys were just waiting for the old lady to go to sleep, so she wouldn't see them go away. And they started and went as fast as thought and got to the edge of the sea. And they turned [in]to two birds[13] that fly fast and went to the sun. When they got there, the sun asked "What did you come for?" They said, "We came after your fire." The sun said, "You can't take my fire. You would burn the earth up. But you can take my ashes and use it for anything." And they took a little of it and went back in a short time.

And when they came [back] they went to kill the fish. And they found that the fish was powerful and could go up in the air and under the ground, so they had to get one [of them] under the ground and the other in the air above the lake. And one turned to a butterfly and the other to a sun. The butterfly got underground and put [ashes] in the pond, while the other poured ashes from the top, and the lake got to boiling.[14] And finally all went dry, and before next morning, they went home to bed. And next morning the old lady woke up and seen [them] still asleep, and she threw the cover off of the boys and said, "You boys told a story about killing that fish. Here you are asleep!" And they told her to look over and see if she could see any lake. And she looked and couldn't see nothing but ashes, with that big fish laying in the middle. And everyone went over and seen the fish, and they gave the boys the wampum.

The boys [once] had to parch corn and eat it by the fire. And now they lived good and had plenty.

Wehixamukes (Strong Man) [Charles Elkhair][15]

Wehixamukes (also called "Strong Man" and other names) has been referred to as the Delaware Sampson, but he is much more than a giant of a man who doesn't know his own strength. He is also a being who does untold damage unless one speaks to him with extraordinary clarity, as he does not share other people's assumptions and has not noticed social norms. Aficionados of children's literature will think of the original Amelia Bedelia character in Peggy Parish's books of the early 1960s.

Stories of Wehixamukes have long been a Delaware specialty. The first attestation of one comes from the Ohio Territory in the early 1800s.[16] Richard Adams told stories of such a character,[17] and Charles Elkhair regaled both Mark Harrington and later another visiting anthropologist, Truman Michelson. In the 1960s, a noted Delaware storyteller loved to pursue these narratives, though by then she called the main character "Crazy Jack."[18] In short, generations of Delawares have been torn between laughter and admiration as they have listened to stories of their Wehixamukes.

This beloved story, like "Ball Player" and "Big Fish," was carefully set down by an amanuensis and sent to Harrington. The handwriting would indicate that it was Fouts's stepson Ray who took the dictation.

This fellow when young was known as a very worthless and good-for-nothing boy, and he would sleep late every morning and wouldn't go anywhere, but stay around the camp with the women. And once the people said that they were going to hunt for scalps, and he wanted to go along. And most of the people laughed at him for they knew he wasn't any good, but they let him go, and whenever they camped any place, they would leave him there, still asleep. And they would not let anyone wake him up. And whenever he would wake up he would catch up with the rest. And one evening the head brave said that "tomorrow we will see some men to fight with." And that morning, this Strong Man got up early and went with the men, and never slept late anymore.

They walked up on the prairie where the grass was tall, and there they seen some other Indians to a distance. And the chief said, "There are too many of them. Let's hide from them. They won't come right this way anyway." And so they hid, and the people passed by and this Strong Man couldn't stand it any longer. And he got up out of the grass and said, "Here we are," and pointed to his breast, and so all of the Indians got up and they told him "now you better throw all of them down because you hallooed at them." So he ran after them and threw them down on the ground. And his people asked him why he did that. He said, "You asked me to throw them down. Well, they told him, "We mean kill them." Well, he took his hatchet out of his belt and said, "Why didn't you tell me that before?" and started to kill them. And this Strong Man killed all of the men but one. And he cut off the ears and the noses and split the hands in between the fingers, and they sent him [the one survivor] home and told him to bring some more people, for he [Strong Man] would be there when they came.

And they went on that evening and camped, and the head Brave said, "We will stay here all day tomorrow and try to kill a Bear to eat for we are getting hungry." And next morning the Brave said, "Now we will go out and try to kill a bear, and if anybody finds a hollow tree, to halloo or whoop and we can get together, and sure there will be a bear in it." And they started out next morning and when they got a little ways, somebody whooped and they went over and seen this Strong Man standing beside a big stem of grass, and he was looking at a hole in the grass, and they told him that was not what they meant. "We mean a big tree." The Strong Man said, "Why didn't you tell me before?" and they started on a little further.

And they heard someone whoop again, and when they got there, he'd found a big tree and the head Brave said, "Now who can climb up there and drive the bear out?" The Strong Man said, "I can." And he climbed into the hole and drove the bear out. And the Bear was killed and they went back to camp. And that day there was one man that had a bucket, and he fried some [bear] grease and took a bark of an Elm tree and made a bucket and whenever he would get lots of grease in the bucket he would Pour it into the bark bucket, and that evening the head Brave said, "Tomorrow we will hunt for Turkey, for it would be good to duck [or dunk] it in the grease." And Strong Man said, "Alright."

And next morning they started out to hunt for turkey and he had not gone very far until he caught a turkey alive and took it to carry to camp. And the Strong Man was there alone and he went to ducking the turkey into the grease until the turkey was nearly dead, and when one of the hunters came back, he saw Strong Man running around one side of the bucket and another, and catching the turkey and ducking it in the grease. And when the hunter came close, the Strong Man said, "Will you duck this turkey a while in this grease? I am getting tired." And the hunter said, "That is not what they mean. They mean to kill the turkey and cook it and when done, eat it and dip the cooked piece in the grease." "Eat it!" The Strong Man said, "Why didn't you all tell me before? I would have had that turkey cooked." They went home from there and when they got home, the head Brave said, "Always say what you mean to this Strong Man. He must be a great man."

[another time]

On their way home, the head Brave said, "We are close to home and now we will hunt and kill the first thing that you see." And they all answered, "And next, everybody can go home." So Strong Man went on and seen one of his men—and ran after him and killed him. And he went on further and seen another one of his men and he killed him. When he got home he said, "I got two men."

And afterwards, he always went by himself anyplace [at all]. They wouldn't say anything to him!

CHAPTER 4

Humans Learning Lessons

In the world that the Lenape lived in and that they wanted to help their young people understand, people made mistakes. They sometimes behaved selfishly or carelessly or arrogantly and thus needed to be taught a lesson. Stories could do this. Sometimes the characters' parents or families taught them what they needed to know, but spiritual beings could also take on this task.

In the Lenape people's ancient hunting culture, it was most often the spirits of the animals whom humans interacted with and learned from. In one story, as we shall see, it was the Bears who were the leading characters. This was the case even though there were no bears in early twentieth-century Oklahoma, nor had there been in late nineteenth-century Kansas. The Bear figure descended from the Lenape people's time in the Northeast, probably extending back to the epoch when they were a part of what scholars have called the "circumpolar culture" that once existed in both the Old World and the New.[1]

Other tribal groups with whom the Lenape had interacted—including the Iroquoians as well as numerous western tribes—believed that Little People sometimes taught humans the lessons they required.[2] Like the leprechauns, gnomes, fairies, and gremlins found in European cultures, these tiny people could interfere in humans' lives in disconcerting, even frightening ways. Just when Mark Harrington was ready to conclude that the Lenape had not had any dealings with them, even after their contact with other tribes, Julius Fouts suddenly told him a highly relevant story, as we will see.

Rock-Shut-Up [Charles Elkhair][3]

This is a story of a human who treated animals abominably, first because of his own fear, and then because of his egotism. The Bears saw to it that he was gravely punished. Charles Elkhair clearly loved this story. Someone—whether Charles or another—started to tell it to Harrington briefly, and then they decided Charley would begin again and offer the tale in a full and rich form. That day, they got through the first part. Harrington's notes show that they continued on another day with a sort of sequel. Then they ran out of paper. The notebook Harrington had purchased at Osage Drug & Jewelry in Pawhuska, Oklahoma, had no more sheets. Unwilling to stop, the narrator continued, and Harrington finished on the inside covers of the notebook. At the very end, someone in the room said that there was another story about Rock-Shut-Up—but that one they left for another day, and they apparently never returned to it.

It is notable that a very similar story comes out of Crow culture: There, a toddler rolls off a travois and is lost, but he does not die, for the Little People raise him. Just as in the Lenape version, trouble ensues when the boy grows up and returns to live with humans again.[4] Elkhair, however, if he had been exposed to the story through a western tribe, had not absorbed the story as being about the intervention of the Little People; in his telling it was all about the Bears. When he told the story to Delaware listeners, he spoke so feelingly of the distress of the boy who thought he would die out in the woods that in later years one of his hearers blurred the story in her memory with his narration of his vision on the Kansas River, when he thought he himself would perish.[5]

[There is a] story of a boy who was shut up in a hole by his aunt & uncle just because the woman hated him.

He was saved by a bear that moved away the rock from the hole. Took him to a she-bear who raised him with her children. The boy thought that they were his family. He lived with them and grew to a good sized boy.

In the fall of every year all the bears would go pecan-hunting. . . . [6]

[Starting again, this time in a notebook]

One time long ago there was a fellow going out hunting with his wife and one little boy, his nephew. After [they] got a ways, the woman does not like this boy, it was not hers nor her man's, all it is, is his nephew. When they eat, they give the boy the skimmings from the soup and nothing else. After a while the woman hated the boy, and finally the man took the boy away from the camp to where there was a hole in the ground—not far from where they camped. He told the boy (a little bit of a boy) "You go into that hole as far as you can go into the ground." So the boy went in there and this man picked up the biggest rock he could carry and set it upon the hole so the boy can't get out. And he went back to the camp and left the boy there. Not very long after that, the animals found there was a boy shut up in that hole. The buffalo tried to push that rock to one side so that the boy can get out, but he can't move the rock. Bear came along and told Buffalo "I can take that rock away with using just one hand." So the bear threw the rock away from that hole. The boy in there was pretty near starved. Buffalo told the bear, "You are the only one who can take care of him and raise him up." Bear took the boy ~~into~~ to a she-bear who had young ones. The boy thought they were children and never knew the difference, where they lived in a hollow tree. The boy never knew any difference, he thought they were his folks sure enough. In the fall of the year all these bears went out pecan-hunting and while they were picking them up there would be a lot of old ones in a bunch. They heard some hounds and someone whooping following the dogs. &, the bears ran every one towards their home, and this human boy and a girl bear and a boy bear ran to their tree and ran into the hole. The mother bear had told the kids they were his brother and sister. There they lived.

Finally the boy was full good size. One time when they were running into their house they saw a little light at the door. And this mother bear went up and licked that light off, and went back to her bed again. She looked up again and there is that little light again at the door. She went up and licked it off again and told the young ones "they will not find us now." In the fall, again they went out pecan hunting. The bear-brother says, "Let's play a trick on these old fellows. When they have a lot of pecans let's go way off from the crowd." They did this and the bear said "I'll bark like a dog and you can whoop." So they did that. All the bears who had been pecan-hunting ran to their holes where they lived and the boys went back to the place where they had been gathering the pecans. When they got there they found big piles of pecans which the big bears had gathered. They took all they could carry up to where they lived, and when they got there the mother asked them, "Did you hear those dogs barking?" They boys said yes—"We did that to get the pecans these old bears grandpas had gathered and give them a scare." She said "You go and tell those grandpas that you did it, so they can get their pecans, and take these back where you got them." The boys did that and finally got out pecan hunting again, and they got all they wanted and went to where they lived.

When they got home the old mother saw the light again on the door. She went and licked it off and went back to bed, but when she looked up again there was another light, which she jumped up, and licked off. She did that from morning until noon. She told the young ones "They will kill us now. I can't put that light off that door. She said the man who was to find them wore owl feathers on his head. So she told the boy yo "When they call us come out, I want you to get out first. Take your little bow and arrow and stick that out with your hand first, so they won't kill us. If you don't do that they'll sure kill us. That afternoon that man came up there and knocked on that tree and said "There are bears in there." So he made a whoop so they the people began coming from every direction. He said "There are two or three bears in here," and they got up there and told them to get out. The mother bear told the boy "Now go out, so they won't kill us, you go first." ~~So~~ But nobody went to get out, and they heard them say outside they are going to build a fire and throw some down that hole and the mother bear told the boy "Get out!. They will throw fire in here. Hold your bow and arrow first." But he could not go. So they threw fire in there, and the mother bear got out but she said "they will sure kill me." Then she got out and they shot and killed her. The other boy bear got out, for they said there were more in there and they shot him. Then there were only the sister bear and the boy. She said "I am not going out, They can burn us up in here but I am not going." So they threw more fire in and then sister bear put it out, but she said "I am not going to put it out any more. You must go now." And the boy got out. He took his bow and arrow and stuck them out the hole first before he came himself.

When he got out they told him to get off the tree which he did. They told him "We never would have killed the others if you came out first." They asked him if there was another in there. He said "yes" my sister is back in there. So they called his sister. She got out and they made her get off the tree. Before she did so one fellow got tobacco and tied it on this young bear's neck. They talked to her, and told her that we would never have killed your mother if the boy had got out first. And they took the boy [back] with them where he used to live. When they got home he knew his uncle's name. He now had the power to kill any game for he knew where they stayed.[7]

When he grew up to be a man, he goes out hunting. He knows where the bears staid. When he finds them he abuses them—breaks their hives lets the bees go, and some[times] he broke their backs. <u>Finally</u> the bears had a council by themselves.

They said, "Asunkepon[8] does not treat us right altho we gave him strength to find us and know where we are all the time." ~~So They bears appoints~~ A little bear ~~said~~ spoke up "I can get him up here, but he won't follow me because I got a little foot. So ~~the~~ another old one spoke up said, "I will let you have my shoes to wear." So she put these big shoes on and went up close to the camp and walked around so people could see its tracks The woman going out getting wood saw this track, and she went back and told the man that she had seen a right fresh bear track, and so the man said "I can get that bear. I don't know why he is monkeying around here. I am going to kill him."

So he followed the tracks. This was done in the forenoon. He ran east to finally catch up with the bear. In the afternoon when he had looked at the track he noticed there was little small tracks. He got so mad, he said, "good." He goes faster trying to catch up, and jumped across a hollow & finaly he saw him sunning and told himself, "I'm going to get you." Finally the bear threw himself down and rolled around, "oh oh oh!" The bears were sitting around, and this little one was in the center. So the man was still chasing after this little bear. When he got there, there were bears all around him. One of them told him to sit down. "I want to tell you something." So they told him, "You have been abusing us for a long time, have broken bear jaws and bashed and hit them when alone. We will stop this right now. We never thought you would do that, when we raised you." One (named Ni-ya-gwe-hon)[9] got up and stepped up to him and got him on the shoulder and snapped his shoulder off, and then got ahold of the other shoulder and snapped it off, too, and got the other leg and snapped that off too, and got the other one and did the same. He was lying there alive with no legs and no arms, but alive. Then they put the arms and legs back on again, and the bears told him "Go home now and tell what we did to you."

So he went home from there. When he got home he got a man to call the people together he wanted to talk to them. The people came to hear him. When they got there, he told them how it was. He told them "These bears killed me because I abused them." After he told them his arms drop off and his legs and he was lying there with no arms or legs. There was some leaves of grass on his shoulder when they had sewed the arms on him.

That is all.

There was another boy raised by bears, too. . . .

Little Masks [Julius Fouts][10]

Julius Fouts told Mark Harrington a story about a friend of his who had passed away years before. The story concerns the loss of a small, precious mask honoring the Misingw. It also alludes to Julius himself having sold a similar mask to the Heye Foundation, which Harrington represented. On some level, Fouts conveyed to Harrington the pain of such alienations, for Harrington later wrote a story in which one of the characters sobs over such sales.[11]

We are not explicitly told who made sure that Julius's friend would be reunited with his necklace, but we do know that it was alive with the spirit of the Misingw. We can draw our own conclusions.

Po-ki-te-he-mun (Breaker),[12] George Wilson, now dead, used to carry three little masks on a string around his neck, sometimes they carried two, oftener one. (Julius carried the one he sold to us[13] for years to give him good luck. This his wife made for him a long time ago.)

Po-ki-te-he-mun used to tell that when he was a boy, he carved three little misingwe (masks) and wore them on a string until early manhood. At this time, he was swimming in a river and lost them from his neck. He felt very bad about it. But that night he dreamed just where they were in the water, then he waked up and remembered [the dream]. Then he went to sleep again. But this time when he woke he forgot the dream. That day down at the river he felt a desire to swim, and stooping down to the water, he recognized the place of his dream, and sure enough, there were the little misingwe. "You can't lose them," said Pokitehemun.

He Is Everywhere (Wē ma tī gŭnīs) [Julius Fouts][14]

**Julius Fouts told another very personal story about a human being who
needed to learn a lesson. This time, Julius was very explicit about which
being was interfering in human life: one of the "little people." In his
view, however, the little people were not entirely independent beings,
as they were in the lore of certain other tribes, like the Crow. Instead,
they were tiny beings who helped the Misingw. It was no accident that
what is recounted below happened to a man when he was out hunting.**

(The small people: They take care of game with Misingw and drive the deer
away.)

Some fellows were going out hunting and one happened to kill a deer.
The others were around but he did not know how far. He skinned it and
packed it on his back, then went on looking for these fellows. After a while
he whooped to call them, and they answered him, seemed like close. He
ran all the time and got across the hollow, but saw nobody, then whooped
again. And so it kept on, the other fellow answering just across the hollow. He threw the deer down and chased the fellow who was answering.

It was a "little fellow" who carried a box with the bark on and he knew
him [that is, knew he was one of the little fellows]. "We'll have a fight right
here," he said. "You were answering me while I thought it was the other
fellows [in my group]!" So the little one said, "All right we'll fight, but wait
while I pull off my ~~clothes~~ coat." When he pulled off his coat the other was
ready to fight. The little one said, "Wait until I pull off the other one." He
pulled off twelve coats this way until he was right small. Then other did
not want to fight him, so small. "But I will give you a name," [he] said.
"You get home, you tell your folks someone give you a [new] name: your
name will be "Answer me!," "NaXko'mīn."[15] This little one said: "I wanted
to see how strong you were,[16] that is why I did that way to you."

The man was Julius' mother's father.

Figure 1. Minnie Young, Charley Elkhair's first wife (NMAI Archive Center, Smithsonian)

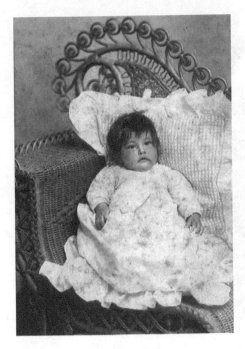

Figure 2. Minnie's and Charley's son, Jesse Elkhair, as a baby (Archive of the Delaware Tribe of Indians)

Figure 3. Julius Fouts (NMAI)

Figure 4. Julius Fouts with a
fire-starter (NMAI)

Figure 5. Minnie Fouts wearing ceremonial headdress (NMAI)

Figure 6. Minnie Fouts with her niece, Fannie (NMAI)

Figure 7. Charles Elkhair (NMAI)

Figure 8. Susan Elkhair (NMAI)

Figure 9. Susan Elkhair posing in traditional clothing (NMAI)

Figure 10. Charley's daughter Sallie Elkhair as a student (Archive of the Delaware Tribe of Indians)

Figure 11. Sallie Elkhair and her sister, Rosa (Archive of the Delaware Tribe of Indians)

Figure 12. Sallie Elkhair camping in her middle years (Archive of the Delaware Tribe of Indians)

Figure 13. The Caney River in Copan, near the Elkhair and Fouts farms (photo by authors)

Figure 14. The Big House ca. 1910 (NMAI)

Figure 15. Susan Elkhair's grave (photo by authors)

Figure 16. Rosa Coffey with her great-granddaughter (Archive of the Delaware Tribe of Indians)

Figure 17. Pat Donnell with her daughter (Sandy Thompkins private collection)

Figure 18. Delaware Tribe of Indians government offices in Bartlesville, Oklahoma (photo by authors)

Figure 19. A modern Delaware woman in traditional clothing (courtesy Nicky Michael)

CHAPTER 5

Talking to the Dead

In the most complex surviving version of the story of the woman who fell from the sky onto the back of the turtle, the universe begins without the existence of death.[1] Eventually, one of the beings who lived in the sky became ill, and none could restore him. From then on, the beings knew death. It brought them great pain, but the fact that life was short also made it possible for them to live to the fullest—to show heroism and value moments of joy. Most Native American religions spent little time theorizing about the afterlife; instead, they helped people to devote their energies to appreciating life on earth. They recognized death as a part of the cycle of life rather than focusing on it as a center of spiritual existence. In this regard, the Lenape were no different from other Indigenous Americans.[2]

In the Lenape world, as the stories show, there was no return from death to life. Yet the dead could sometimes communicate with those living people who still remembered them. They could do this indirectly, by causing them harm (perhaps keeping the game away or making them ill) if issues from life were left unresolved. Or sometimes they might simply visit a particular person in a vision, in the same way that an animal spirit could—and from then on that person would sometimes be able to talk to the dead.

Perhaps what is most striking from the Lenape tales on the theme of death that Mark Harrington collected is that women seem to have been the keepers of the tradition. Three of the four stories were definitely told by women, and the fourth is unattributed but is about a female figure. At first glance, women's centrality in this realm is not obvious, as men were the ones who led the prayers and ceremonies at funerals. Charles Elkhair was known for his skill in this regard, for instance.[3] Indeed, most of the Lenape people's ceremonial life involved communing with people of the past in the sense of revivifying their ancient knowledge, and men led such ceremonies. But providing food for the dead was a key element of honoring them, of letting them know they were remembered, and women were always charged with this task, one that was both thought-provoking and memory-stirring for all who were involved. Many of the most important traditional Lenape funeral rites that are still followed by some families in the early twenty-first century[4] were also observed by David Zeisberger in the late eighteenth. But Zeisberger was blind to the importance of food. He said only, "After the ceremonies described above had been completed, and all had partaken of a feast, the exercises for the day were at an end."[5] No one reading the stories that follow could make Zeisberger's mistake of minimizing the importance of feasting in communicating with loved ones who have been lost.[6]

Whether it was because they were charged with feeding the dead, or connected the act of giving birth to the act of laying out, or simply had strong desires to talk to the people they had loved, Delaware women in the early twentieth century seem to have been the primary keepers of stories about communicating with the dead. These were not frightening "ghost stories" in our modern sense of the word. Rather, they were full of affection.

First Cause of the Feast for the Dead [Minnie Fouts][7]

Minnie Fouts told the story of the "first cause," or origin, of the tradition of the feast for the dead. Knowingly or not, she hearkened back to the ancient creation story of the Woman who Fell from the Sky, and the first appearance of death among the beings who inhabited the universe. In her telling, a key feature that made it possible for the new mortal to accept death was the knowledge that those who loved him would remember him as they enjoyed the blessings of food (implicitly, of life itself). She then moved into the more recent past and reversed the perspective, speaking of a young boy who loved another person so much that he wished to die when his friend died. He had to learn the hard way that it was his duty to live life to the fullest until it was his turn to go.[8]

Judging from the handwriting, Minnie Fouts seems to have dictated this story to the same person who acted as scribe for her husband— most likely her son Ray.

It was told by the old people of my tribe that the first-born in this world never knew that anyone died, and one time there was a certain man [who] got sick, and so they doctored him and tried to get him well, but they failed in everything they knew. He was so sick that he would not breathe for

=2=

long times at a time. The last time he lost his breath in the morning and never regained it until in the evening. There were a lot of people around him all the time, because they never seen anyone die before. When this man came to, he told them that he knew now that people had to die at a certain time, which was fixed by god.

=3=

"The only reason that I don't want to die is I won't get to eat any more—and I know now how you people can do to feed me after I die. You people feed someone and say, 'I will give you this food in remembrance of my relative who has died.'" He says, "Now I am willing to die if you people

=4=

will do for me that way. And also do this for everyone that dies from now until eternity, And now when I die bury me in the ground and put bark around me when you put me in the ground, and put my head toward the east." And this man died and they done him that way, and now the Delaware

[*marginal note* the bark forms a coffin][9]

=5=

People still believe in that way of burying the dead. So they quit burying in that way at a certain time. They quit for about 5 or 6 hundred years—Finally there was two boys that liked one another. One of the boys got sick, and so the other boy stayed with him and wouldn't leave him and felt sorry

=6=

for him every day. And finally the sick boy died, and they buried him. And when the other boy went to the burial, he had fine clothes on when he got there. They were digging a grave. He says, "I want you to dig a large grave. I have been with my friend a long time before he died, and now I want to be put with him

=7=

in this grave. I want to go with him. And his relatives told him there was
no use in doing that. "It would look too bad to bury you alive, and we do
not live here long anyway. What is the use to hurry?" The boy said, "I think
too much of my friend." And when they put his friend in the grave, he laid
down beside him.

=8=

And so they put dirt over them and commenced to bury him. And so he
staid in there a long time and when he came out of the grave, he said, "I
couldn't go with him because I couldn't die. He would bring me food to
eat when I was in there. He said to me that I couldn't go with him because
I was still alive."

=9=

"You better get out of here and go where your relatives are, and you tell
them what I told you. Tell them when you get there I wish my relatives
would feed me in form of a feast. You tell them how to have a feast. Feed
someone in remembrance of me." When this boy left the grave for his relatives, they couldn't get

=10=

near him. Only a few [could]—for his face and meat [flesh] was moulded
[rotted]. He told them of the story which commands them to still believe
in feasts. That's what I have heard long ago.

Talking to the Dead [Susan Elkhair][10]

Susan Elkhair's story about death shares some important elements
with that of Minnie Fouts. She, too, begins with some background—
in this case, an explanation of the fact that a young man's coming-of-
age vision could consist of an encounter with the dead—before moving
on to a set of events said to have happened more recently. Her story,
like Minnie's, also revolves around the love and abiding friendship
between two young men who could hardly bear to be separated by
death. This common element was not a coincidence: the Lenape had
long made it a cultural practice to encourage such connections. David
Zeisberger wrote of observing such friendships; when one of such a pair
died, it was the survivor's greatest wish to avenge him, just as in this
story.[11]

Mrs. Elkhair, as Mark Harrington called her, told her story to the
anthropologist, presumably through a translator. The exact phrasing
has every mark of being Harrington's, but not the content: that was
undoubtedly hers.

Some people were helped by the spirits of the dead while they were children,
in the same way that some were helped by different animals.

One old man named Secondine[12] was one day [as a child] driven
out by his parents into the woods, in the hope that he would receive a
helper.[13]

He found refuge in a hollow tree, and made this his home. Before
long, he was visited by the spirits of the dead, who talked to him, and
brought him food taken by them at night from the houses of the living, in
which way the departed are accustomed to get their food.

The ghosts finally told the parents where their son was, and they came
and got him.

People with this sort of helper were able to talk to the dead.

A story is told of two Delawares who were bosom friends and companions. One time they went to town and got drunk and coming home, lay down beside the road and slept. One of them woke and discovered that it was morning, and that he was sober. But when he tried to rouse his comrade, he found that he was dead, that someone had killed him.

The survivor felt very badly, not only because his friend was dead, but because he did not know who had killed him. He thought he might have done it himself when he was drunk and did not know what he was doing. But he promised himself that he would find out who did it. If it was himself, he did not want to live anyway.

Then he went to the nearest house and told them the man had been killed, and that he might have done it, but that he would not have done it if he had known anything about it.

He then inquired for someone who could talk to the dead, and found an old man who had this power. He then told this man about it, and asked him to talk to the dead man. He did so, and reported that the dead man had said that a third party whom he named had killed him, and that the tomahawk with which the killing was done, still lay under the head of the murderer's bed, with the dead man's blood and hair still upon it.

So they went to the house designated and found the man and the tomahawk, as he had stated. So they took the murderer out and killed him; but before he died he confessed to what he had done.

LOST BOY [CHARLES ELKHAIR'S DAUGHTER?][14]

A young woman in Charles Elkhair's house recorded this story on February 21, 1911. It was the same day as she wrote down the narration titled "The Disappearance of Corn." We cannot be sure who the person was, but the handwriting is in a style often found among young women in that era and the phrasing reveals a typical elementary education combined with knowledge of popular magazines. (The writer uses words like "clairvoyant," for instance.) Hence the person was almost certainly one of the family's daughters—Rosa or Sallie, who had been to Chilocco. The amanuensis attributed "The Disappearance of Corn" to Charles Elkhair with a dramatic flourish. For this story, on the other hand, she gave no author. It may have been her own work, or it may have come from Susan Elkhair; in either case it would have been thought that no attribution was necessary.[15]

The story reaches deeply into Lenape lore—at one point alluding to an elder who had communicated with the dead in his vision quest, and at another point calling to mind the story of the Girl Who Sounds the Thunders and other narrations about marriages to water beings. Apparently, the years at boarding school had not succeeded in cutting the young writer off from these traditions. There are Westernized insertions—like the use of the terms "clairvoyant" and "mermaid"— but at root the story comes from a Lenape imagination.

2/21 011

There was once upon a time when three boys, in crossing a large stream [illegible—got swept away?]. The stream was normally shallow. But when they entered a great wave of water came washing speedily down the river. The boys seeing their possible danger, they hurried. But one of the number was over taken by the rushing water and was supposed to be drowned. No more was seen of him, which led to a search for his discovery, and there arose great mistery as to whether he was dead or alive. He was not found.

This boy leaving [being?] the only child of his aged parents, some asistance was sought leading to his discovery, the parents learning that there was an aged man living near, whom possessed some misterious power, clairvoyant perhaps. They went to consult the man concerning their son.

This misterious man was part-blood Shawnee and [part] Delaware: Suddenly, upon learning the custom of the mistic man, the father of the missing boy had taken one [gallon?] of good whiskey, and one lb. of chewing tobacco, and after an interview with the man, the father was told that, he [the mystic] would meditate, and in two days he could come back and he would tell him whether his son was alive or dead, and where he was. Upon the father's return, the aged man told him that he had taken the one half gal[lon] of whiskey and the tobacco into the forest and drank thereof and smoked, and communicated with the spirit of the departed numbers of the tribe and was told that their son was alive had been taken by a woman to abide with her to rejuvenate at the mouth of a great river. There on the evening of the second day when the announcement was to be made to them, the aged man told the father of the missing boy [that he] was asked to announce to the Tribe they should all, or anyone wishing to see the mystery, was to encamp on the bank of the great river opposite the mouth, and that after sunrise they would see the missing boy. Before this hour a great crowd gathered at the destined place and the misterious deep began to roll, and throw forth, great whearl pools. And thunder or rumbling like sound burst into the air of sunrise. Behold, they seen on the waves of the great river, the son. At his side was, a beautiful humanlike personage and said to be a mermaid, so this boy could not communicate with his parents, but greatly to their satisfaction they seen the son and confidently knew it was the departed son; they left the boy in the deep misteries of the river.

Unto this day, they do not know, but it is supposed that he still remains there.

Otter Hide [Charles Elkhair?][16]

For many years, in order to ward off illness, the Delaware had performed the otter hide dance. Some elements were reminiscent of the Big House ceremony, but in key regards it was different, as the celebrants begged the animal spirit to believe that it was remembered, missed, and loved and not to torment the living. Comparable traditions dated back centuries. When the people were about to leave Indiana, an observer wrote, "They make a feast of a piece of the first good fat animal that they kill as sacrifice to some of their Deities or to the spirit of some one of their deceased friends who they suppose has the power of keeping the game out of their sight. . . . It is a token of thankfulness for the favours they have received, and that their good luck may be continued—if they have not had good luck it is for the purpose of reconciling the Deity or spirit of their deceased to them."[17]

The key element of the otter hide dance seems to have been the idea that unrecognized pain and contention from the past could make itself manifest in the body and cause ill health. Modern medical practitioners would agree.

In his notes, Mark Harrington did not record who was telling him this story, but when he later published an account, he said that it was an informant in Oklahoma, and he implicitly connected the material to what he had gleaned from Charles Elkhair. Still, the teller was selling the otter hide to Harrington, and that would have been unlike Elkhair. Perhaps it had belonged to a different family line and Elkhair had inherited an object he felt he could not care for properly. "The exact details and order of the ceremony were not remembered by our informant," wrote Harrington.[18]

Otter hide = kû nuⁿXäs

meeting= aᶜ'kcŭᵐqua mûh'tīⁿ = "Compulsory hog-eating."

Many years ago the people had a young otter as a pet for a small girl about 10 years old. They kept the otter until it was pretty good size The girl ~~got tired of keeping~~ felt that she had better not keep him longer, because she came to think ~~she found~~ that he ~~became~~ was pilsu[n] ("clean," sacred) & somebody above us likes all wild creatures.[19] The old folks told the girl to tell the otter, "I will turn you loose now. I have got you raised and now you can return to your own Way."

So she took him down to the creek, and the old folks told her to tie a little tobacco on his neck and turn him loose. And when she did that, before a year had passed, the girl ~~got~~ began to get sick. So when she got sick, the Indian doctors told her that her pet otter caused it. Doctor told the girl, "The otter wants something to eat." And that she had to kill a hog and cook the whole hog and call for a lot of men. So the men called for ate the hog and the soup and said the child would get well. She got well after they did that.

When the girl was sick they got this hide[20] and put their minds on it that it was the same otter and that they fed the same one. They fed the otter every two years

So that hide came [to us] that way. When the ~~hide~~ keepers of the hide died, it was passed on to others.

Finally it came into someone's hands who did not follow it anymore, so it got sold.[21]

They called [for] anyone willing to go to the big [tent? house?], [both] men and women. Began at night and quit next day, about noon. The head man, owner of the hide, wears it over his head, the head on his breast and the tail hanging behind. The day after the feast, all night they walk around the fire singing and shaking the turtle—one man, and then another, they keep the hide right there. At noon they talk to the hide. Talk to the hide and tell it that in two years they will feed it again.

Harrington apparently asked a question and got his answer:
They do not talk to the otter hide at first because it seems to know what the meeting is for.

CHAPTER 6

The Coming of the Whites

It is not surprising that stories about white people figure in Lenape lore as it existed in the early 1900s. The Indigenous narrators refer to the newcomers as "whites," "settlers," "palefaces," "colonists," "big knives"— and by other names in their own language, as will be seen. Such stories are far from the oldest or the most important in their cultural repertoire, but they are nevertheless significant. The white settler population had been responsible for more than two centuries of constant displacement and loss. This was a profoundly painful subject. The Lenape used story-telling to speak of their historical experiences with the whites in a way that would be more psychologically helpful than hurtful. Sometimes they made themselves laugh; sometimes they ruminated about good and evil, or the moral worth of people who broke promises compared to that of those who kept them.

Julius Fouts told two stories about whites—one that was essentially political and concerned the first appearance of whites in Lenape country, and another that was primarily religious and concerned the reason for the appearance of whites on earth. Charles Elkhair, on the other hand, told a story that blended political and spiritual elements so deftly that they can-not be separated. The stories of both men exhibit startling continuities with the past: in one case actually repeating a tale that had been told for at least a century and a half, and in another case accurately referencing historical details from the colonial era. When we consider how little most of us know about the lives of our ancestors of more than two centuries ago, unless we have read about them in a book, this is truly remarkable.

The Coming of the White Men [Julius Fouts][1]

This story of the Dutch arrival at Manhattan is one that has been loved
by the Lenape people since at least the late 1700s, probably earlier. It
appears in almost all of the places Lenape stories were recounted over
the years.[2] The richest, most detailed version dates from the early 1800s,
recorded by the Moravian missionary John Heckewelder. (See appendix B.) The tale always contains two notable elements. First comes a
humorous tall tale about early cross-cultural interaction, claiming, for
instance, that the warriors who received the newcomers did not know
what to make of metal axe heads and thus wore them bizarrely as necklace pendants. (In the past, some historians have taken this story seriously as evidence of cultural misunderstanding, but it is a mistake to
think that men who used tomahawks on a daily basis would not have
known what to do with an axe. Rather, younger generations were simply having fun imagining the strangeness of the Europeans in their
forebears' eyes.)[3] Second, the story always includes a version of the
tricking of Dido, borrowed from the classical tales of the *Aeneid* told
by early missionaries. (See the introduction.) It is noteworthy that
Julius Fouts included both elements but also two additional features
that were more overtly expressive of anger: the kidnapping and rape
of a woman and the sense that the whites might drive the Indians west
endlessly, until they were pushed into the sea.

Yet even as Fouts alluded to feelings of rage, he seems to have been
intent on sparing Mark Harrington's feelings in some regards: he told
Harrington that white men were currently called "salt" men, a literal
rendition of "white," rather than "long knives" or "muhXcigun." There
is a bit of a mystery related to the latter word. In his notes Harrington
assumed it meant "big knives," known to have been a common term
for white men, and it certainly has had that crystallized meaning in
modern times. "X ci gun" was Harrington's effort to render *kshikan*,

or knife.[4] But the phoneme *muh* or *mah* does not convey "long" or "big." *Maxke*, on the other hand, means "red," implicitly "bloody." Was another meaning papered over by informants long ago? We will probably never know.

mu hoX ci gun[n]
white man

The Delaware knew of the coming of the whites 7 years before they came and were camped at the place.[5] [When they came] one man could talk to them then altho' he had never seen them. This was the man who had sung about them seven years before. His song said, "I saw somebody coming smoking. He had a knife in his hand. He was swimming on his back."

When the Delawares met the boat at the shore, they took the whites up to the camp. The whites had lots of knives and dishes, hoes, axes, etc. He [the white man] showed the Indians these things, and he stayed around and told people to "come and look at my boat." So they went and looked at it. There was a young girl in the crowd, and the white people caught her and took her away. A year from then the man returned with the girl and she had one child. When he came, he brought more axes, hoes, knives and plates and gave them to the Indians. They did not know how to use them, but ran a string through the eye of the bright axes etc. and hung them on their necks. Then he told them how to use them, and then he told the people "I would like to buy a piece of land from you."

And they asked him how much he wants [to pay] for a very little patch. They won't sell it at first, but he says all he wants is "as big as a cow skin." The Indians said "yes, you can have that much," and they made the contract. Then he began to cut the cow hide into a small string. I tell you that string went around a "hell of a big piece of ground." So he began to cheat them (the Indians) first jump, and he's still doing it. The whites will drive the Indians into the water before many years, I think.

———

Cu wa nuck = white man (now)
(salt man)

ORIGINATION OF WHITE MEN [JULIUS FOUTS][6]

Julius Fouts seems to have arranged to have someone take down his story of the appearance of white men on earth. The handwriting is not that of his usual amanuensis, and the narrative contains nonstandard spelling that would be typical of someone who did not often write, at least not in English. Toward the end, he insisted that this story was not his own, that he had heard it from elders, who themselves had gotten it from their elders.

We have every reason to believe him. At first glance, the story seems to be an imaginative rendering of certain Christian elements: the struggle between God and Satan, and perhaps also the tension between Cain and Abel. But considered in another light, it is a profoundly Indigenous tale, containing elements found in numerous ancient Indigenous stories—the creation of life from sea foam; one sibling who chooses to hurt his parent, and another who does not; dramatic action at the edges of a river or in a canyon. Moreover, scholars have found evidence even in colonial records of a Lenape belief in an evil manito, one who spread disease.[7]

1ST

In the early life of the Delaware Indians was the origination of white man. When the white man was first created, it is said that there was no other nation then on earth existing but the Indians. They were visited by a man of an unknown nation. This stranger then began to teach the Indians a religious training, telling them how they should live, and this stranger resembled these Indians themselves in color, perhaps, and disposition. The stranger departed from the Indians, going toward a nearby stream. When he reached the stream it was flowing nicely, in the stream eva he seen great heaps of fome, accumilated on the water. Took notice of the large heaps of fome. He studied over the situation. This man was sent by god to the Indians, to teach them the way to live. After meditating for a time he decided that he could create man himself out of the heap of fome.

2ND

He then gathered some of the fome and created man in their own image. At the finish of his creation of this being, he looked better, in every way, showed to be farer in coller, and therefrom there were men of this class, of this image. They were rou[g]h in and strong in physicke, and fastly increased. When there came to be many of them, he had no further influence over them, they would not hive to the teachings of the creator. He could not determine who how he could induce them to observe his command. They became boistrous and mean, very unruly. He could not controlle them.

He then decided to go back to god, and when he had journeied until near to his destination, he beheld there was a great canion before him. And there fortunately he met his brother. He told his brother that his nation of people had been unruly and disobedient to him.

3RD

"I taught them the way to live, but they would not hive to my command," he said to his brother. "They killed me." and

The brother then told asked him if he would give his people over to him. "If you give them unto me I shall teach them the way of loving and teach them every meckanical trade, [a] benefit to mankind, and make them a wise nation, and all things for their future use hensforth.

The brother then consented to give these people unto his brother for him to teach and command them to the best of his ability. And power. He['d] then taken charge of these people, and the taught them all useful trades, and industry, and then that people who are Palefaces began to fastly learn, by practice, the better means of progress, and success followed, and social life and happiness was soon established among them.

4ᵀᴴ

And this man also taught them how to scheme, and that he could mislead his brother, to his own satisfaction.

The creator of these people discovered that his brother was very much wiser than himself, it was thereafter observed that his brother had been, dieh condemn[ed]—and by god—because he was selfish and strong[ly] disobedient to god. False to him. It was for this reason that he met his brother to offer his service to take command of the people he had created on earth. Unto this day we find that same evil exists, greater than [the] richous, throwout the entire world. We find that evil is all the more strong in every respect. This condemned man was <u>Saten</u> who was so false to god he could no further [arange?abide?] in the home of god, or richous men. He was sent out of the home [of god] unto earth where he went to his brother at the great

5ᵀᴴ

gorge in the canion. This tradision came from our fore fathers of ancient times, handed down from generation to generation, until it is now with us, this present day. That is why I can relate this story so thorough, as I hereby do.

Yours Truly,
Julius Fouts

WHITES & INDIANS [CHARLES ELKHAIR][8]

In his story of his people's early relations with whites, Charles Elkhair addressed both political and spiritual issues. He seems to have had a very clear understanding that when the Lenape lived on the East Coast, they were at war with white men for many generations. The story offers a vision of both natives and newcomers. We learn that the newly arrived whites had what in effect were floating forts, against which the Indigenous were relatively powerless. This was indeed the case: when a ship went upriver and barraged villages with grapeshot, it was a devastating force against which there was no countermeasure. We also learn that white men had a strange love of digging, of mining the earth for any and all riches it could produce—surely an apt description of the Europeans' primary relationship with nature.

The story also calls to mind certain historical realities as they would have been experienced within Indigenous villages centuries before Elkhair's time. During the colonial era, young warriors and aging statesmen really did disagree, often dramatically, about which was the best course to take, just as in the story. Women really did serve as intermediaries, fulfilling an ancient political role, just as in the story. And when more immediate expedients failed, Indigenous doctors and prophets really did attempt to use "medicine" (or spells) against the whites, just as in the story.

Elkhair sent his story via a scribe. In the end, the political commentary was somewhat muted. Indians had kept their promises. He implicitly comments that the whites had not, but he does not say so explicitly.[9]

The head Brave of the Delawares said, "I wish someone could find how far the 'big knives' are." And they appointed 23 men, 20 old men and three young men. And these twenty-three men started to the east. They walked ten days and got to a big river. And that evening, they seen lights across the river. And they said that they'd found the Big Knives. And the [head] Brave said, "We will go back tomorrow. We know where they are." And two [of the] boys heard what the Brave said, and they said they ought to go and get some scalps to take home, instead of going home without them, and made fun. So the third young fellow told the Brave what the boys said. "Well," the Brave said, "Alright. I call myself a Brave, and I will fight until I die." And that night they built a big fire and all of the old men went around the fire and said that they would fight until they died.

When the young fellow got up, they told him not to do it, for he will live a long time. And next morning they went to fight and the two that was making fun went home, and the other staid and seen what would happen to the old men. Along in the evening, they all were killed but this one young fellow. So he started home, and when he got home he seen those two young fellows there. And he said, "Those old men are killed that went with us," and [he] said that "these two fellows was the cause of their fight," and "those Big Knives are across the river." And they all said, "Let's go after them," and they found where the old men got killed by the Big Knives. And they went and fought the Big Knives. So they whipped the Big Knives right along.

And they sent after a sea captain to fight us. So the sea captain said that he couldn't come, and the Big Knives said he had to come or they would behead him, and that captain finally came. And [now] the Indians couldn't do anything with the Big Knives. They found it was a big fish that was in the way, and made a sort of a fort. That captain turned into a fish and got between the Indians and the whites, and the Indians' arrows would glance off, and they couldn't get over the fish to kill the whites. And that evening the Brave said, "There is a fish in our way. How can we kill him—that is, the sea captain?" And a Shawnee said, "Let's look at him, I know of a medicine that will kill him." So they went off and made the medicine and they made a small bow and arrow with a little flint tip. And they sang for the sea captain's spirit, and it came and they took the little arrow and dipped

[it] into the medicine and shot at the captain's spirit. But it didn't take effect on him. And then they took a short stick and dipped it into the medicine and put the stick over the captain's spirit and dropped the stick and nocked the spirit down. And next day about noon the Captain was coming from dinner, and he stopped under a tree and took a paper and sat down to read, and a limb from the tree fell on him and killed him.[10]

And when that happened, they went to fighting again, the whites and the Indians, and there were women from both sides looking, and the women said, "We will look [at] our sons fight." They fought so hard that it made a roaring sound, and the streams were flowing with blood. And the women said, "We ought to try and get our sons to quit fighting, for they have fought against each other lots of times." And so the Big Knives' women told their men to stop fighting, and the Indian women said to the Indians to stop fighting.

The Big Knives and Indians went back to camp, to the Indians' camp to the west of the Big Knives. So the Indians' brave and the Big Knives' brave met and made peace. And the Indian brave told the Big Knife brave that he wanted him to "come up to my camp." "I want to eat with you tomorrow noon." And next morning the Indians went hunting and killed some bear and roasted it, and [got] everything good to eat. And next day at noon they sent over a boy to tell the Big Knives to come over and eat with them, and about 20 Big Knives came over, and 20 Indians dined together. The table was set so the Big Knives sat on [the] East side, and the Indians on [the] West. When they were through, the Indian brave got up and shook hands with the Big Knife brave and said, "Now we will talk about relations between us," and they went off to sit down and smoke and study how they will fix the relations and the Indian Brave said, "Now, what do you think about our relations?" The Big Knife Brave said, "I think we ought to make a big hole and bury all of these men, so we won't see the bones of those people that are dead." The Indian Brave said, "You like to make holes in the ground. You might someday dig where those people are." And the Big Knife said, "What can we do then?" And the Indian Brave said, "You see that sun, you see grass growing, and that river running? And as long as that sun rises and grass grows and river runs, we never will ever fight."

And the Big Knife said, "Alright. And I will treat you as my brother, and always protect you from anyone else that wants to fight you, and protect you as if you were in my arms, so they will get me first." And until this day the Indian has not broken this peace.

(Big Knife is a name given to white men or white people because they carry swords in war.)

CHAPTER 7

Tales of Ordinary Life

Julius Fouts spent many hours talking to Mark Harrington about all sorts of subjects. Harrington's surviving notes provide a written record of the time they spent together. It is likely that Harrington, in the role of anthropologist, asked many questions; but it is also more than possible that Fouts was frequently the initiator. In either case, it was Fouts who did the talking and who thus decided what could be included in the record. And as he spoke of real-world issues, he often interwove bits and pieces of stories. This happened especially often when he spoke of subjects related to raising children and when he explained the Lenape people's ancient clan divisions.

A Child's Life [Julius Fouts][1]

Given that Julius Fouts's own father died when he was young, one suspects that what he said on that subject, and most likely on other subjects related to childhood, was at least partly autobiographical. (We must remember that it was Mark Harrington who was writing down what he said; so it is that "Julius" appears throughout in the third person.) The Delaware customs he remembered closely mirror customs among numerous other Indigenous ethnic groups, in other times and places. Hundreds of years earlier, for instance, Mesoamericans were burying the umbilical cord in different places and with different prayers, depending on whether the child was a boy or a girl.

Naming a child:
The way a child is named is this: If anyone dreams that somebody, named so-and-so is coming, when the child is born he is called by this name. Thus their name came in dreams.

They don't give Indian names any more.

Julius' name is "Pē ta ni hink.°" "Throw him over here."

The navel string custom:
The Delaware took the child's umbilical cord, and after, it was dry buried it in the ground in the garden or under the rocks near the house for a girl; in case of a boy they would bury it out in the woods. This would make them like to hunt. Julius said as a joke that if the cats or dogs got it the children would fight all the time!

They used to tell children who were pulling over the contents of baskets continually that they must be hunting for that string!

The tree swing:
A bark baby holder was used when children were first born, but how it was shaped is not now remembered. Afterwards a board was used.

Sometimes these were hung in trees to swing while the mother picked berries. Chains [of flowers] were hung on the bow but just what kind are now forgotten.

Losing one's baby teeth:
Take the teeth and black the inside of them below with charcoal, and throw the tooth to the eastward, saying "come back quick—I want to eat sweet beans!" The charcoal they throw west, and tell it not to come back. This must be done before sun up in the morning, and it makes the children's teeth come in quick and strong. (It made a child's teeth strong all through his life if he was made to bite a live black snake all along from head to tail, the snake being then turned loose.)

The scratching punishment:
If the boys used to steal anything from the gardens (a roasting ear [of corn] or such as that), the owner of the patch or the parents used to take a gar-fish bill and scratch them once—say, on the arm. If they did it again they were scratched twice and so on.

The death of a father:
At evening of the night that they are going to play moccasin,[2] they take the widow of the dead man out to the west of the house where the corpse lies and fire off a gun twice. Leading her by the elbows, in the morning they take her out to the east and do the same. This is to frighten off the spirit of the dead so it will not come in the house that night. They wake all the children before they shoot so as not to scare them. They do this with man or woman. They always shoot, even for a child's death.[3]

The Three Clans [Julius Fouts][4]

Lenape society traditionally was divided into three clans, known in English as "Turtle," "Wolf," and "Turkey," though as will be seen the translations are actually significantly more complex. Each had its own spiritual chief, though others acted as communal war chiefs. In the past, before the Indigenous population dropped so dramatically, each clan was further divided into sub-clans or kindreds.[5] Some of the sub-clans still existed in the early 1900s, but they were rapidly fading away, along with knowledge of them. Here is what Julius Fouts told Mark Harrington about the subject, recounting little stories as he proceeded.

Wolf Clan, Tûk sīt
"dog foot" or "round foot"

Turkey Clan, Pĕ lä
"They don't chew."
Charley Elkhair is Turkey chief now, there are no others left.

Turtle Clan, Poko ungo'
"dragging along"
Julius belongs to the Turtle clan.

They say that the three persons or man-like animals who started their clans argued about who was the best. One time they came to a big river, on the far side of which they could see food. Now, the turkey said he could go across and get the food, and the turtle said he could, but the wolf could not. The turkey took a running start and flew. He gave out close to the opposite branch and fell into the water, but finally got ashore. Meantime the turtle just walked across under water! (laughter) While the wolf could do nothing but run up and down and howl. So they decided the turtle was best, the turkey next and wolf last.

There used to be small divisions to the tribe in each clan, but that is all being ended now, but still remembered. They (the clans) used to live in different towns, but now they don't do this. A man can marry in his own clan (Turkey or Turtle or whatever). The clans occupy separate parts of the *Xingui kao* (Big House). (There was no clan division in games.) There is maternal descent. A man who is a (maternal) turtle and (paternal) wolf is regarded as a turtle but he can sit on the wolf side [in the Big House]. But if he marries a turkey his children can sit on the turkey or turtle side only.

Each clan had its own chief (sa ki ma).[6] There were other officers in each clan called braves or warriors (ila). There was no head chief. The election [for each clan] was held by the candidates standing up and whoever voted for him would go to his side. If chosen he might stay chief as long as he lived, or if the people got tired of him, they might put him out and put another chief in.

Turtle chief = "Pokoungo wi sa ki ma"

Each clan chief had a councilor called "sa kǐma ĕlkī gaᶜkī," or second chief, who did his work when he was not at home.

"Buying into" clans
Old Miz Elkhair[7]

She is said to have been offered kinship in the Wi sac het ko[8] clan for five strings of corn, and accepted, thus "buying into" the Wi sac het ko kindred and becoming one of them.

The people of the sub-division (or kindred):
It is said they were originally named from some peculiarity of themselves or the place where they lived. They really formed clans as they were

considered kinfolks and could not marry in their own clan (subdivision or kindred). Children, also followed the clan of the mother every time.

On speaking of these things they always say—I (or he) belongs to P
as Pasa ka nŭm dě lī wī hī lai'ī—I belong to P
Pasa ka nŭm lī wī hī laiir—he belongs to P

They say the Pasakwanuma were so called because they were always stealing other people's roasting ears from the fields at night!

"They are just like families. That is how they grew," Julius thinks—"[from the] kinfolks of one person." "Or they [the names] are taken from the places they used to live."

Harrington showed Julius Fouts a list of subdivisions mentioned by Lewis Henry Morgan in the 1850s, and Fouts helped him make a new list, including only those still in existence, and adding some:

Turtle group

1.	Oke ho'ki.	Bark country
2.	E ko ong weta	Under the hill
3.	Ol ha ka mi' kaᶜso	Hollow where a lodge has stood[9]
4.	Wi la nog' si	Carrying off something under the arm (beggars)

Turkey group

1.	Li o'li wai yo	[not interpreted]
2.	Nuk wing gwe ho'ki	Rubbing the eyes
3.	O ping' ho'ki	Opossum country
4.	Mux ho wi ka' kon	Old leggings
5.	Mux am hok si	Blood red land
6.	Ku we ho'ki	Pine country
7.	Mun' hat ko wi	Easy mad, cranky

Wolf group

1.	Mun sit	Big foot
2.	Wi sac het' ko	Yellow tree
3.	Pa sa' kwa nu ma	Snapping corn
4.	O la' ma ne	Red paint
5.	Mun ha ta' ne	Scratching ground
6.	Max so' ta	[not interpreted]
7.	A li ke	Stepping down

"Easy mad" and "Stepping down" are new kindreds. "They used to joke each other about their clans."[10]

The Origin of Stories[11]

Mark Harrington's notes offer no hint as to who told him this little story about stories. Perhaps more than one person did, for the central idea remained vibrant among the Delaware of Oklahoma for generations to come, as the interviews included in the afterword make clear.

A man returning from hunting found a curious hole in the ground. He looked into it and somebody spoke to him. The hunter asked, "who is it?" But the thing did not tell him, only said he was a grandfather. "If anyone wishes to hear stories let him come here and roll in a little tobacco or bread [bead?] and I will tell him a story." So the people came and that is the beginning of the stories—which we do not know are true or not. This grandfather told them never to tell stories after it begins to get warm in the spring. If you do, he said, the snakes, bugs and all kinds of little creatures will get after you!

An Afterword in Three Parts

I. WHAT HAPPENED TO THE STORYTELLERS?

Charles Elkhair and Julius Fouts liked the project they did with the anthropologist from the East. They must have, for in 1912 Harrington sent an acquaintance, Truman Michelson, another former student of Franz Boas, to interview them and obtain stories for the Smithsonian's Bureau of American Ethnology, and they seemed happy to participate. Besides talking about the history of the Big House, Elkhair gave new renditions of the stories of the snake scales, the doll dance, and the otter dance, Wehixamukes, the Big Fish, and the Delaware and the White People.[1] The stories were very similar to the versions he had given to Harrington, but in some cases they had yet more detail and dialogue. The talented storyteller was enjoying himself, and he threw himself into the performances.

By now, Charley was in his sixties and Julius in his fifties. They were no longer young, and over the next decade they faced the same problems as everyone in their world: young men leaving for the Great War and then, in 1919, the scourge of the Spanish flu. At the same time they attained economic self-sufficiency. Oil had been discovered in the Bartlesville-Dewey area in 1907, and in the 1910s it was confirmed to be present beneath the land of Julius Fouts.[2] Meanwhile, although the Elkhairs did not have access to oil profits, they had a relatively large and successful farm, though they were unable to help their children much.[3]

Despite the money, Julius's last years were somewhat sad. He died in August 1926, and just two years earlier, in the fall of 1924, his community had celebrated the last Big House ceremony and then "put it away," as they said. They made the decision to do this for multiple reasons, but most importantly because there were no longer enough elders who had had visions as youths and thus could lead the prayers and stories, and because it was impossible to have the deer hunt at the heart of the festivities, for the ancient quadrupeds were approaching extinction in their region.[4] Those who were children at the time had yet to realize the seriousness of the situation. "The Xingwikaon churches took place each year. Each autumn

I camped with my family. I watched the elderly ladies and the elderly men. They cried, and I wondered why. I was young. I was happy. I thought this way of life would go on always."[5]

In 1927, with Minnie still reeling from the loss of Julius, some members of the community attempted to save the Big House, at least in a physical sense. They proposed to perform a version of the ceremony one last time for the Moving Picture Company of Oklahoma, which would profit from the film they would make but would then pay the Delaware a substantial sum, to be used to renovate the dilapidated building. Nothing came of the idea, possibly because people like Fred Washington, a relative of Susie Elkhair, was against any such public exhibition. He wrote, "I am . . . against a disposal of historic customs of my People as well as the disposal to the movie firms, also destruction of the Big House. I am for rebuilding the old Delaware Church, and [to] be kept private . . . as [a] Historical event."[6]

In February 1928, Fred Washington's cousin, James Charles War Eagle Webber, decided to take matters into his own hands. He traveled east to the University of Pennsylvania Museum, for which Harrington had once collected materials. Although Harrington had moved on, Webber was directed to the office of Frank Speck. Speck was another former student of Franz Boas, and he was dedicated to the preservation of Eastern Woodlands cultures, including that of the Delaware. For several years, Charley Webber worked with him, first in person and then by mail. Their labors led to the writing of Speck's 1931 book, *A Study of the Delaware Indian Big House Ceremony*, which included a lengthy transcription of Webber speaking in Delaware about the Big House and re-creating the ceremonies. In 1932, Speck came out to Dewey and interviewed a number of War Eagle's friends and acquaintances, including Charles Elkhair. Later, Speck managed to obtain a five-hundred-dollar donation from the Pennsylvania Historical Commission. The funds were deposited into the bank account maintained by the Big House Committee.[7]

Charley Elkhair, still with his strong interest in cultural preservation, was a leader of that committee. His whole circle remained deeply invested.

Other members of the committee included his wife's kinsman, Fred Washington; his daughter's husband, John Falleaf; and Minnie's first husband, Willie Longbone.[8] One of their most pressing concerns was their continued subjugation within the Cherokee tribal political structure. They wanted the independence they had been promised at the time of removal. Without political or economic sovereignty, they did not see how they could ever successfully preserve the tribe's cultural identity. In early 1935, a group of elders signed a petition and sent it to the Commissioner of Indian Affairs in Washington. "We the undersigned Delaware Indians of Northeastern Oklahoma, believing our best interests would be served by being organized as an Independent Tribe, respectfully request that you use your efforts to have this accomplished for the 'Lost Tribe of Indians.'"[9] Charley, listed as age eighty-five, was the third signatory. Above him were Elizabeth Beaver and Minnie Britton, ages seventy-eight and seventy-four, respectively. Elizabeth was Susie Elkhair's sister. All three were known for being among the very last survivors of the trek from Kansas, who grew up speaking and living entirely within tribal customs.[10]

Placing his mark on that paper was one of Charley's last acts. In February 1935, Charley died. Susie—like his friend Julius—had preceded him. And at the time, Minnie Fouts was desperately ill, though she survived.[11] War Eagle began to take it upon himself to send Speck more stories along with his letters, a number of them strongly resembling the stories that Charley Elkhair used to tell.[12]

The Depression was in full force, and a few years later the nation plunged into war and young Delaware men enlisted. In the spring of 1942, in the bleakest of times, War Eagle and Minnie Fouts arranged to have a Big House ceremony in a bark tent built on Julius's and Minnie's farm. Fred Washington wrote about it to Frank Speck: "We had a praying meeting for 12 days and nites in the month of March. The Lenape people held a meeting some[what] like the Big House way of holding ceremonies. The whole purpose of this praying is asking the Great Spirit to stop this Bad Thing going on, as This War should be stopped and make some peace."

They sang and told stories. And they prayed for the whole world. That had always been the purpose of the Big House ceremony. Charley used to say they could save the world that way.[13]

The war ended, and people moved forward into the future. Minnie died a few years later, on Christmas Day 1949. She was buried in the same Delaware cemetery near the town of Copan where her husband and the Elkhairs lay, as close in death as they had been in life. By then Minnie's son Ray had already died, without children, though her niece Fannie, now Fannie McCartlin, still lived. Charles and Susan Elkhair were survived by his son Jesse and the two girls, Rosa and Sallie. Jesse had married Josie Bullette, and when he died at age eighty in 1961, he was survived by his three sons (Earl, Mack, and Ray) and two daughters (May and Thelma), along with twenty-one grandchildren and twenty great-grandchildren. Rosa had married Dennis Frenchman but had no children, while Sallie had married John Falleaf and had four daughters and six sons, as well as many grandchildren. Sallie's years at Chilocco weakened her ability to speak Delaware, but with a supportive, traditionalist spouse like John Falleaf, she was able to maintain many customs. In keeping with her people's belief in expressive names, when her fifth son was born (after Fred, George, William, and Richard), with a smile she named him "Numerous." Sallie died in 1951, Rosa in 1969.[14]

By the end of the century, some of the specific cultural knowledge that Charles Elkhair and Julius Fouts had worked so hard to preserve had come to reside only in the pages they orchestrated the writing of, so as it turned out, their work had been truly important. They were not forgotten. Elders interviewed in the 1970s spoke of them all frequently and fondly.[15] In the sixties, seventies, and early eighties, a fluent Lenape speaker, Nora Thompson Dean (1907–1984), worked with her adopted nephew, Jim Rementer, to record many stories that she remembered. Today the world can listen to this rich oral tradition online, through the Lenape Talking Dictionary.[16] Some of the tales are the direct descendants of the stories told at the turn of the century, in the era when Nora was growing up. The stories live.

II.   Four Elders at the End of the Century

In the 1990s, Nicky Michael, a young scholar of Delaware heritage herself, approached the last generation to have experienced the Big House or to have been raised in households where Delaware was spoken. In seeking such elders, she activated personal networks. She visited the two churches where much of the traditionalists' energy was then focused: the New Hope Indian Methodist Church and the Rose Hill Baptist Church. She was also welcomed by two local women's groups—the Bartlesville Indian Women's Club and the Delaware War Mothers Society. One of the women she spoke to, Rosetta Jackson Coffey, was a great-granddaughter of Charles Elkhair through her mother, and like her, the others all lived within the vicinity of Bartlesville.

In those years, Nicky was studying Delaware with Lucy Blalock, one of the last remaining fluent speakers of the language. But by then the language used for the interviews had to be English. Nicky asked questions and the elders answered. Here, we have transcribed only the answers, embedding enough of Nicky's questions in the topic sentences of each paragraph for readers to understand what was asked. The tapes and full transcriptions are available at the Tribal Archives in Bartlesville, for those who want to hear the questions, or the parts omitted, or the women's laughter.

It is striking how many of the old traditions found in the stories told by the Elkhair and Fouts families were still present. We are in familiar territory when the speakers mention their way of holding funerals or communicating with the dead. The latter subject still seems to have been a special interest of the women, along with foodways and craftwork. The Lenape still thought of naming as being connected to storytelling, and Elkhair's great-granddaughter Rosetta specifically mentions the storytelling tradition as having been a winter activity, just as Fouts and Elkhair had once described. The speakers were sometimes serious, but often made jokes. Like Fouts and Elkhair, they even remarked on how annoying and yet how useful "those academic people" could be.[17] The interviews are richly revealing in many ways, perhaps most of all in that they demonstrate that the act of telling a story continued to be a way to connect with others on a profound level and to make sense of the human experience. All of the women had attained the stature of community elder largely because of their overwhelming love for their Lenape communities. And one of them, Joanna Nichol, was a talented storyteller in her own right—one might say, her generation's equivalent of Charley Elkhair.

Rosetta Coffey (September 17, 1997)

A lot of people say, "Well, what is a vision?" And you can kind of go into a trance yourself and you see these things. Just like myself—a lot of times I can close my eyes and see [the old-timers]. I can see the eyes looking at me and it's kind of scary in a way. It's like anything else, time changes. The grandmother, the mother, or the great-grandmother, they have their own things that they do. Everything that's within the house, that's their responsibility to raise their children and to teach them the tasks that they have to carry out when they are going into their own lifehood. And then the father's way is that he has to provide. He is the provider of the family. He would like to get out. He would get out and till the garden and get the spot going. But it was up to the wife to do the planting and to do the harvesting. If it was large quantities, well then, the family . . . the children were there to help. They start teaching these children these things within, you know, the family, and they don't go from family to family. It's just the immediate family that they teach their children all these things.

And as to naming, now, the grandmother or the mother has a right to do that. They do not have to go through anybody, do not have to give anybody anything, unless they want to . . . I have named, I think, two great grandchildren . . . three. I have another one that I will probably give a name. But I don't come up with these names right now. I think about them, and I try and give them a name that fits them. The first great granddaughter,

I gave the name to her, *Kёkilёkshinkwe*. And she's half Delaware and half Navajo. But I gave her the name of "Laughing Eyes" and she knows how to say that. *Kёkilёkshinkwe*. It means "laughing eyes," and the reason I gave her that name is because we have had her ever since she was about three years old and first thing in the morning, when I would wake up, she would wake up and she would look at me and she would smile. She never has ever been in a bad mood. To this day, when she wakes up, she looks happy. Her little eyes used to just roll around, you know, and just full of . . . mischief, I guess. That is the reason I gave her that name. And I had thought and thought for about four months. I kept thinking about different names and then as I was standing there . . . well we live out in the country and there's a spring that runs and I was standing there one day and that name—it just came to me. I had no idea because you know there seems like there was a lot of names, I had thought about but I wasn't satisfied with those. So, I held off until this came to me. So that's what her name is. The naming, some people say, "Well you know, you got to fill out an application, you got to do this, you got to do that." You don't have to do nothing. You don't have to have no fees. It's all up to you. Because my grandfather named me and that was a long, long time ago. And my name, I kind of forget it because it's not really the name that I really had. But my mother's gone, my aunts are gone. So, I had to talk with Jim Rementer to get something like my name [in Lenape]. And it was "A Flower That Blooms." So, with the help of him, I have been able to do this for my great grandchildren. And now I need another one. The mother wants me to name her a Delaware name because she's so many different other tribes. She's got a voice on her that could almost sound like she's whistling, it's so loud. So, her name will be Screaming Eagle. And I know a lot of other people who are named Little Bird or Little Chicken or Chickadee or something like that, you know. It's alright as long as you're named for something. Of course, everybody has their own ideas of this, as to how. . . . But that is always the mother or the grandmother's duty to always do that. Well, I guess you probably know that my clan is Turtle, and all my children are Turtle. So, they follow the mother's clan.

It was a long time ago. You know there were all these Delawares around here that were Turtle and Turkey and Wolf, and you weren't allowed to marry in your own clan. Because in one clan everybody is kind of related, you know. That's one of the things that by my own mother and my father . . . the way it turned out, after they had married, and my mother's father had remarried—it put my dad and my mother as almost cousins.

. . . I don't know what all you want to know. There's some things that I probably won't tell. But there's a lot of storytelling. Now, my dad, he believed in telling those stories and all those stories that he tells are about birds and they're about animals. And he would only tell us those stories during the winter months. And people say, "Well, why? Why does he do that?" Well, I don't know. But one summer we were all out of school and everything and I asked him if he would tell us a story. And he said no. He wouldn't tell us one because sometimes it would take maybe two nights to tell one story. But he said the reason why they didn't tell these stories, only in the wintertime, was because those stories were about the birds and the animals, and they didn't want the insects to hear those stories. I have never ever heard a story about insects.

So, that was one of our beliefs, you know. But I do see people and I heard them tell stories. Which I had to correct one of my sisters[18] about that because she wanted to be a storyteller and I told her it was wrong. But I don't know whether she is going to heed it or not . . . I don't think she really knows; you know. She's probably about seven years younger than I am. So, a lot of this took place because I was the oldest daughter. I have a brother that's older than me. . . .

Our parents spoke Delaware real fluently but they didn't talk very much around us. We grew up only knowing a few words. My mother, when she started school, she could not speak English. So, that was real hard and they were punished for that. And I never realized how hard that would be until

I went to a workshop where tribes from all over came. I really don't remember the purpose of that meeting that we had. We had it for one week. So, we had the Yakama, the Creeks, the Cherokees, the Navajos, the Apaches and who knows how many different languages that we had there. They told us to pick out a language. Well, I picked out Yakama and so that was the class that we had to go into. I thought oh boy, here I'm going to learn some words in Yakama. I could have chosen Creek because I know quite a few words in Creek. But I chose the Yakama language. When you went into that room, you sat down, and nothing said. Then your teacher comes in and speaks to you in Yakama. And she expected us to learn. She didn't write on the board and that was hard. She would talk to us in Yakama. The whole week, I never knew what she said. [Laughter] That was really hard.

I never did get to see the doll dance, but I do remember them talking about it later on.[19] But I never did ever remember one. I might have went but I was probably too small to remember. There is some kind of dance that I can remember. I can remember seeing ribbons. Seemed like to me they were blue and white ribbons. The only thing I can remember is like them blowing in the breeze. So, I don't know what that was. There's a lot of different dances from every tribe.

My dad talked about the long house [i.e., Big House]. I never did hear my mom talk too much about it. My dad was something within his clan where he was the person that sat for. . . . Each clan had their own door. And he was one that sat by the door where his clan was. . . . That's about all I know of it. They did want to make a long house and have meetings in it. I was against it because that wasn't what it was used for. A long time ago they had their meetings there and to carry on. . . . But they never talked to us about it. I really don't know where it's located. There's two different places that say this is where it is, and somebody else says well no, it's over here. So, I don't know.

I think it is best that way because it's all now in the past. I told them I wouldn't have no part. It's just a memory and I think that's where it needs to be left. . . . The last thing we need is somebody who doesn't know what they're doing to make up something. . . . If I don't know anything then I just say that I don't know. And I'm not going to make it up because I don't want it to be wrong. I guess that's the way we were taught. . . . There's too many things that's going on, that's not right. We have told them once before that when they didn't know about something to ask. And I don't think anyone has been asked anything since then . . . that's one of the reasons things aren't going good. There's too many wannabes that want to be it, you know? And they don't know. And I think that a lot of things are backfiring on them. They're not getting along. People are getting embarrassed and worse. . . . They need to listen. That's what they need to do. It's like the procedures my mother did during a funeral . . . I had to tell my children how my mother carried on these because she carried on a lot of them. Each clan does theirs a little different. I know my dad's clan; they didn't really go through the stages that my mother did. And there's this thing that happened the other day when they had the dinner. And I don't think it's right because I have never seen it done before. . . . But all and all, that is good. When my mother died, though, I was determined to carry out [the funeral preparations] the way that she did. And my mother used to get criticized by different older people. Well, not really older. But she used to be criticized for "you should have done this," "you should have done it that way." And those very people never did anything like that! So, we decided that when my mother died that we were going to do that for her. . . . No one ever criticized me for doing it that way because we did it the way she did it.

It was a long time ago. . . . The last night, they would bring the body to the house around four o'clock. Leave it overnight and there was always someone there with it. That was the thing we carried out for her like she carried out for others. We didn't get no criticism. . . .

We [women] made all of our clothes and my clothes . . . I don't have a Delaware costume. I wear a Comanche costume because its more simple to make. [laughter] I made [a Delaware] one for my granddaughter and

I tell you I ripped that collar out a hundred times. I almost didn't put one on. It's hard. I never made another one.

Well a lot of people, whether they are in that [Plains Indian] tribe or not, you'll see them coming out with that [outfit]. A lot of people do that and they don't get permission to do it. So, they suffer the consequences when someone from that tribe approaches them and tells them, "You, take that off. You cannot wear that." Or asks them, "Who gave you the right to do it?"

Speaking of my parents—My dad was real spiritual. Where I am living now is where we were raised. Of course, we had a farm. We had cows and everything. Horses. That was mostly what we did is ride horses. . . . All of us older ones, from my two brothers and me, we were the oldest. We knew what we had to do, every day, seven days a week. So, our dad always told us, "You do those things first then you can play." So that's what we were told to do, and we always kept our bodies clean because you never know when you're going to die. They said keep your bodies clean . . . I was told always to be good to people even though sometimes people act bad towards you. I was told just to walk off and leave them but sometimes that's really hard to do. In this day and age, people will come up and say anything to you out of the blue. I find myself just popping right back. The older you get, you get mean, I guess . . . I don't like to hear people do that and it makes me feel sorry for the ones that are maybe underneath them. I guess I have always been the one, when there was any ball games or anything comes up. . . . Even today I root for the underdog . . . I'm just betting on them because they don't win very much.

We had a big family, there was eight of us. . . . We always had someone who was staying with us. Whether that was an uncle or . . . it was mostly uncles and my grandfather. My [Comanche] grandfather named me, and he named our two boys . . . there was no big deal over that. There was no paper writing. So, he named my two boys. He passed away before my daughter was born. Her Comanche name—I can't say it in Comanche—, but it means "Black Hair." And one of my son's names is like a spider, it's got long legs [laughter]. And then my grandson . . . his name is [Tin Bear?], and that is an original name of a [Comanche] chief.

Pat Donnell (September 20, 1997)

Well, my mother never had much of a family. Her parents were divorced when she was so young, and her mother died when she was a young girl. She went to Chilocco Indian School. My mother and father both did. Although my father had both of his parents but back in that era people were so poor. So, when Chilocco opened up, a lot of families sent their children to Chilocco. And she was one of those. She was kind of raised by our aunt. So, when she had children of her own, it was so important to her to try and keep the family together and keep them close. There was three of us children and we were very close. And I give her the majority of the credit for that. That was something she always wanted but never had. Of course, you know, back then they tried to take your culture away from you. She really hated that. So, when she had children then she tried to . . . then they were allowed to learn more about her culture and everything. So, she tried really hard to learn all she could and to encourage us kids to learn more about our culture. She was just always there. She was just my inspiration to do anything. She had bad eyesight and couldn't sew or anything like that. So, she encouraged me to do that. I guess I did a lot of things because she couldn't. I did those things because I knew she couldn't. She was just the greatest woman that ever was. I wish you could have known her. She was just a wonderful lady, very supportive. She was the type of person that, no matter how bad she felt, she made you feel better when you were around her. She was just a great lady. I hope that some of her has rubbed off on me. Of course, I'll never be quite like she was but maybe a little bit has rubbed off.

It was my aunt who raised her who got me started sewing. Even though my mother went to boarding school and lived over there, she did come home on the weekends, and mainly holidays. They could afford to let them come for the holidays. But I spent a lot of time with my aunt. She taught me how to sew. It was like sewing little squares of materials together to make a quilt or something. She took the time to sit down, because she loved children, and that's what her and I did a lot. Just anything us kids wanted to do; she would show us how. She was a real neat Indian lady. She had her hard times too, but she loved children. So, we spent a lot of time with her when we were growing up. I learned a lot from her. My mother couldn't sew but she (her aunt) could and so she helped me. So, that's how I learned to sew and that's how I really took an interest. My children decided that they wanted to do the Indian dancing and things. There didn't seem to be anybody else to do it and we couldn't afford to pay someone to do it. So, you were kind of forced to learn how to make things and do things. So that's basically how I really got involved in that.

I do it for my children and grandchildren. And you just get so much enjoyment out of seeing them wear it and perform in it or whatever. I just love it. I like doing it. I've always said that I never was very good at it, but my children and grandchildren think it's great. So that's what thrills me. My family really seems to be involved in tribal things and I think this is really good.

What do I like to do? Well, I like to fish! [laughter] Of course, my mother was never able to do that, and my father never cared much about fishing. But when I married Walt, he was quite the outdoorsman. A Fisherman. He's taught me a lot. We used to [break in recording]. We used to fish a lot, and we still do every once in a while, but not like we used to. We had campers and we'd go camping . . . stay maybe for a whole weekend. So much fun. Just he and I sometimes.

Went up there to this big lake and just had the best time. Just he and I. We got in some scrapes.

There was the time that we almost sank our boat. We went to this lake and the rain came. And of course, this lake was down low, and we left our boat tied up. We didn't pull it out of the water, and it started raining. I had never seen it rain like it rained. And Walt got to thinking, "I better go check on our boat." He went down there, and you could just see the front of it. It had filled up with water so deep! So, we started baling the water out. It was an experience. . . . Our motor was under water. We had to take it to the shop and get it all dried out. But that didn't stop us! We got that fixed and went on to another place. It was fun. Those experiences were really fun. We've done a lot of different things since we've been married.

I think probably, like 1980 was when I joined the Indian Women's Club. They do a lot of good things. I really got acquainted with a lot of different women and we have all different tribes. They do a lot of good things for Indian students. They have scholarships. We work hard for our scholarship money. But we enjoy it too. Got involved in the style shows that they put on to raise money for scholarships. When I got involved in the Indian Women's Club, that's when I met Georgeanne Robinson, and she was one of my big inspirations to do ribbon work. She taught me how to do ribbon work. We learned how to do a lot of different things in that club. If I hadn't had joined that club, I probably wouldn't have learned all those things. They would have classes. She was a wonderful lady and taught me a lot. She was there to help you. . . . She was thrilled to be able to show you her talent and help you learn it. She was the one that really got me interested in that. . . . They encouraged you all to make some traditional clothes. You know, if you were Delaware, Cherokee, Osage, whatever tribe, to do that [style]. The majority of the women did, and they'd help each other. They learned a lot about their tribes and the way they do things. How their clothes are made, how their outfits are made and why they do it that way. It's very educational. They've done a lot for students and have fun doing it.

It used to be when we first started the style show, we didn't have the nice clothes that they have today. It was funny. Some of the little things that we've done and some of the places that we went to have our style shows . . . I remember one time. . . . Well we didn't all have clothes so whatever Georgeanne and whatever someone else had—it just sort of got put together and we'd have a show. And she had a lot of contemporary clothes too that we'd throw in there. But one time, Georgeanne had a buckskin dress and so she told me to wear this and model it. So, I did. It was getting closer and closer to show time, and I couldn't find the leggings and the moccasins to this dress. So, they said just put on anybody's moccasins because we don't have much time. I think it was Mary Crow who had a pair of moccasins, and I think they were size ten. And I wore a little smaller than that and they were so big! I couldn't walk. I just had to scoot along. When Georgeanne came up and saw me coming, she just almost lost it. But she was so gracious and always adlibbed so well. She always narrated, most of the time. You just wouldn't believe. Sometimes we just grabbed whatever we could find. [laughter] That was just one of the instances that happened. There were many more . . . little things that happened. You could probably write a book about some of the places we've been and some of the places we had to get dressed.

We went to San Antonio one time. Took a bus down there and we had to put on a style show in one of the missions down there. It was like a hundred degrees. So hot! We had to make our changes and do our style show. I thought we were going to die, it was so hot down there. We just made a good time out of it. Some of the conditions were just not the greatest, but all the girls were just so great. We always had a good time. So, we've been a lot of places and done a lot of things. I've enjoyed that. We do a lot of cooking. That's one of our ways to make money. I enjoy doing that. Helping them make the fry bread, and so I have been involved in that too. I don't particularly do just one particular thing. I do a little bit of everything. It's kept me pretty active. But I'm slowing down some. [laughter]

. . . My mom wasn't real fluent with her language. . . . Now her aunt spoke some Delaware. But she was like twelve when she went to Chilocco, and she would have liked to learn more, but they weren't allowed to. As a result, she didn't learn a whole lot about it. Times were just so hard back then. They didn't really encourage you to learn about your culture and everything. You were punished if you tried to speak your Native tongue. So, she was scared to death to try to learn it. That's just one of the negative things that happened back then. As a result, we didn't learn it. Nowadays they're trying to learn all that now, and it's very hard because so many of them can't speak it now. So, they're trying to learn. My brothers have been very involved in their culture, and I have just been real proud of them. But we didn't know that much about it because we weren't taught that till we were older, and everybody was trying to learn all about their ancestors. We're learning a lot now.

When I was younger, my aunt who I was telling you about—everybody called her aunt Kate—she would take me to these gatherings that they had. They used to have a gathering up here in Dewey, and they called it The Old Settlers. And all the cowboys and the Indians would all come together, and they'd eat, spend the day together, visit, and do different things. It was quite the deal. Of course, I was young and didn't realize what was going on. Us kids would just go up there and play together. I remember back then . . . if you were an Indian you got in for free and you got to eat. Back then I didn't think anything of it. I remember now. It was a pretty neat deal. You know, if you were an Indian you got to get in there and eat and everything for free! [laughter] It was quite a neat situation. You had a big rodeo. The Indians would come and perform and stuff. I never thought too much about myself being an Indian. I thought, "Oh, those people are really neat." [laughter] Of course, I always knew I was. They just never stressed that. I guess because of the fact that back when my mother was growing up—I wouldn't say they were ashamed of the fact that they were Indians—they just never. . . . But from her experience at the school, they never wanted them to be very proud of it. As a result, she wanted her kids to not be victimized by that. Later on in life, it's been different.

I think we've come a long ways. I just think that history always repeats itself. I think it's just wonderful that the Indian people are learning their Native language now. It's just sad that it had to happen that way. So, I think we're in pretty good shape. [laughter] I don't want to get involved in politics or anything like that. But if the tribes will stand their ground and try and keep teaching their children about their heritage and stuff. . . . We'll survive. It's never been easy for the Indian people anyway. All the modern conveniences and things that they have nowadays, I just think they're wonderful. [laughter] I think of the things we have now, and the things we had when my kids were being raised, and my mother when she was growing up. . . . Some of these children nowadays have no concept of the things that we grew up with. For instance, hanging your clothes out to dry or using a ringer type washing machine. They have no concept of that. [laughter] But you just kind of forget about those things. I talked to one lady. I said, "What do you think about going to these powwows and dancing on carpet?" [laughter] And she said, "Hey, I think that's wonderful." [laughter] So, those are just some of the things that I think back about. And the games we used to play! Kids just don't really know. We used to make our own toys and now they think everything has to be bought. We used to just have some good times with some of the things that we made. Always played outside and never watched TV because we never had a TV. [laughter] I just wish that kids could kind of go back to that. I think modern conveniences are wonderful, but they're getting away from the family, from doing things together as a family, and kids playing together. Like I say, TV is wonderful and it's a good educational tool when you use it that way. But some people use it for babysitters and stuff nowadays. Our kids have been brought up with a little bit of that. They played outside a lot and didn't watch much TV. They had some good times playing together. And I'd give anything for families to spend more time with their children and do outside activities. That's how you really have fun and learn about one another. That's really important. So, I don't know. Not sure where we're headed. But maybe if we can try and instill that in our children and our grandchildren then maybe there's hope for them yet. But we've really tried to do things that our kids like to do, and go along with them whether or not we really did enjoy it or not. If they were getting enjoyment out of it, that's what's important. Do things you can do as a family. Sometimes people are a little selfish. They want to do what they want to do. But I think I've talked too much!

Joanna Nichol (October 11, 1997)

I was born September the 12th, 1919. My mother was pregnant with me when my brother died.[20] I would have had a brother that was two and a half or three years older than I had that not happened. I also had a sister who was older than him, but she only lived two weeks. I have a sister now that was born October the 12th, 1924. From the time I was five, I had somebody to take care of with her. Then my mother and father separated when I was ten and she was five. So, I took over as being a listening post for my dad and taking care of my sister. Mother thought that dad could make a better living for us than she could. She worked in the laundry, a place down on Second Street for Joe Brooks' dad. She worked there the whole Depression. She never missed a week. She worked all through the Depression, and my dad had a hard time. But when I was young, before my sister was born, I remember going to sleep to Stomp Dance songs.

When I was five, I was at the . . . last Big House meeting that we had. I don't know what happened at that big house. But you know it is recorded. It is in the Library of Congress.[21] One of the Senators had one of those cylinder recorders and the Chief gave him permission to come do that. So, it's on tape and you can hear Charlie Elkhair sing his vision in Delaware on there. And you can hear the singing of the women and the men and everybody in the big house. Every time I hear that, without even thinking about it or anything. . . . In fact, the first time I heard it, it was caddy corner from the school room from me. And they were playing it over there and I was doing research on a bunch of rolls. I was looking for names. All of the sudden, I realized that there were tears running down my cheeks. I thought, "What's causing that?" Then I went over, and Greg [Shaf?] was over in the corner with another friend of mine there in California. . . . We were up at DQU.[22] So, I said, "What is that you're playing?" And when they told me what it was . . . I know I was there, but I don't remember much about it. I guess I got in trouble or something about it makes me cry. They said they wondered why I was crying. I wondered too! [laughter]

Mother would take me out of school for anything that was done. Like uncle Dutch White Turkey. . . . When he died, we had his feast after the twelve days of feeding at his grave. I used to go with mother to go feed at his grave and leave food. I would always be so excited when we'd go up there the next day because the food would be gone. I was too little to think that it might be animals or something, but I just knew that it was Uncle Dutch that did that. I remember taking the food up religiously. I either went with Aunt Kate when she went, or I went with mama. . . . My age must have been eight or nine when I remember the last Snake Dance. There are very few people alive now a days who remember that the Delawares used to have a Snake Dance. But my mother took me out of school and said we had to go early because she had to cook. They had to serve the dancers a soup of some sort. I don't know what it was, but it was soup of some sort that made them so . . . the snakes couldn't hurt them. So, we went, and I got to just horse around in the kitchen and the women kept giving me little bites of something to play around with. Then I saw them put up the rope around the dance ground. Daddy and Uncle Roy, my mother's brother—(There was four girls[23] and one boy. Uncle Roy was an only boy. Spoiled rotten! But I was his favorite niece.) He was about the color of an old penny, but he had the bluest eyes I ever saw. Blue, blue eyes. He would blow all the money he had. He worked as a cowboy, and he'd go to town and get drunk and blow all his money. Then when he went broke, he'd show up to the big house out at Aunt Kate's. But he and daddy were out at this Snake Dance, and they were all dressed. They had just a regular Delaware outfit. I don't think that had anything on the upper part of the body. But I know they had a little bridge cloth on, front and back. So, they were dancing out there, and they all had a snake. I was out leaning against a tree and the rope went around the tree and went over to the next tree. I was standing pretty close to that tree, and you wouldn't believe how many ladies came out from Bartlesville to see this dance. The women would just push to get a closer look at these Indian men dancing. I knew my daddy very well. My dad was very strict but if you obeyed all his orders, you were like home free. I saw my dad and uncle Roy talking and Uncle Roy was giggling. I thought, "I wonder what my daddy's going to do. He's going to do something." But I didn't know what it was going to be. The next time they came around, they both turned around with their back to the ladies and they mooned them. You know, they [those women] almost killed me! They almost knocked me down and stomped on me, trying to get away from that rope. [laughter] I never will forget that. That was so funny. [laughter]

All the women said that my daddy was so handsome. Even when I came this time [from California]. . . . Daddy had been dead for many, many years, [since] back in the early forties. . . . But when I went to Potawatomi Meeting, and they asked us to identify ourselves by our last name . . . I got up and said my last name and said that my father was Potawatomi and that my mother was Delaware. . . . There was some old lady talking about our last name and she was so old that she had to wait for her daughter to bring her over. So, when we sat down to eat, she wouldn't eat until her daughter brought her over there. And she came over and she said, "Oh you're Alec's daughter!" And I said, "Yes, ma'am." And she said, "Oh, he was so handsome. He was the handsomest man I ever met. And he was so courteous. I remember when he used to run across the parade ground at Chilocco with his coattails just a flying!" [laughs] I never forgot that. I thought that was so great. So, then when I came to move back here . . . the first language lesson I went to was with Lucy Blalock. She wanted to know who we all were. Our maiden names for us women and stuff. So, she can trace them that way. When I said I was Joanna Pambogo, she said, "Pambogo! Oh, you had a good-looking dad." She said, "If Josie hadn't have had him, I would have had him." [laughter] And she told me how he used to tease grandma all the time. He would tease grandma until he'd make her cry. He told me this later. He said when she'd cry her little mouth would form a box. Just a square little mouth. [mimics crying] And he'd like to see that, so he used to tease her. But anyway. Daddy moved up here like a good Indian man does when he marries an Indian woman. It used to be the custom that the man moves in with the lady. Unless you stole the lady and then you brought her back. That was not unknown in those days. They'd move back.

Another thing I was at and didn't know it and didn't find out until I was telling [my cousin] Leonard about it. For once, Leonard had on his hearing aids and could hear everything I said. [laughter] I told him. I said, "I remember when we had Uncle Dutch's funeral feast. I remember the ladies put a blanket out there and a rock on each corner of the blanket. There were young girls coming and they were bringing little loaves of bread. They put their little loaves of bread on the blanket." I started to keep talking and he said, "No. No that wasn't Uncle Dutch's funeral feast, that was the Doll Dance." I said, "Really?" And he said, "Yes, that was the last Doll Dance we had." I was about six or seven. Mama took me out of school again and we did it in the fall. At first, I was really aware of the men. One was turning a whole cow and the other was turning a whole pig over the coals. A bed of coals. They were cooking it and I watched them for a long time. Mama made me report back every five to ten minutes, so she'd know I didn't go anywhere. So, I watched them. Then when they put the blanket down all I wanted was one of those loaves so I could just taste it. The girls came and kept throwing their loaves there and then they went to work helping. When it came time to eat, there was four older ladies. Each took a corner of that blanket, and they snapped that blanket. It sounded like a rifle shot. Pop! They knew just how to do that, man. Snap! Make that blanket snap. . . . Loaves of bread were flying through the air and all the men were running for a loaf. When I saw that they were all going to get loaves, I lost interest in that. So, then I went and got in line to eat. I remember I was so little, I had to hold my plate up high. I got all the way to the end and pulled my plate down and there was a pig ear and a pig tail and that's all. Oh! My heart was broken. I cried so hard. I ran behind the cellar. The cellar was not completely underground. There was a big, rounded top and I spent a lot of time behind that reading or playing with toys. I went running out behind there and just cried my heart out. Mama came and scolded me for crying. She said, "You shouldn't cry. The ladies were just trying to tease you. Now you go back, and they'll give you something real good to eat." So, I went back sniffling. I remember that so well. I went back and they gave me a real nice dish full of food and some candy and pieces of the loaves of bread. That was nice. I liked that.

But she [my mother] was adamant about me leaving school to go to any Delaware celebration, even if it was just a Stomp Dance. They always took us to the Stomp Dances. I don't remember when we went in wagons, but I remember after daddy got a Model T Ford. I don't remember riding in wagons hardly at all. But when dad got the Model T Ford, then we never missed a Stomp Dance. He would put my sister to bed, down on the floor, because she was just a baby. I was five, six, or seven years old and he'd put me to bed on the back seat. We had a touring car, a four-door touring car. He would always tell me, "Don't you sit up now at all. I don't want you watching because you never know when somebody's going to get drunk and start shooting around here." Which was true. Usually someone would make eyes at someone else's wife and most guys carried a gun in those days. I remember when Jim Buffalo. . . . He was the great womanizer and I know this only from hearing daddy and mama talk. But I heard him running through the corn, down the hill. That husband had a big ole' shotgun. Jim was running for dear life and that guy was shooting at the noise in the cornfield . . . a drying cornfield in the fall. He was shooting at the noise, and he was kind of close, I guess. Jim was really. . . . You could hear him. All the way up from the car you could hear him. So, I knew my daddy knew what he was talking about. But my daddy was a real good singer and leader. And Dean [a cousin] takes after dad on that kind of thing because he has a good voice.

My dad sang . . . over the radio. He got a job over there after he and my mom divorced. He had us boarding with the Tates. . . . Just before you get to the bridge, you look to your left up on a hill—that's the Tates' house. That's where we stayed. We only stayed there about two weeks. My sister fell out of one of those trees down below and broke her leg which cut daddy's singing career short. He had to come back home and take care of us. I mean, to this day, I don't know how I did it because she was a good sized five-year-old kid. I carried her. . . . When I picked her up when she hit the ground . . . I didn't know her leg was broken. But, when I picked her up, I put one arm under her knees and the other arm around her back. She put her arms around my neck, and I climbed that steep hill. We couldn't even drive a car up that hill, it was so steep. Getting from that tree down below to that house. . . . But I made it. I got up there with her. I told Mrs. Tate, I said, "She hurt herself." And so, Mrs. Tate took her and when she took her, she put her arm under this part of the leg and the leg bent just like it was a knee. And she said, "Oh God, she's broken her leg." So, she told me to get in the back of their car and she laid her in my lap. So, we went to town—to the hospital. Then she called dad. So, dad had to come to town, rent an apartment, and get ready to take care of us all on the same day. I was so mad at the doctor. I could have just killed him. He wouldn't let me wash her foot before they put that cast on her. They put a cast on that whole leg and around her waist. They didn't want her moving that leg because that break was so clean. It was only one little sliver that would hold it while it healed.

In the meantime, my dad met my stepmother. So, he became an absent father. He came home long enough to get clean clothes and dress to go to work. He always had food in the house. But he would leave the whole day, working. Then he'd go straight to her house. He would come to our house with coney islands. He would buy each of us a coney island and then he'd go. He'd drop them off and go straight to her house. I had to play at a tree behind the house we lived in, which was a boarding house. . . . We lived on the second floor in the back corner. If she [my sister] called me, I would have to run up there because she either had to go to the bathroom or she was hungry or something. She got to a point where she could spin around on the middle of that bed, pushing with one foot. Even though her whole leg was straight. But she could tilt that back part of her cast and just go. [laughter] So, I used to laugh at her. Then when mama found out that daddy wasn't coming over. . . . She was work-ing and living across town, and Bartlesville was not that big then. So, then she started coming up and bringing us food and helping us in the evening.

Meantime, I was trying to learn to cook beans . . . I was a reader back in those days too. With her bed rest, reading was my only occupation or whatever you want to call it. I would sit there with my feet in the oven so I could hear when those beans went dry. And I still scorched them! So, mother took care of that.

Mother left us some bananas one time. She left the bananas on top of the chest of drawers next to the bed where she was at. Well, mom didn't think she could reach it. So did I. I went downstairs to play that evening and she started crying. I went up there to see what she was crying about, and her little belly was sticking up and she was almost blue in the face. She couldn't breathe. She was full of gas from that banana. So, I had one of the ladies that lived there call the doctor and ask him what I should do. He told her to put me on the phone and he told me I had to give her an enema. The landlady said she had an enema and showed me how to do that. My sister wouldn't let her touch her. So, I had to do it. It relieved her. I never forgot how to give enemas. [laughter]

And then we had a windstorm . . . I have not seen a windstorm that bad since I've come back. It was just a windstorm, not a tornado. The size of these big trees—they were bending over and touching the ground and then bend over the other way and touch the ground. That house was just rock-ing. I picked her up out of that bed and took her down the stairs. And the stairs went down this way then went down that way. But I got her down there without a crack in that cast and we stayed in that room down there with that lady. Until the storm was over, and dad came home. Anyway, we lived there for a while.

Dad wasn't that strict about culture, but every time mama got a chance, she fed me culture. Before my sister was born, my [maternal] grandfather had two wives. The first wife was barren. That was grandma Pomp. So, he took a second wife. The second wife had all the children. The first wife was boss of the house because she was the first wife. So, grandma Pomp was my playmate when I was about three or four, before my sister was born. But, after my sister was born, she became my responsibility most of the time. But grandma Pomp, she was a character. She could not speak English and I could not speak Delaware. There was no Indian spoke at our house because two tribes. So, grandma Pomp would take me for a ride in daddy's stripped-down Model T Ford. He had a stripped-down one that was a lot of fun to ride in. We used to go tearing through the fields because there were no fences back in that time either. Then my dad used to always pay me with puppies. Every time I did something extra good, he would either get me a new puppy or if one of my puppies died, he would always replace it. So, the night my sister was coming [to be born]. . . . I had an old horse that was so old that I had to mix mash for him. No teeth. But that's all daddy would let me ride. He was very careful with me because he had already lost two children. He didn't want to lose anymore.

So, Uncle Nort had the forty acres that was right alongside the . . . high- way. Mama's allotment, her hundred and twenty took over there and went on over the hill. In fact, there's a mansion close to her property back there, now. Kate owned the rest of the section and Uncle Nort had another piece. He had about seven pieces. That's one of the first things I did when I got back here in '89. I went back and looked at where all the allotments were. I knew where mama's was but I wasn't sure about Aunt Cass's. Her allotment was right across the road from Uncle Roy's. Then down next to her was Aunt Rosie. Next to Aunt Rosie was her two boys' allotment. Then grandpa owned that south side of the road before you get to Shooter Creek Bridge. That whole section, he owned. And grandma owned clear up to Glen Oak if you crossed the road on the other side of the bridge. Grandma Pomp had bigger than anybody. I don't know how she managed that, but she had almost a full section. Hers was on that road that the Tates' house was on and that Kate's house which was just across the road from the Tates'. You go down along the road of that section corner and grandma Pomp

owned the northwest corner of that next section. . . . It was big. The Curly
Heads owned all that and both sides of that rode. We all sold out eventually. Mom and dad sold out when I was about seven. I had gone to kinder-
garten in the country and then first grade through second grade in the
first year. So, dad said that we better get me in town to a school that was
going to work me a little harder. That was one thing my father and grandfather would not give up and that was education. If you didn't learn, you
got a whipping. Boy, I never will forget the "d" in the alphabet. I got a whipping because I kept forgetting the "d." I might forget another one, but
I never forgot the "d" after daddy got through spanking me and then
standing me back up on my little stool where I had to stand on when
I recited for him.

But back in those days we had great big snows. My mother made the
first snow suit that I ever saw. Nobody else had a snowsuit like mama made
for me. She made that for me to wear to school. To walk down through
the snow to school. I had to walk a mile to go to school. I remember
I walked down the hill and mama would watch me. She always made red
snow suits so that she could see me. She could watch me all the way to the
corner. She watched me fall one time and stay down. So, she called the lady
down there and asked her to go see what was wrong. I just got so cold that
I was ready to go to sleep. That lady took me in and rubbed my face. . . .
She took me in and fed me some chicken soup. Then she dried me out and
wrote a note to the teacher and sent me off to school. By that time enough
wagons and horses and cars had come by that I could walk through the
mud then and go to school.

Mom and dad loved to dance, and they had a player piano that they
used to pay Leonard with cake and ice cream . . . because he's, my cousin.
They used to pay him to come up and peddle the player piano so they could
all dance. All their friends would come over and they would have cake and
pie and whatever. That was nice. Mama wasn't against the new things, but
she just didn't want me to forget the old. So, she always saw to it that I had
access to all of those kinds of things. Another thing that scared my cousin,

really scared my cousin. And that was—in our family, the old folks come and gets us a few days before we die. I used to take Sandy's grandmother [Aunt Cass], I used to take her gowns to her. When she divorced Ace Barry—Well, she didn't divorce Ace. Ace divorced her. Ace's wife just literally walked in there and stole him away from her and snowed him under. Then she wouldn't let him see his kids. So, whenever I'd see Lilian and Arlene and Roy coming over to our house, I knew Ace Barry was going to come by and see his kids. That's the only way he could do it. To sneak around and do it. Aunt Cass started drinking and she met Claude Morrison and she married him. They'd get drunk and fight and he'd beat her up every time. She'd wind up in the hospital. The first-time mama told me about this, people coming and getting us. . . . I took Aunt Cass her gown while she was in the hospital. The old hospital, Memorial. I took her clean gowns to her, and Aunt Cass gave them back to me, except one. She said, "Take these back to Josie and tell your mom that I won't need them." I said, "Oh, but you're going to go home." She said, "No, I'm not going home. Just tell your mama I won't need them. But I'm not going home." I went home and mama was there and so was Aunt Kate. When I told them that, they both started crying. Mama told me to go outside and play and go next door and see the cookie lady. This lady would give us cookies every time we went to see her. So, she told me to go see her. I didn't often have permission but this time I was legal. [laughter] I didn't know why mama was crying but it's because Aunt Cass knew she was going. Sure enough, she went two days later. . . . She had a clean gown that morning and kept another for the next day. She sent the other two back.

Mama took care of Lillian, that's Sandy and Patty Kay's mother [her niece, Cass's daughter]. Took care of Lillian from the time Lillian got pregnant with Dean. Mama and I lived with Lillian and [her husband] Lou and [her kids] Sandy and Patty Kay. Sandy and Patty Kay were little kids then. Lil wasn't supposed to have Sandy. But she went ahead and had her and I understand that she almost died. Aunt Kate fainted on the floor [during her labor] and the doctors said, "Don't bother with her, we have more problems right here. Just, step over her." Then when she had Patty Kay. . . . She had a really hard time having her. When she did have her, Patty Kay had a lot of hair on her arms and on her legs and stuff. So, the doctor said she wasn't in there for long enough. Of course, Lillian took one look at her and said, "That's not my baby." [laughter] The doctor told her not to worry and that it would come off and that that happens to a lot of women. So, when she got pregnant with Dean, the doctor gave her everything that was legal to try and abort that baby. Dean wasn't going nowhere. He knew where he was at, and he was going to stay. [laughter] He stayed right there. When she went into labor, I sat in a chair outside the door. Right by the bedroom, where she and Louis slept, the front bedroom. I sat there for about an hour and a half, almost two hours. The doors were open, and the doctor dropped this dripping baby in our hands and told us to do something with it. He said, "I have a lot of work to do in here."

I took him into the kitchen, and I used Crisco, you know, cooking grease. I greased him down and then I wiped him all off. I put a little dia-per on him and a little shirt and wrapped him up tight in a blanket. Held him and sat in the chair by the door. He was tired because he had been busy getting born. So, he slept like a good little boy. He was my boy until I left and quit living with them. I slept with him on my chest, and I would get up. Lillian nursed him. . . . Don't let me get ahead of my story.

So, Louis found a house to rent over on Santa Fe [Street] which was right behind where we were. . . . Louis started working—and Louis is still alive, he's still around—Lillian insisted that Mama go out with her friends and play cards. You know how much the older folks love to play Pitch around here. Well, that's how mama was. She had a crew she loved to go play Pitch with. And I was going out. I was running around with Edith and Rosalie Horner and Dale and Wayne and Goofy Taylor. We had a whole little gang, just a bunch of Indian kids. So, I was getting dressed to go out too. . . . Well, Lillian was bathing the baby and I was getting dressed to go out. They called me from the hospital and told me to go there and pick her [my mother] up. I said, "What could have happened, Louis?" He said, "I don't know but I'll take you down there." So, I went in there and got mama. She said, "Oh baby my head hurts." It had only been about ten minutes since she left the house! I said, "What happened?" And she said, "Well, we stopped at that honky-tonk. . . . We had one beer and then we got in the car to go to so and so's house over on Highway 60." Down there, there was nothing but red clay because of lead. . . . It had killed all the plant life out there. But there was a short cut there and they were really barreling going across that flat out there. It had rained a couple of nights before and no one had noticed it or paid any attention to it or traveled on it at night. Half of the road was taken away by water and when their wheel went down into that hole, it threw mama out of the roof of the car and into the field. Her head had hit the only rock that was in the damn field. The doctor tried to tell me she was drunk. I said, "How could she get drunk in ten minutes?" I fought with him about that. He gave her pain medication. That's all he gave her and then he sent her home. He wouldn't even examine her or look in her eyes or nothing. He smelled the one beer, and he was a fanatic on drinking. So, that was it. I had to call a couple of days later. I had to call for more pain medication because she had run out of what they had given her. She was really hurting. My mom didn't scream because when we lived on third street, she passed a kidney stone that was the size of a robin's egg . . . and she did not utter a sound.

She said, "My children were playing out in front of the little porch." It was an outhouse, but it was real close. It was dug beside a porch. She said, "I couldn't scream because it would have scared my children." So, Mama didn't scream even though she was hurting so bad. But I could tell by the way that she was acting. She couldn't raise her arms up. From her elbow to up this way she could. But like this way, she couldn't. She had a big ole bruise . . . and another at the back of her head. It just looked horrible. I called up to get some more pain medication. Lillian had brought [the baby] Dean in there because the kitchen was in the front room. She was washing him, bathing him.

All of a sudden, while I was talking to mom, she started talking Delaware. She said, "Excuse me, baby." And she started talking Delaware to the foot of her bed. I know she had forgotten how to speak Delaware because there was no need for her to speak Delaware anymore. I was in my teens, late teens then . . . I remembered what she told me. I said, "Who are you talking to, mom?" And she said, "I'm talking to grandpa and grandma and Cass. They've come after me." I said, "Oh, Mama. No, not yet." You always try. I told her, "Not yet." She said, "Oh honey, don't act that way. You know, it's time."

Lillian took one listen to that, and she grabbed that baby and back in the bedroom she went. She didn't come out until Louis got there. In the meantime, I went over to the neighbors and called Rosie and asked her to bring her car over and take mama down to Claremore. When I got back from Claremore, Lillian and Lou had moved to Penn Street! Lil would not stay in that house. She didn't believe in ghosts, but she heard mama speaking Indian and she knew something was happening. When I told her what was happening and who it was. . . . She took that baby and went. She told Lou that he better find another house if he wanted to keep her. "And we're going to move tonight." So, that happens. I was there when it happened to Aunt Cass, and that's when mama told me that that happens.

. . . Well mama was there for two days, and we took her at the end of the second day to Claremore. They put her in Claremore, and she died the next morning. They called me up and told me that if I wanted to speak to my mom that I better get down there right away. Before I finished dressing, they called back and said it was too late. It gives you a certain amount of security to know that you are going to have some more time before you go. I firmly believe it. That was something that really stayed with me.

I find it strange that when my mother died . . . I think I was one of Arnold Moore's first customers. Arnold Moore was here then. That was way back in. . . . She died, and we were having the services. Aunt Kate, bless her heart. She came through and was looking in the casket and acted like she was fainting. She fell. I was watching her, and I saw that she held her head up until she got her body on the floor. Then she laid her head down very gently. I got tickled. I'm sitting there, the front row, with a handkerchief over my nose, and I'm laughing. They think I'm crying. Then I heard mama say, "Kate, for heaven's sake, get off that damn floor!" I could hear mama so plain. I looked around and was waiting for somebody else to react. Nobody else reacted. I had sat with mom all night long at the funeral home. Kate got up and went and sat down. It was just so funny.

Then I buried mother and then I went to California in '39. Same time that Hitler was passing the line into Poland, I was crossing the line into California. I made the remark then, "I wonder how long Hitler is going to be in Poland? I wonder how long I'm going to be in California?" Turns out I was going to be in California for fifty years. Hitler didn't stay very long in Poland. [laughter] Too long in the long run. But it wasn't really a long time. Then I became aware of another strange thing that I do which I didn't know I did.

Well, when we were young, we used to go swimming at a creek . . . to the best swimming hole, and we were down there swimming. Lillian and Arlene were playing in the water and so was I. They were older than me, like I said. Lillian was four years older than me, and Arlene was two years older than I was. But daddy had taught me to swim, just like my daddy always taught me things. He threw me and said, "Swim." You'd be amazed how fast you could learn that way. Lillian was in trouble first. I pushed her to the edge of the creek so she could grab hold of a root and pull herself out. By that time Arlene was in the trouble. I went back and got Arlene. In the meantime, I saw my sister got in trouble. So, I got Arlene and had to hurry up and come back and get my sister. After I got her out, I didn't have enough strength to get out myself. I just drifted underneath the water. I remember it was so nice feeling that way. I could feel the pebbles on my back, and I could see the sun shining into the water and it was so beautiful. I was just kind of floating down the creek and my back would periodically touch the pebbles. I thought to myself, "I'm just going to stay here.

I'm so comfortable." The next thing you know, I was being rolled back and forth on a log and I was throwing up water. I never really thought anything about it right then. Although I was aware that I was a little older when that was over. In my mind, I was a little more settled. I was a little better about noticing things around me. But it didn't register because I was only about seven or eight.

It wasn't until I went to Chilocco that I realized that this thing happened. We were told to go down into the basement and get our uniforms after we had been lined up. . . . As we checked in, we were told to go put our things in the room we were going to be in and then go down into the basement and get our uniforms. There was about six of us girls that were sent down to go get our uniforms. I was in a room with four at that time and then there were two from another room. When we walked down into the basement, there was nothing but a row of doors all the way down our left side and all the way across the other end. It was all windows on this side and just a wall back here where you came downstairs from. One of the girls said, "How are we supposed to know what door to go to?" What I thought I was going to say was to just try doors until we come to it. Instead, out of my mouth came, "The first door is to the showers . . . the next door is whatever it was. The next door is. . . . The next door is where we get our uniforms." I told them where every door went, and I didn't even know I knew it. I thought, "Where'd that come from?" Well, I never thought anything more about it afterwards. The girls said, "Oh, you must have been here before." I said, "No, I haven't. I have never been here before."

So, then the next time it happened was when I crossed the line into California. The ride that we had. . . . Back in those days you could hitch hike anywhere because it was safe. There was none of those kooks. . . . When we drove into Los Angeles, the people that were driving the car. . . . A man and his wife. She said, "Oh, look at that pretty building over there. I wonder what that big, tall, white building is?" Without thinking, I said, "That's the Lincoln Heights Jail. It's a brand new building in Los Angeles. They finally voted for a new jail." And that's it. Up here, I'm thinking, "Oh, here

we go again, kid. Where in the hell did that come from?" We went there.
We were going to visit [my friend] Virginia's boyfriend at his mother's
home in Hollywood. So, we went to Hollywood, and I knew everything
like I had been there before. All the way when we were getting there.
I started looking in the newspapers because my mother was already dead,
and I wasn't going to go back to living with my father and my stepmother and be the janitor for that group. I was living with [my friend]
Josephine Hamilton over at [inaudible] at that time.

So, I got a job as a governess for a little two-and-a-half-year-old boy.
One of the reasons that I did that was because Josephine had an elementary school family, and she had a college school family [that she worked
for]. She had told me to "go ahead and go to California with your friend
and when you come back, we will go to the World's Fair in San Francisco."
Then she said when she gets done getting these kids through school, "then
we're going to travel the world." I thought, "Oh my god, I'm too young to
be tied down like that." She had just talked me into coming to visit her
[while she was at her family's house] and I had stopped . . . on the way back
from seeing my new baby half-brother that I had up there. I had money
for a cab to take me out to the Indian village and visit the Hamilton house.
They knew exactly where to go.

I went on to California without any real plans. But I was thinking,
"We'll go out to the World's Fair, but I'm going to tell her [my friend,
Virginia] that I can't stay very long. I don't want to tie myself down here
very long." I would have liked to have gone to college. But at the time there
was no way because I was making my own living. When Virginia asked if
I was ready to go home, I said, "Yeah, but I'm not going because I have a
job that I start next Monday." She said, "What did you get a job doing?"
I said, "Taking care of a little kid. They call it 'governess' out here." So, she
looked for the same thing and got a job. She stayed for about six months.
During those six months, she got lonesome for her mama. But we hitch-
hiked back here at least three times during that time. [laughter] In fact,
we brought a footlocker and a little Boston bull terrier dog and got out

there to hitchhike from LA to Oklahoma. Virginia's mother lived up in Dewey. . . . I don't think Virginia was Delaware. Her dad might have been, but I don't know. Anyway, we'd sit on the side of the rode with magazines. Both of us would have a magazine. When a car would stop and it was someone we didn't think we should be riding with, we'd just tell them, "No, we like to sit out here in the sun and read." [laughter] And tell them to go on. At night, we'd usually get a ride with truck drivers because truck drivers could pick us up at night because they couldn't get caught. They don't bother you. They're on a time schedule so they never bothered us. The extra driver would get the back and go to sleep. We'd have the big wide front seat to ride in. We'd stop to eat at a restaurant, and they wouldn't let us go into the restaurant with them, but they'd bring us back something to eat. So, that was the thing. Then I came back here. But I was always a Delaware. . . . I've held a lot of jobs. I've been an entertainer. I've sung for a living, vocal. My favorite place to work was hotel bars because you're close to your people, and you know what they like. It's nice to do. But I was always the Indian. In fact, that's what they called me in LA—"the Indian." People speak to me and call me and say, "Hi, Indian." I know where I knew them. Later, when I got married and went to live in San Francisco . . . then I became the Stanford grandma. They're the ones that started calling me "Mama Joan." And they got me a license plate that said, "Mama Joan." [laughter] I loved them people. Yeah, I did.

[The remainder of the interview describes Joanna's years in California.]

Bonnie Thaxton (August 19, 1997)

I'm very proud that my mother was full blood Delaware—and my dad was Irish. But I'll guarantee that he knew just as much about the Delawares as anybody! He could talk Delaware and went to all the funerals and all the things. He used to really be traditional. He knew all about it, more than a lot of people. They would always call on my dad. We lived five miles north and three miles east of Dewey. I went to the school out in the country.

When I graduated from the eighth grade, I went to the Indian school at Haskell. I went there four years until I graduated. I really loved it up there. We weren't allowed to talk our language and all that. . . . And we didn't go around where they were talking Delaware back when we were children. . . .

Anyway, I loved arts and crafts. I loved bead work, and I did weaving. This teacher was really surprised at some of the patterns that I'd come up with. When I wouldn't be at school, then a lot of times, I'd be around there with that weaving or bead work. I had made some rugs and the head principle up at Haskell came around and looked at the weaving and all that. . . . He couldn't believe that some of us had made those rugs. He asked who and she told them. He bought the rugs, and boy, he gave me twenty dollars. Twenty dollars was big bucks back then! After graduating from up there, the teacher begged me to come back. I probably should have gone back but when you're young you don't think those things. They begged me to come back, and I probably could have been an instructor. But I decided to stay at home. I went and worked at Philip's and I went and worked there for about two years. . . . Later we moved to Tulsa and had to work down there. I've powwowed all my life. The shawls that the elders used to wear are not like the ones we've got now. They had the real bead work on them. They were very heavy. You can imagine.

[Brief exchange follows about various specific handcrafted items.]

You know it's a real religious thing to have powwows and Stomp Dances. A lot of people used to think that it was just to go over there and get drunk. That's not at all what it's all about. I remember thirty years ago, a burial. And they don't know how to do that this day and time. If someone would die, they would take him to. . . . I remember when my grandma Lucy died, and they brought her out to our house. . . . And they would appoint two ladies to cook and they would cook all night. There would be a man to help the women lift these big pots and so on and so forth. And get water for and all that. Then I remember in the evening they would go and shoot in the direction of the body . . . and then they'd shoot the next morning. By golly, we were scared silly, us children. Jump and whatever . . . I used to always think. . . . Go to the cemetery and they'd stay up all night with the body and then they would leave at midnight. People would sit there all night long in the homes and then take them to the cemetery and everything they used to have there. They'd have a feast out there. . . . Everybody would eat, and they would sit down and eat and all that. I don't see that anymore. You know when they'd come home from the funeral, you'd have to wash your hair. . . . We'd have to ruin our hairdos. [laughter] I remember they used to—when they had the body there, they would cover all of the mirrors. It was a few days after the funeral when they would have another feast.

I was about nine years old when my grandma died. It seems like I was going to others they had. . . . But it seems like it's been forgotten, I guess. . . . I've heard of the big house. Mother used to talk about it. I really didn't know all that much about it. I know that it was real sacred and everything. . . . I don't think they could revive it. I just don't think it's going to happen. . . . The thing is I just don't think anybody knows enough about it to revive it.

My mother spoke the language, very much at the time, and my grandmother could not speak English. She talked Delaware. My mother, her brothers, and sisters all talked Delaware. If I could hear some of the words, then I could understand what they were talking about. I took my mother to see her sister at Shawnee who lived down there. They started talking and laughing and carrying on. I thoroughly enjoyed taking my mother to visit her sister, and her sister would come up here and stay with mother a week or two. And they just talked Delaware all the time.

I tried to learn [Delaware]. I went a few times especially when Lucy Blalock was teaching. She was good. . . . She would tell you if it wasn't right! . . . I just loved Lucy. She really could talk Delaware.

It's hard [to speak Delaware] because you gotta keep talking to people or you forget a lot of it. If you are going to learn how to speak it then you have to have someone to talk to everyday. I think I'm glad they're trying to talk the Delaware language. Then again, there's people that don't have anyone to talk to. And I think that you do need someone to talk to everyday.

[More brief back-and-forth about specific people.]

I'm proud of being Delaware. I'm very proud of my children, knowing that they are proud to be Indian too. I was real thrilled when Bucky started dancing, and he said, "Mom, I think I want to start dancing." I said, "You are?" And he said, "Yes." And I said, "Well what are you going to do?" He said, "I think the Straight Dance." And I said, "Well, you have to make up your mind if this is really what you want to do." I was just real happy about it. Of course, he'd been in the Navy and everything. He said, "Mother, do you think that you could make my outfit out of my Navy uniform?" And I thought, "Oh boy." That material in that Navy uniform is really difficult material. I mean they are so together that they don't splinter anything when they're wearing them. So, I ripped that, did that and did that and made his outfit out of it. . . . I made him his ribbon shirts and the hand-kerchief that they have on their back and all that. On the night of the pow-wow, he came over and he hugged me and said, "Mother, I bet I'm the only one that can say that my mother made my outfit."

I have different ones that always wants to dance with me and this and that. Even different young men! There's a boy from Pawnee, Eddie. . . . Do you know him? . . . He is a sweet person. He took a liking to me. He's prob-ably younger than Bucky. I don't know that. And I just really think a lot of Eddie. And every time he's the headman dancer, he's always wanting me to come and be there with him. Then he has the giveaway and he's always giving me something. He gave me a Pendleton and a shawl. He's just a wonderful guy. He hadn't been dancing for quite some time and he's really a good Straight dancer. I wondered if he got married and this and that. Finally, here at our powwow in May, we were dancing, and someone poked me with their dance stick. I turned around and it was

Eddie. I said, "Well, where have you been?" He came over and he sat down, and he said he was a policeman over at Pawnee and that he was very busy. . . . I told Eddie to be sure and talk to one of our Delaware War Mothers. He said, "Oh I can't do it because I'm heading to Connecticut because they pay real big money up there." I said, "Well, good for you." He said, "Next time I'll be there." I said, "Okay." He told me that he was studying to be a highway patrol man. But he did come up to the powwow again. . . . I think a lot of my friends and relatives realize that I'm getting old or something. [laughs] Like I say, I love to go to the dances, and I always have. And I will as long as I can!

[More back-and-forth about specific people. They look at a feather-decorated outfit.]

I put the feathers up there. I got an eagle about . . . a couple of years ago. It was real money. When I got it, they called me from the post office. Wondering if I'd be home and so on. They said, "You got a package that's in hot ice." And I would have to be at home . . . and everyone down at the post office was wondering what on earth was in this package. The guy that delivers my mail is really a nice young man. If I get a package or whatever, you have to go down and get it usually. But he will bring that out to me and bring it here to my door. He's just really a nice person. One day he wasn't even working but he came to put up the mail for the next day and my check came in. . . . And he saw that and knew I got it the third. So, he came out and brought it out to me. He's just a nice young man. Anyway, when he delivered that big ole box he said, "Bonnie, what is in that box?" I said, "It's an eagle." He said, "Oh my gosh! We were all wondering at the post office what could be in that box, in that hot ice." I said, "Well, that's what it is." He said, "Oh goodness, what are you going to do with it?" And I said, "I'm going to eat it." [laughter] He looked at me so funny, "Bonnie! You're not going to eat it." I said, "No, I am going to have me a fan made [for an outfit], and Bucky will probably get a fan out of the deal." He said, "I'll be darned. How did you get it?" I told him. He said, "Oh, you have to be Indian to get it!" I said, "Yes, sir." He thought that was really something. I thought, "What am I going to do with this thing?" I opened that box and I called Bucky. I said, "I don't know what to do with this thing. I might just go ahead and marry it." He said, "Oh, no!" [laughter] I went over there. I didn't have enough room in my freezer to keep it. I had too much in that freezer, and he told me to bring it on over. . . . So I took it over there and he has a friend that loves to make fans and this and that. Of course, Bucky gets the . . . Indian guys over. He was going to have it mounted with, I think, a flag. It was really nice. Of course, we went ahead and took care of the inside and everything.

I got my order in about six months, at the time. Then I got those papers. You have to have a written deal to show them that you received them, and what you're using them for. You need to take that when you're powwow-ing because they can come up and say, "Where'd you get that eagle feather?" And if you don't have that paper . . . you're fined.

I got it in here. You wanna see it? Someone else gave me one, and I thought, "Well, I don't know anything. . . ." But one time Bucky and I went to . . . a powwow and he called me. He lived in Kansas then. He said, "Mother, you wanna go?" But it's so hot up there! He said, "Do you want me to bring the trailer?" I said, "Don't do that. Just bring your tent." He said, "Okay. . . ." Just bring your tent and he and I could sleep in that tent. It was very little. We went over there and had the best time at that pow-wow. There was that fella, and I hadn't seen him for a long, long time. They came up there where we put up our little tent. He was an elder man from Little Rock, I think it was. So, they drove up there and they had some young guys with them. His grandson and his friends and so on and so forth. Pretty soon that fella wanted to put up a tarp so there would be shade next to their tent. Oh, that old fella was having a time. Bucky and I went over there and asked if he needed some help. He said, "Oh, I sure could use some." Bucky did all the work. That old guy just thought Bucky was the finest person. He said, "Oh, I haven't run into too many fellas like you." And he wanted to know about his name and this and that. . . . After all that, Bucky was just really glad that he offered a hand. Bucky was really good at helping people like that. That evening that fella called Bucky over there and he said, "Bucky, I've never seen a young man quite like you." And he said, "I've worn this dance outfit for a long time . . . I'm going to give it to you." And Bucky said, "Oh, I don't want to take your eagle feather." And he said, "Yes, I want you to have it. I think you're a mighty fine young man." I just couldn't believe it and Bucky couldn't either. . . . He thought his grandson and his friends would help him with their stuff, but they disappeared. He just couldn't believe that this young man came over and gave him a helping hand. He just went on about Bucky. So, anyway he gave him a beautiful feather. We do have a lot of feathers . . . I'm real happy I got that eagle.

III. TODAY

The Elkhairs have many living descendants in Oklahoma and beyond. Among them are those who continue to take a special interest in maintaining tribal traditions. Through the line passing through Charley's son Jesse comes Michael Pace (Xinkwilënu), a former assistant chief and chair of the Cultural Preservation Committee, who has been a noted dancer and storyteller for many years, regularly invited to perform at museums in the United States and even overseas. Mike grew up going to powwows and stomp dances; his uncle Ray Elkhair taught him as a boy, and those memories became part of his childhood happiness.[24]

Through the family line passing through Charley's daughter, Sallie Fall-eaf, descends John Sumpter. He has been active in the tribe's political life for many years, serving on varied committees, working on cultural preservation, land management, Native American Graves Protection and Repatriation Act (NAGPRA) work, and veterans' affairs. He even made it his business to learn how to make the wampum that his forebear, Charley Elkhair, once deemed essential to the Big House ceremony, and he has worked on reenactments for the National Park Service. He has been to almost every one of the powwows that happen annually in Copan, on what was once Falleaf land.[25]

In 2022, in the wake of interruptions due to the COVID-19 pandemic, the annual Copan powwow was held just as in the past.[26] On the eve of the wider gathering, to which all tribes and other guests are invited, the Delaware always meet on their own to hold their traditional social dances. On this Thursday evening in May, as the sun grew low, Levi Randoll, a young Elkhair descendant, used the same kind of fire-starter seen in the old photos of Julius Fouts. He made the kindling begin to smoke, struggling with the dampness that came with a week of pouring rain. He persisted, explaining to the interested people gathered around that the fire for such an occasion should be *pilsit* if at all possible. They nodded, understanding him.

Dusk fell and the fire leaped. The people gathered in the cleared arena at the edge of the wooded campground. Different families clustered behind the various benches. In the star-studded darkness, the drums throbbed and voices rose in song. First the people did the Bean Dance (Malaxkwsit-kan, they explained on a handout), the dancers winding around the field like a vine, tighter and tighter, until they ended laughing in a jumble. They did the Stomp Dance (Nikantkan), legs pounding in the same patterns as they had for centuries. Then came the Woman Dance (Xkweyok Naxkuhë-maok). The accompanying song originated in the deep past as a call-and-response story about a woman who died and asked her husband to let her have her little son—which of course could never be.[27] Women and girls came forward, wearing beautiful skirts they had made in the traditional style, or which someone had made for them, with bright colored shawls drawn over their blouses. Sarah Boyd, a young woman, led them as they wound through the darkness, starting and stopping in response to the men's singing. Trailing at the end came a bevy of very little girls who did not yet know the steps. They crashed into those in front of them at every pause. If Charles and Susan Elkhair, or Julius and Minnie Fouts, were watching, they must have smiled with pleasure: those young girls didn't yet know the dance, but they were learning.

The Turtle's Back

(IROQUOIAN AND MUNSEE VERSIONS)

In the 1890s, anthropologist John B. Hewitt, who was himself of Tuscarora descent, interviewed several elders of different Haudenosaunee nations (that is, the Iroquoian nations of Oneida, Mohawk, Onondaga, Cayuga, Seneca, and Tuscarora) to obtain their renditions of their people's creation story. They spoke in their own languages, and he transcribed the words, then produced a word-for-word translation, and finally a colloquial one. He later published all the versions together. The version given here was provided by Seth Newhouse (Mohawk) in 1896. The story demonstrates how closely the Lenape origin myth (surviving elsewhere in fragments) resembled that of the Haudenosaunee. It also serves as a reminder of how much complexity and detail was lost when Mark Harrington (and other outsiders) took down the Lenape stories in English, working through a summarizing interpreter.

In the same year of 1896, Hewitt also interviewed a man named John Armstrong who lived on the Cattaraugus Seneca Reservation. Although Armstrong lived there and spoke Seneca, he was himself Delaware and was part of a small community of Delaware people. He told the creation story in Delaware, in the northern dialect called Munsee. It is impossible to know how much his Delaware rendition was influenced by the Iroquoian rendition that he also knew well. It was certainly distinct in some regards. Its deep value to us now lies in

---

the fact that it was transcribed in Lenape; we can hear the rhythm of
the Lenape storytelling.

Seth Newhouse (Originally in Mohawk)

In the regions above there dwelt man-beings[1] who knew not what it is to
see one weep, nor what it is for one to die; sorrow and death were unknown
to them. And the lodges belonging to them, to each of the ohwachiras
[families] were large, and very long, because each ohwachira usually abode
in a single lodge.

Within the circumference of the village there was one lodge which
claimed two persons, a male man-being and a female-man-being. Moreover, these two beings were related to each other as brother and sister, and
the two lived in holy seclusion. . . .

After a time, it came to pass that the female's parent perceived that,
indeed, it seemed she was in delicate health; one would indeed think that
she was about to give birth to a child. So then they questioned her, saying,
"To whom of the man-beings living within the borders of the village
are you about to bear a child?" But she, the girl child, did not answer a
single word.

At last the day of her confinement came, and she gave birth to a
child, and the child was a girl; but she persisted in refusing to tell who the
father was.

In the time preceding the birth of the girl child, the man-being at times
heard his kinfolk in conversation say that his sister was about to give birth
to a child. Now the man-being spent his time in meditating on this event,
and after a while he began to be ill. And moreover, when the moment of
his death had arrived, his mother sat beside his bed, gazing at him in his
illness. She knew not what it was; never before had she seen anyone ill.

[The family experiences the grief of mortality for the first time when the
man-being dies to make way for the new life. They place his preserved body

in an alcove that they reached by climbing a ladder. The child—who was his daughter—becomes an adult. At first her weeping is boundless as she realizes her father is dead, but she becomes reconciled to having lost him when she finds she can always climb the ladder, sit by his remains, and communicate with him, sometimes even laughing at the stories he tells. Eventually her father informs her she must marry. She embarks on a difficult journey, and finally marries a man who is cruel to her, though he provides her family venison and corn. She endures her experiences with fortitude because her father's spirit regularly advises her and guides her. At length her husband becomes ill.]

When they failed to cure his illness, his people questioned him, saying: "What should we do so that you may recover from your illness?" Then he answered them, saying: "I am thinking that, perhaps, I would recover from my illness if you would uproot the tree standing in my dooryard." . . . When they had uprooted the tree, he said to his spouse: "Do spread for me something there beside the place where stood the tree." Thereupon she did spread something for him there, and he then lay down on it. And so, when he lay there, he said to his spouse: "Here, sit you beside me." She did sit beside his body as he lay there. He then said to her: "Hang your legs down into the abyss." For where they had uprooted the tree there came to be a deep hole, which extended through to the nether world, with earth all around it.

Truly it came to pass, that while he lay there his suffering was mitigated. . . . When he had, seemingly, recovered from his illness, he turned himself over . . . and looked into the hole. After a while he said to his spouse: "Look thither into the hole to see what things are occurring there in yonder place." She bent forward her body and looked in. Whereupon he placed his fingers against the nape of her neck and pushed her, and she fell into the hole.

. . . She kept falling in the darkness. After a while she passed through it. She looked about her in all directions and saw on all sides of her that everything was blue in color. . . . She knew nothing of the thing she saw, but in truth she now was looking on a great expanse of water, though she did not know what it was.

This is what she saw: on the surface of the water, floating about hither and thither, like veritable canoes, were all the kinds of ducks. Loon noticed her, and he suddenly shouted, "A female man-being is coming up from the depths." Then Bittern spoke, saying, "Indeed she is not coming up out of the depths. She is falling from above." Whereupon they held a council to decide what they should do to provide for her welfare. They finally decided to invite the Great Turtle to come. Loon said to him: "You should float your body above the place where you are in the depths of the water." In the first place, they sent a large number of ducks of various kinds. These flew and elevated themselves in a very compact body and went to meet her on high. And on their backs, thereupon did her body alight. Then slowly they descended, bearing her on their backs.

Great Turtle had satisfactorily caused his carapace to float. There upon his back they placed her. Then Loon said, "Come, you who are deep divers, which one of you is able to dive so as to fetch up earth?" Thereupon one by one they dived into the water. It was at this time that Beaver made the attempt and dived. The time was long and there was only silence. It was a long time before his back reappeared. He came up dead, his breathing having failed him. They examined his paws, but he had brought up no earth. Then Otter said, "Well, let it be my turn now; let me make another attempt." Whereupon he dived. A longer time elapsed before he came to the surface. He also came up dead in his turn. They examined his paws also. Neither did he, it is said, bring up any earth. It was then that Muskrat said, "I also will make the desperate attempt." So then he dove into the water. It was a still longer time that he, in turn, was under water. Then, after a while, he floated to the surface, coming up dead, having lost his breath. They examined the inside of his paws also. They found mud. He brought up his paws and his mouth full of mud.

It was then that they made us of this mud. They coated the edge of the carapace of the Great Turtle. Now it was that other muskrats, in their turn, dived into the water to fetch mud. They floated to the surface dead. In this way they worked until they had made a circuit of the carapace of the Great Turtle, placing mud thereon, until the two portions of the work came together. Loon said: "Now there is enough. Now it will suffice." Thereupon the muskrats ceased diving to fetch up mud.

Now this female man-being sat on the carapace of the Great Turtle. After the lapse of time she went to sleep. After a while she awoke. Now then, the carapace of the Great Turtle was covered with mud. Moreover, the earth whereon she sat had become enlarged in size. At that time she looked and saw that willows had grown up to bushes along the edge of the water. Then also, when she woke again, the carcass of a deer, recently killed, lay there, and now besides this, a small fire burned there, and besides this, a sharp stone lay there. Now, of course, she dressed and quartered the carcass of the deer and roasted some pieces thereof, and she ate her fill. So when she had finished her repast, she again looked about her. Now, assuredly, the earth had increased much in size, for it grew very rapidly. She saw another thing: she saw growing shrubs of the rose-willow along the edge of the water.

Not long after, she saw a small rivulet take up its course. Thus things came to pass in their turn. Rapidly was the earth increasing in size. She looked and saw all species of herbs and grasses spring from the earth and also saw that they began to grow. . . .

Source: J. N. B. Hewitt, "Iroquoian Cosmology," in *Twenty-First Annual Report of the Bureau of American Ethnology, 1899–1900* (Washington, DC: Government Printing Office, 1903), 255–295.

John Armstrong (in Munsee, translated into English)[2]

a-wă-çagămäu'   dallao' çoăk
above the sky   they lived
They [the beings, the spirits] lived above the sky

Gï'-gai' in   lawodänai-ä' we'-gin
headman   in the middle of the village
and the chief lived in the center of the town.

we-wo' in
he has got a wife
He had a wife.

woak 'in ne dja-no'   o'-gwäsis 'in
and he's got a child   a girl
And he also had a child, a baby girl.

da-çe' in   wu-notce'in ma'-o-lallendamo-wi'
sometimes   he began   to be dissatisfied
At some point he began to feel out of sorts.

Niskhallendăm oin
he feels bad   he said
"Something is weighing on my mind," he said.

in manaso' in
he was jealous
In fact, he was jealous.

in winginäu
he wants something
He wanted something.

wä-mä'-in	a-wän	gwĭ'-gje	windaumowawall
every	body	they tried	to tell him what he wanted

Everyone tried to tell him what it was.

maha	in	awän	gwize	iwĕn	da-nät	gwäk	ayăndăñ	wa-ge'-gai'
it can't	who		can			whatever anything	what he wanted	this chief

No one could tell whatever it was that the chief wanted.

da	in	lĭk-iq	gwe-o'	nall in	mai-a-o-tho	lino	o-in
some		time	after	then	one	man	he said

Then some time later, one man said,

ni-ha-mĭⁿtc	dĭlli de-ha	yo-nät	wŭᵏdă-yaⁿ-damĭn
I think so	I really think	might be	he wants

"I now think that this is what he probably wants:

lit-dä-hä-wät	wŭn	mĭ'tkum	am	mă'-kină
he thinks	this	my tree	then	to pull up

He probably thinks, 'This tree of mine should be pulled up,

pale	wam nipalla
another place	set it aside

and set to stand someplace else.'"

nallin	wämĭ'	a'wän	in	pä-ŭ'
then	every	body	perhaps³	come

Then everyone came.

Nall'in	wä-ma'-wän	nă o'-dall na-wŭl	yoll	mĭ'tkwull
then	every body	they took hold of the tree	this	the tree

Everyone took hold of that tree.

nall'in   gwese'   ma'kinawawăll
then   they did pull it up
Then they succeeded in pulling it out.

pallewĭ'in   winipallawawall
another place   they set it
And they stood it someplace else

nall'in   ktcĭ-pkwĭ'-läl   wĕñ-djĭk-kde-nĕⁿt   wŭn-mĭ'-tuk
then   the bottom dropped   they pulled it out   this tree
Then the bottom of the hole dropped out where the tree had been taken out.

nall'in   wä-ma'-awän   in   pĕnamin   yon   ändăpkwak
then   everybody   perhaps   looked   this   where the hole is
Everybody looked at the place where the hole was.

Än-da'   wä-mă'-awän ända   wäme' gi-sĭ   pĕnŭñ-gĕ
Whenever   everybody   whenever all finished   seeing it
When everybody had finished looking

nall'in   wa-gĭ'-gai   odĭlla-wal   wewăll
then   chief   told   his wife
then the chief said to his wife,

nyo'hă   ambeä'   mawe'   pnummōdok
well   we must   go   see it
"Well, let us go look at it, too."

nall'in   wa'-o'-gwä-o   onatnawul   w-unitcanăll
then   this woman   she picked up   her child
Then the woman picked up her child.

djañ-go'-gwä-sǐs
little girl
It was a little girl.

wonaiyomawǎll'in
she placed her on her back
And she carried her on her back.

nǎhin bä-ya'-di-de'   enda wallagǎk
they two reached there   at that hole
When they arrived over where the hole went in,

nall'in wallinoq   pěnǔminliallau-ming
then   this man   looked far into it
The man looked down into it.

nall'in pǔskwin
then   he stood up
Then he stood up,

dǐllawal   wiwall
he told   his wife
and said to his wife,

yo'   ge ambeä   gi   pǐnaX   yon   pkwǎgamiñkw
well you too   you   look   this   hole
"Well, you too, you look at this hole in the ground."

o   ino'   wa'-o'gwä-o
Oh   she said   this woman
"Oh," said the woman,

gĕⁿ'-lă ĕⁿ-gwi'damin
truly   I am very afraid
"I am truly afraid of it.

djipina-kwŭt
it looks ugly
It looks frightful."

nall'in wapaça-nai'   ye 'in dellnomin
then   her blanket   thus it is said
Then she did this with her blanket [demonstrating]—

o-çak-gănt-dămin-'in   nĭn   wa-paça-nai'
she bit it, it is said   then her blanket
She held her blanket in her teeth.

nall'in   yulak'in wŭndakweo'   odallno-min nä'-a'-gĭ
Then it is said this side side of a thing she seized it on the ground
Then she put her hand on the earth on the far side

wak'in   yulak'   wŭndă-gwe-o'
then again   this side side of a thing
Also on the other side.

the'-in yo'-dĭllnomĭn
         she did this
So then she did like this [demonstrating]

o'dăn-zen-min'in   yo'-ă'-ge
She seized   this earth
She grasped a handful of earth.

nall'in   dalle-ni-mi-k'in
then   she stooped down it is said
Then she began to bend forward.

nall'in   wun-lino   o'-çăk-gāt-dăb-hā-wŭl
then   this man   her legs he seized
Then that man seized his wife by the legs,

o'dillipena-hä-nul   yol wiwŭl
he pushed her in   his wife
and pushed her in.

ä-li'-pĕnĭ'lat   nall'in wŭn ne'nindawäs   pä-tcĭ-lau
while she was falling   then this fire dragon [comet]   it came
As she was falling, a Fire Dragon came flying.

yolhawa'   mänā-lat-djil   wagĭgai
this one   he is jealous of   the chief
This was the one the chief was jealous of.

nall'in wŭn nĕnin-dawäs in   mīlāwăl yol o'gwä-wal wilohāgăn
then this fire dragon   it is said gave her this woman   ear of corn
Then the Fire Dragon gave the woman an ear of corn

mi-at'-in-sŭk
just one
It was just one.

nallwak'in   djuñ-gĭ-ho-sĭs
then again it is said   a small kettle
And he also gave a small kettle,

nallwak'in   djuñ-gĭ-tcgwă-hă-gănĭs   wak'in   a-mo'-gwi-u   wa'-găn
                     small mortar   also   beaver   bone
And a small mortar, and a beaver bone.

nall'in ausdä-o   yok-a'-kiñk   ä-pe'dit   manĭt-do-wăk   o, wak'in
then   next   beneath   they live   spirits   they said
Then for their part the Manitous of the earth said,

yo' pnauwallindamōk
now you must think of something
"Alright, you must think over in your minds

gīsa' widahämawa   nano'gwäo'   gätma-ksit   inowak
whether you can help   this woman   wretched   they said
whether you would be able to help this poor woman," they said.

Nangä'   mo'gwa-tcĭl-es
It must be   sunfish [rock bass]
Some said, "Let Sunfish do it."

inoq nila nça-gi-hä   nan   linapäo
I can care for   the   people
And he said, "I could look after the people."

nallin   nik-dă-gă-nik   o wak'in
            the others   they said
Then the others said,

mo'gwă-tcĭl-es   maha gis   gwäkw   ça-kĭ-duiwĭ
sun fish   he can't   anything care for
"Sun Fish couldn't look after anything.

mäd-çiçit
too ugly looking you are
Ugly as he is."

inowăk   ginho'-gwĭ-ç-aum
they said   pike   maybe
And they said, "Maybe Pike could do it."

nallwak'in   wakgătc owak ktă-ga-nik
              they said   the others
Then others said, however,

aluwenă   ma-de-çe-çu   gin-hō-gwĭç
he is worse   homely thing   pike
"The Pike is even uglier."

nallwak'in kda-ga-nk   owăk
            the others   they said
Then others said,

da-gwaX-aum   mĭñga-çă
turtle may be   he is better
"Turtle would be better.

muç-ga-nĕ'-çu
he is strong
He is strong."

nall wämĭ'in   dilliwullinominau
then all it is said   became of one mind
Then everyone was in favor of it.

nall'in wa' dä-gwăX   nĭn   o-ça-gi-Xi-nin
    this turtle   this   it showed its back
Then the turtle stuck its back out [of the water].

tckau-we-wĭs   o'dĭllĭ   pĕnĭ'lan   o'dĭllĭ   ma-dä-ᵃX-i-niñk
slowly   on   she fell   on where she fell supine
Slowly she fell down and landed there.

nall'in   ne'o'dĭllĭ   lĕmăt-ă'-pĭn
         on it   she arose and sat
Then she sat up.

nall'in mĭs-hā-da-min   o'dĭllĭ klĭnmän   nä ă-gi
       she thought   she held it   this earth
Then she remembered that she had that earth in her hand.

nall'in o'dille   si-pi-aX-don
             she spread it
She spread it around there.

the-in äle'   ok-djok-o-niñk   gatc-a-lum-mi-kĭn
it is said   . spreading it   it began to grow
As she moved it around, right away it started to expand.

nallha'in   allu'e'in   o-e-a-moXgnŭmin
         more and more   she was stirring it again
Then she stirred it all the more.

nall'in ma'da miqgău   nall'in gatc'in miäXhaç-kwŭll gi-se k-nol
      not long   truly   grasses   they grow
Then not long afterwards grass began to grow,

wak'in mĭ-kwŭ-çal
      bushes
And also bushes.

nallwak'in ma'da-mĭ'-kau unämin wun oXgwä-au   le' a'lum-i-k'in
wä-mă-kwäk
           not long   she saw this   woman   truly grows
all things
Then not long afterwards the woman saw that everything was growing.

[Story continues with daughter's marriage, birth of twins, etc.]

Source: J. N. B. Hewitt's papers are preserved in the National Anthropological Archives
of the Smithsonian Institution. However, we used the excellent, carefully edited version prepared by Ives Goddard in "Three Nineteenth-Century Munsee Texts: Archaisms, Dialect Variation, and Problems of Textual Criticism," in New Voices for Old
Words. Algonquian Oral Literatures, ed. by David J. Costa (Lincoln: University of
Nebraska Press, 2015).

APPENDIX B

Dutch Arrival at Manhattan

(JOHN HECKEWELDER'S VERSION)

In the mid-eighteenth century, the eleven-year-old John Heckewelder arrived in Bethlehem, Pennsylvania, with his Moravian missionary parents. In the 1760s, when he was in his early twenties, he went to Ohio Territory to work with the Lenape; he became quite fluent in their language. Later, he wrote a book about Delaware history and customs, and he included this version of their cultural memory of the arrival of the Dutch at Manhattan. Though it has sometimes been treated as a serious account, it bears all the marks of a humorous tall tale. Toward the end of the book, he added comments about the arrogance of presuming to understand a people whose language you do not speak.

A great many years ago, when men with a white skin had never yet been seen in the land, some Indians who were out a fishing, at a place where the sea widens, espied at a great distance something remarkably large floating on the water, and such as they had never seen before. These Indians immediately returning to the shore, apprised their countrymen of what they had observed, and pressed them to go out with them and discover what it might be. They hurried out together, and saw with astonishment the phenomenon which now appeared to their sight, but could not agree upon what it was; some believed it to be an uncommonly large fish or animal, while others were of opinion it must be a very big house floating on the sea. At length the spectators concluded that this wonderful object was moving towards the land, and that it must be an animal or something else that had life in it; it would therefore be proper to inform all the Indians on the inhabited island of what they had seen, and put them on their guard. Accordingly they sent off a number of runners and watermen to carry the news to their scattered chiefs, that they might send off in every direction for the warriors, with a message that they should come on immediately. These arriving in numbers, and having themselves viewed the strange appearance, and observing that it was actually moving towards the entrance of the river or bay; concluded it to be a remarkably large house in which the Mannitto (the Great or Supreme Being) himself was present, and that he probably was coming to visit them. By this time the chiefs were assembled at York island, and deliberating in what manner they should receive their Mannitto on his arrival. Every measure was taken to be well provided with plenty of meat for a sacrifice. The women were desired to prepare the best victuals. All the idols or images were examined and put in order, and a grand dance was supposed not only to be an agreeable entertainment for the Great Being, but it was believed that it might, with the addition of a sacrifice, contribute to appease him if he was angry with them. The conjurers were also set to work, to determine what this phenomenon portended, and what the possible result of it might be. To these and to the chiefs and wise men of the nations, men, women and children were looking up for advice and protection. Distracted between hope and fear, they were at a loss what to do; a dance, however, commenced in great confusion. While in this situation, fresh runners arrived declaring it to be a large house of various colors, and crowded with living creatures. It appears now to be certain, that it is the great Mannitto, bringing them some kind of game, such as he had not given them before, but other runners soon after arriving declare that it is positively full of human beings, of quite a different color from that of the Indians, and dressed differently from them; that in particular one of them was dressed entirely in red who must be the Mannitto himself. They are hailed from the vessel in a language they do not understand yet they shout or yell in return by way of answer, according to the custom of their country; many are for running off to the woods, but are pressed by others to stay, in order not to give offence to their visitor, who might find them out and destroy them. The house, some say large canoe, at last stops, and a canoe of a smaller size comes on shore with the red man, and some others in it; some stay with his canoe to guard it. The chiefs and wise men, assembled in council, form themselves into a large circle, towards which the man in red clothes approaches with two others. He salutes after their manner. They are lost in admiration [stunned surprise]; the dress, the manners, the whole appearance of the unknown strangers is to them a subject of wonder; but they are particularly struck with him who wore the red coat all glittering with gold lace,[1] which they could in no manner account for. He, surely, must be the great Mannitto, but why should he have a white skin? Meanwhile, a large *Hackhack* [gourd] is brought by one of his servants, from which an unknown substance is poured out into a small cup or glass, and handed to the supposed Mannitto. He drinks—has the glass filled again, and hands it to the chief standing next to him. The chief receives it, but only smells the contents and passes it on to the next chief, who does the same. The glass or cup thus passes through the circle, without the liquor being tasted by any one, and is upon the point of being returned to the red clothed Mannitto, when one of the Indians, a brave man and a great warrior, suddenly jumps up and harangues the assembly on the impropriety of returning the cup with its contents. It was handed to them, says he, by the Mannitto, that they should drink out of it, as he himself had done. To follow his example would be pleasing to him; but to return what he had given them might provoke his wrath, and bring destruction on them. And since the orator believed it for the good of that nation that the contents offered them should be drunk, an as no one else would do it, he would drink it himself, let the consequence be what it might; it was better for one man to die, than that a whole nation should be destroyed. He then took the glass, and bidding the assembly a solemn farewell, at once drank up its whole contents. Every eye was fixed on the resolute chief, to see what the effect the unknown liquor would produce. He soon began to stagger, and at last fell prostrate on the ground. His companions now bemoan his fate, he falls into a sound sleep, and they think he has expired. He wakes again, jumps up and declares, that he has enjoyed the most delicious sensations, and that he never before felt himself so happy as after he had drunk the cup. He asks for more, his wish is granted; the whole assembly then imitate him, and all become intoxicated.

After this general intoxication had ceased, for they say that while it lasted the whites had confined themselves to their vessel, the man with the red clothes returned again, and distributed presents among them, consisting of beads, axes, hoes, and stockings such as the white people wear. They soon became familiar with each other, and began to converse by signs. The Dutch made them understand that they would not stay here, that they would return home again, but would pay them another visit the next year, when they would bring them more presents and stay with them awhile; but as they could not live without eating, they should want a little land of them to sow seeds, in order to raise herbs and vegetables to put into their broth. They went away as they had said, and returned in the following season, when both parties were much rejoiced to see each other; but the whites laughed at the Indians, seeing that they knew not the use of the axes and hoes they had given them the year before; for they had these hanging to their waists as ornaments, and the stockings were made use of as tobacco pouches. The whites now put the handles to the former for them, and cut trees down before their eyes, hoed up the ground, and put the stockings on their legs. Here, they say, a general laughter ensued among the Indians, that they had remained ignorant of the use of such valuable implement, and had borne the weight of such heavy metal hanging to their necks, for such a length of time. They took every white man they saw for an inferior mannitto attendant upon the Supreme Deity who shone superior in the red and laced clothes. As the whites became daily more familiar with the Indians, they at last proposed to stay with them, and asked only for so much ground for a garden lot, as, they said the hide of a bullock would cover or encompass, which hide was spread before them. The Indians readily granted this apparently reasonably request; but the whites then took a knife, and beginning at one end of the hide, cut it up to a long rope, not thicker than a child's finger, so that by the time the whole was cut up, it made a great heap; they then took the rope at one end, and drew it gently along, carefully avoiding its breaking. It was drawn out into a circular form, and being closed at its ends encompassed a large piece of ground. The Indians were surprised at the superior wit of the whites, but did not wish to contend with them about a little land, as they had still enough themselves. The white and red men lived content- edly together for long time, though the former from time to time asked for more land, which was readily obtained, and thus they gradually pro- ceeded higher up the mahicannittuck [Hudson River], until the Indians began to believe that they would soon want all their country, which in the end proved true.

*

The language, then is the first thing that a traveler ought to endeavour to acquire, at least, so as to be able to make himself understood and to under- stand others. Without this indispensable requisite he may write about the soil, earth and stones, describe trees and plants that grow on the surface of the land, the birds that fly in the air and the fishes that swim in the waters, but he should by no means attempt to speak of the disposition and characters of the human beings who inhabit the country, and even of their customs and manners, which it is impossible for him to be sufficiently acquainted with. And indeed, even with the advantage of the language, this knowledge is not to be acquired in a short time, so different is the impression which new objects make upon us at first sight, and that which they produce on a nearer view. . . .

There are men who will relate incredible stories of the Indians, and think themselves sufficiently warranted because they have Indian authority for it. But these men ought to know that all an Indian says is not to be relied upon as truth. I do not mean to say that they are addicted to telling falsehoods, for nothing is farther from their character; but they are fond of the marvelous, and when they find a white man inclined to listen to their tales of wonder, or credulous enough to believe their superstitious notions, there are always some among them ready to entertain him with tales of that description, as it gives them an opportunity of diverting themselves in their leisure hours, by relating such fabulous stories, while they laugh at the same time at their being able to deceive a people who think themselves so superior to them in wisdom and knowledge. They are fond of trying white men who come among them, in order to see whether then can act upon them in this way with success.

Source; John Heckewelder, *An Account of the History, Manners and Customs of the Indian Nations Who Once Inhabited Pennsylvania and the Neighboring States* (1819; repr., Philadelphia: Historical Society of Pennsylvania, 1876), 71–75 and 321–322.

APPENDIX C

The Woman Who Wanted No One

(AS TOLD TO TRUMAN MICHELSON)

In 1912, an anthropologist named Truman Michelson went to Oklahoma to interview Charles Elkhair, following in Harrington's footsteps. The stories Elkhair told to Michelson are very close to the versions he gave to Harrington. And Michelson, like Harrington, wrote them down in English. However, in one case, he did something different: as Elkhair—or conceivably some other storyteller[1]—spoke, he transcribed the sounds in the original Delaware. Then he worked with the people who were helping him with the project to place a translation of each word immediately below. He did not provide a colloquial translation, but we have done so here, after which we provide a facsimile of Michelson's Delaware transcription together with its word-for-word translation. This text gives us a wonderful sense of the linguistic playfulness that was used. Remarkably, it also shares some elements with the Munsee creation story told to John Hewitt about the same time more than a thousand miles away (appendix A).

One might make the argument that by today's standards this story is what we would call sexist, in that a young woman is pushed to accept one of her suitors and is harshly punished when she refuses all of them. But at root, what she is being pushed to do is to accept a life with others. It also seems that she would have been allowed to reject her suitors, like

194

many Indigenous heroines before her, had she refrained from insulting and demeaning others.

There was once a good-looking woman. The men, they liked her looks. But she would not have any of them. Several animals held a council. "I sure would like to have this woman," the animals said. There was a Beaver, a Skunk, and an Owl. Then they said, "Now, we will try to get her, this woman." They told the Owl, "You go first to see her. See whether you can get her or not, this woman."

The Owl went to see the woman. She told him, "I wouldn't have you, because you are ugly and have big eyes. I wouldn't have you." So he went back and when he got there he said, "I could not get that woman." Then the Skunk went next to see this woman. But no, she said to him, "I would not have you, because you are too ugly and you also stink." So he went back and he said, "Me too. I could not get this woman." Then the Beaver said, "Now in truth I will get her, this woman." When he got there, he started to talk to the woman. But like the others, he could not get the woman. She told him, "I will not have you, because you are an ugly thing. Your teeth are wide and your tail is long and broad. It looks like a stirring paddle, this tail of yours." Then the beaver left and went back and when he got there he said, "Well, I, too could do nothing with this woman." Then he said: "How could we do her so we can get her?"

They talked it over, how they could do it, how they would be able to get that woman. Then the Beaver said, "Way over here in the creek, where she gets water, right there, a log runs into the water. Now, I will go and gnaw it nearly in two, that log in the water. Then when she goes to fetch water, the log will break with her weight. The woman will fall into the water. Then it's us she will send for, call to help her, so she can get out." When the woman fell, she said, "I wish the Owl were here. Maybe he would help me so I could get out of the water." Then she began singing out. She sang [untranslatable lyrics follow]. "I like the Beaver!" Then he said, "No one

will like the looks of me because I am ugly, because my teeth are wide and
my tail broad, and it looks like a stirring paddle, that tail of mine." But
the woman was still singing out. She said, "I like the Skunk!" Said the
Skunk, "Not me, no one would like my looks because I am so ugly and
because I stink." Then again, the woman began to sing out. She said,
"I like the Owl!" Then said the Owl, "Not me, no one likes the looks of me
because I am ugly and because I've got big eyes." So then, she went down
the creek and nobody would help her. In the end, this woman drowned.

Source: Truman Michelson field notes, MS 2776, folder 5, National Anthropological
Archives, Smithsonian Institution.

1

kutimâ âli cïkixkwē·u naĉ́ 4
There was 1 good looking woman then

lẹ̃owạkᶜ wïaki tâli wulïnawâ·u
men they liked her looks

naĉ́ kōwiⁿgi anâⁿi wi'tēĕ·l·l
then not anyone will she have

naĉ́ ai·š́ïsạkᶜ kẹx̄ā tẹtowānĕ·u
then the animals several councelled about her

kẹlâ·ᵉ nuwiⁿgi wï'tcēyō naⁿnixwē·ᵉ
I sure would like to have her this woman

naĉ́yukʷᵉ ai·š́ï·sạkᶜ naxā·lᵘᵉ kuti
the now animals three 1

tamâ·ᵗkwᵉ âxkutïĉkakᵘᵉ
beaver and 1 skunk

ōkᵉ kutïkukus naĉ́ tẹla wä·nĕyō
1 1 owl then they said

yōkwē ā kwïtei mecenâ·ona
now try we will get her

naⁿnixkwᵉ naĉ́ lāⁿ wäⁿi·
this woman. then they told this

kuꞌkus kï lïtani māi ꞵẹnâ·ō
owl you go first and see her

kâxane eta·ᵉ kaski mecena
see whether you can get her or not

naⁿnixkwᵉ naĉ́ mōwiꞵenâ·un
this woman. then he went to see her

wäⁿi kukus netxkwē yu.
this owl that woman.

tḗk̇ṓ táwalaḳi kwísgi wītcī—
she told him   I wouldn't   have you

waˀluˤu sáˀmi ḳamaxai-
because   you are

inák̇s̩i sáˀmi ḳamasgckisgú-
ugly   because   you have big

ci tá walaḳi kuísgi wi tcī—
eyes   I would not   have

waluˤu nacī́ ḳutkin
you   then   went

náni ḳúkus i ḳa pī́yắte
this   owl   when he got there

luiˀḗ ḳōtawalṓḳi ngaṣki
he said   I could not get

mecenaˀi náni x̣kwḗ nacī́
that   woman   then

wa ckắk̇ʷ acite moi penā́ʼung
this   Skunk   next   went to see

nˀéli xwéyō walaḳi ōk̇ náni
this   woman   not   and   she

tḗk̇ō táʼwolaḳi ḳwísgi
said to him   I would not

wītcī walúˤu ḳéˀifoe sáˀmi
have you   you   because

ḳamaxaiti nák̇usi ōk̇ sóʼmi
you are too ugly,   and also

ḳaˀtci mák̇ʷ cici. nacī́
you stink   Then

ōk kạnạn wundji kĭk tạ̈kin
and   he went back,

luē mai aita nếpe gwila liha
he said yes   I alm, I could not

nâni ×kwē. nạcé â cite get him
this women   then   to him

wâni tamá'kwe teliān yú'kwe
this   beaver   said   now

a cíte namái penấon nani
in bush I will get him   this

×kwē iḱạp̣ey̆ā̃te nạcé tôleti
women, when he got there then he started

kĕkō lân nēl ×kwēyȯ ulaki
to talk to her this women. I think really

ōk nani kwīlạlihấō nếlị
also her   could not get   that

×kwēyȯ. tetko ahiyawalimātā
women   she told him   I will not

kwisgi wi'tciwaluhi sōmi
          have have you   because

ka maxai hi nakw cĭci
you are an ugly thing

kamamaṇgi pa kanikạci
your talk are broad

ōkena nạ kacu kwanāi ×wisgi
and also   your tail   a big

paᵏka´cu a laci´ pimwika⁻
and brood — it looks like — stirring paddle

linaᵏka´t̯icu na´ni ᵏcuᵏunai´
it looks — this — tail of yours.

nace´ wundjai ´aiya lum²ikan
then — left & went back

na´ni tama´kwe iᵏapiya te
this — beaver — when he got this

lue´ maiai´ita´ ne´pe gwi´la
he said — well — I don — I could

li´ha na´ni ×kwe nace´ ta´ni.
do nothing with — this woman — then, how could

hetca´ yuᵏwe ka̯teli´nala⁻na⁻
me — do her

wundjia̯ ka̯ski mekena´ngr
so we — could get her

na´ni ×kwe nace´ to k²ka nota mane´⁻
this woman — then — talked it over

yo a¯i⁻namonitet´ wundji ka̯ski
how they should do — how they would

mecena´ tit ne´l xwe¯yi
be able to get — that woman.

nace´ wa̯tama´kwe teliwa⁻n
then — this beava — said

ce´ nata wa̯li si¯pung e´heli
way over here — in the creek — where

m binating nace⁻
she gets water — then

na táli táxan tcá pâ mä
night then a log   runs into the water

natci yukwe náni na mái
then now   I will go + knew the

katcéta man náni táxan
nearly in two   that   log

m bing táli nacé xú unda
in the water . then then when

m bi ná ting náni x kwé
goes fetch water   this woman

nacé xú pök" hika man
then   she will break with her weight

náni táxan . na cé xú
that   log .   then

tcá hí puihi lán náni x kwé
she will fall into the water . this woman.

na cé xú kilóna kwén djí-
then us she will

m könän k téli ā wí tci mä-
send for us   so we could help her

nän . téli ā ka pán jí na cé
so she could git out then

únda tcá puihi lät náni
when she fell

x kwé na télnän yukwilahä
woman she said I will

yúkwe kúkus tōʻjin tám ʻsē-
now   owl   hue   maybe

hā wíngi witcimuk͏ʷ ka͏li
   he would help me   so I

ā ka pán nacé tōlōmi
could get out of the water.   Then   she began

a ʻšōwin lué pē′pē′ kuán ʻsā
singing   she said Pē pē kwan

pē′ pē′ kuán ʻsā yuká núhā
             name

nóʻli hā tamā kwē ba nacé
like   the beaver   the

tēlüän taẋa lá͏ᵉ nōlí na ḳōwi
said   will not like the looks of

nū aciwän sā′nu na maẋahi-
me anyone   because   I am

nak͏ʷ cĭcĭ sā′nu na ma ma-
ugly [=mák"aci] because   my teeth are

ṇgu pa kani kōci ā′k alaci
too wide & my tail broad, and Etc.

ʻjim X kwikan lí na ḳā ta cu
a thin long paddle   it looks like

yóni X ukwenaiṇi, nacé
my X tail.   Then

kw=ākwi ĭli aʻšō witᶜ nami X kwē
yet was   stinging.   this woman

lué pē̃ pē̃ kwán'sa níha
  he said

nōli'hā cekā 'kōwi'sā pē̃ 4 pē̃4
  I like   the skunk .

kwán·ʿsa lué nóni cekā·kᵘ
            said   that   skunk

taxā́ lō'ᵉ nī nōli na kō'wi'
  not   me would like my looks

awän sā́'mi na maxa·í·nā
  any   because   I am so ugly.

Ku cící ā'k' sā́'mi ᴀdjinā̈k-
        and   because   I stinke

cíci . na cé lapi tōlamā-
        then   again , she began

i-cwin lué pē̃ pē̃4 kwán'sa
  sing   she said

nī̈hā nōli hā kúkᵘsa na cé
  I   like   owl   then

tiluän nóni kúkᵘs taxā̈'lō²
  said   this owl   . not

nī nōli ᴮia kōwi awän
  me like the looks of   any one

sā́'mi na maxa·í·na kúcíci
  because   I am so ugly

sā́'mi na máng ckingō̃ cᴀ
  because   I 'm got big jeys

8

naʿcé   yᴜta tǟli nä·hi·ilän
then   she went down the creek
nä́ka̱ xwē̆yō̆ kü̆ walä́ki
dead woman   nobody
wlⁱsgi wi·tcamᴜkᵘ sí́yi
        would help her   her
xand̄k̄ī ap̓ta̱ p̄ı̄yō̆ naka
she finally drowned the
xwē̆yō̆.
woman·

Elected Leaders of the Delaware Tribe of Indians, ca. 1800–Present

Chart compiled by Clayton Chambers, Jim Rementer, and Nicky Michael, based on U.S. government documents for 1778–1867 and surviving minutes of the meetings of the General Council of the Delaware Tribe, 1867–present.

Title	Name	Dates
Chief	Machingue (& others)	1778–1805
Chief	Hokingpomskan (& others)	1805–1813
Chief	William Anderson	1813–1831
Chief	William Patterson	1832–1839
Chief	Nat Coming	1839–1849
Chief	John Ketchum	1849–1856
Chief	John Connor	1856–1872
Chief	James Ketchum	1872
Chief	James Connor	1873–1877
Chief	Charles Journeycake	1877–1894
Chairman	George Bullette	1895–1921
Chairman	John Young	1921
Chairman	Joseph Bartles	1922–1951

Chairman	Horace McCracken	1951–1970
Chairman	Bruce Townsend	1971–1978
Chief	Henry Secondine	1978–1983
Chief	Lewis Ketchum	1983–1994
Chief	Curtis Zunigha	1994–1998
Chief	Dee Ketchum	1998–2002
Chief	Joe Brooks	2002–2005
Chief	Jerry Douglas	2005–2010
Chief	Paula Pechonick	2010–2014
Chief	Chester Brooks	2014–2021
Chief	Brad KillsCrow	2021–present

Acknowledgments

The authors have incurred many debts as we worked to bring this book to fruition.

First, we wish to express our gratitude to the Delaware Tribe of Indians, including the late chief, Chester "Chet" Brooks; the current chief, Brad KillsCrow; the past assistant chief, Jeremy Johnson; the current assistant chief, Tonya Anna; and the rest of the Tribal Council (Rusty Creed Brown, Larry Joe Brooks, and Homer Scott), who welcomed the project and reached out helping hands.

At Rutgers, which stands on Lenape land, many students have put their shoulders to the wheel. History graduate students Peter Sorensen, Hal Crouse, and Raven Manygoats worked on the transcriptions and the search for sources. A long list of undergraduates eagerly contributed in small and sometimes big ways to the research: Lauren Baker, Alexander Coty, Elizabeth D'Alosio-Schmunk, Kate Dobbs, Keval Gandhi, Cailyn Higgins, Mitchell Johnson, Sam Jones, Robert Kaiser, Tyler Klecan, Gabriel Landi, Randon Lyu, Elayne Milan, Megan Nigam, Kimberly Olmeda, Meliton Rulloda, Adam Rusak, Ishan Shah, Kevin Stephens, Melaina Valente, Quinlan Van Es, and Yousrah Younous.

Visits to numerous archives were useful only because the staff there made them so. At the Archive of the Delaware Tribe of Indians, we wish to thank Curtis Zunhiga and Anita Mathis for their tireless work in preserving their people's past, and thus safeguarding their people's future. At the National Museum of the American Indian, we wish to thank archivist Nathan Sowry and curator Paul Chaat Smith, who are both talented scholars. At the American Philosophical Society, Brian Carpenter made a fly-by visit profitable, and at the Penn Museum Archives, Alessandro Pezzati went above and beyond in collecting together every possible file where Harrington's work might have left traces. The Kansas State Historical Society made it feasible for us to consult the Pratt Papers even without traveling there. At the Bartlesville Public Library History Room, Kim Inman and Leslie Calhoun were the personification of friendliness and helpfulness, and at the Bartlesville Area History Museum, the indefatigable Debbie Neece made it possible to consult even those records they have not yet been able to digitize.

Camilla would like to thank her colleagues at Rutgers from various arenas. The Humanities Plus teaching development program under David Goldman made it possible to encourage undergraduates to participate in this project, and the Faculty Research Council helped defray research expenses. Peter Mickulas at Rutgers University Press was the one who first invited us to do this book, and he has been an inspiration on numerous occasions since. Colleagues in the History Department have made life a joy.

In Bartlesville, Perry Haynes provided Camilla with a true home away from home in his extraordinary Bardew Valley Inn. Sarah Boyd, who works for the tribe, helped in key regards. Jim Rementer answered endless questions: his knowledge of Lenape language and history is breathtaking. The work he will leave behind him in the Lenape Talking Dictionary is invaluable.

Nicky would like to thank her father and mother for raising her to value her Delaware nation; her children for carrying on those ways; and her husband and traditional Indigenous peoples who continue to support her growth and love of her Lenape people and of all Indigenous peoples. To those Elders who trusted her with their emotions, stories, and Lenape ways, she gives her most heartfelt thanks. Her colleagues and students at Bacone College remind her daily what is beautiful about doing the work of educating Native American youth. To all the many people who have made a Lenape identity possible: Wanishi.

Glossary

All terms are listed as they appear in Harrington's notes and thus in this book. In brackets we have added other iterations as found in David Zeisberger, Frank Speck, or Charles Trowbridge.

Ashkas [ashakash singular, ashkashak plural]	Attendants of Big House ceremony
Dagwoch [tachquoch]	Turtle
Gamwing [ngamwin]	Big House ceremonies and feasting
Gicelemunkaong [kishelemukonk]	Creator; "he who created us by his thought"
Hominy [English, from Powhatan]	A food made from dried and ground corn
Kahamagun [kohomokan]	Coarse pounded corn
Kekir [kak, singular]	Wampum
Kinnickinnick	Sumac
Kshikan [schikan]	Knife; choanschikan, "Big Knife," used to describe the early settlers
Manito [manitou]	Spirit, divinity
MaXcikak	Snow and ice spirit; possibly related to the word for "bad" or "mischief" as the word for "snow" is not embedded

Misingw [mesingw]	Spirit mask, spirit of the hunt
Ogweyuk	"Those above"; apparently used by Harrington's informants instead of "manito"
Pela [pele]	Literally, one who doesn't chew; used to refer to Turkey phratry
Pilsit/ pilsuw	Clean, pure
Pokoungo [puk-kah-wung-ah-me]	Literally, "dragging along"; used to refer to Turtle phratry
Sakima [sachem]	Chief
Saungque [sanquen]	Weasel
Tuksit [tookseet]	Literally, dog foot; used to refer to Wolf phratry
Wehixamukas	The name of a culture hero appearing in numerous stories; called "Strong Man" by Harrington's informants, but this is not a translation
Xingwikan [xingwikaon]	Big House; used to refer to the central ceremony of Delaware religion
Yahquaha [possibly from an Iroquoian term]	Naked bear, a dreadful beast

Notes

INTRODUCTION

1. Spelled "Anishee" in the original text. Charles Trowbridge, "Account of some of the Traditions, Manners and Customs of the Lenee Lenaupaa or Delaware Indians," appendix 3 in C. A. Weslager, *The Delaware Indians: A History* (New Brunswick, NJ: Rutgers University Press, 1972), 498. In 1823, Trowbridge, working for General Lewis Cass, went to the Delaware settlements in Indiana to obtain supplementary information for the "Account" then under preparation. The main body of the Delaware Tribe had recently moved to Missouri Territory, but he was able to talk at length to the trader and interpreter William Connor, who had been married for many years to a Delaware woman named Mekinges, daughter of Chief William Anderson. When the tribe left for Missouri, they separated. She and their six children went west; he remained and married a white woman (Weslager, *Delaware Indians*, 334, 362; Charles Thompson, *Sons of the Wilderness: John and William Conner* [Indianapolis: Indiana Historical Society, 1937], 109–111, 128). Though the incident above is recounted in the third person, it is likely that Connor spoke autobiographically, given that he himself traveled in this period on tribal business. A Quaker traveler who earlier visited Connor's household reported that the women who lived with him spoke only Delaware. John Dean and Randall Dean, eds., *Journal of Thomas Dean* (Indianapolis: Indiana Historical Society, 1918), 53–54. Trowbridge later produced a study of the language, which has been transcribed and printed: C. C. Trowbridge, *Delaware Indian Language of 1824*, edited by James Rementer (Merchantville, NJ: Evolution, 2011).

2. Weslager, *Delaware Indians*, 498. Connor said that "they will entertain each other for a whole night." All observers of the Delaware in the colonial and early national period commented on their superlative oratory and their storytelling

tradition. Connor's brother, John, also married to a Delaware woman, expressed similar enthusiasm for their celebrations and storytelling traditions to incredulous missionaries. Lawrence Henry Gipson, ed., *The Moravian Indian Mission on White River* (Indianapolis: Indiana Historical Bureau, 1938), 614.

3. The Bartlesville Public Library contains an extensive collection of handwritten notes collected by Ruby Cranor in the 1980s concerning the family trees of the area's Delaware residents. Documents 1960.6304 and 1960.6332 both mention Charles Elkhair's parents and his siblings. The Cranor notes contain errors, but the elements mentioned here can be confirmed by other documentation. In the U.S. national censuses of 1900 and 1910, Elkhair stated that his parents were born in Ohio Territory (later Indiana). In 1858 in Kansas, a man by the name Mo-se-ha-kund had one wife and four children, his stage of life rendering it likely that he had been born prior to the 1820 move. (See entry 110, 1858 Delaware Indians per capita pay, facsimile of original document in Bartlesville Public Library history collection, document 1960.6943.) Such entries continue for the remainder of the tribe's time in Kansas, except that two of the children die. See per capita pay lists through to 1868 preserved in the John G. Pratt Papers, microfilm roll 6, of the Kansas Historical Society. In 1866, Charles Elkhair was listed as one of the heirs of a recently dead mother. (See entry 1101, Delaware Indian Diminished Reserve, July 4, 1866, Pratt Papers, roll 11.) However, his father Mosehakund lived for many years, until 1904, rendering it easy for him to pass on his memories and knowledge.

4. The name can also be translated as "Someone who walks along slowly, then turns around in the opposite direction." See "Delaware and English Names," appendix to Robert Grumet, ed, *Voices from the Delaware Big House Ceremony* (Norman: University of Oklahoma Press, 2001), 197.

5. Translation by Jim Rementer, who is certain of it because he found the name in his notes from a 1969 conversation with Nora Thompson Dean.

6. Less is known of the family of Julius Fouts, but some information is recoverable. He later stated that both his parents died when they were young, his father in Kansas and his mother just after arriving in Oklahoma. In 1867, on the eve of traveling from Kansas to Oklahoma, the Indian agent made a list of every tribal member, including full names of all adults and children. (See Pratt Papers, roll 8, notebook at end.) The head of household given is his grandmother, Nelachenow. (There is no age given, but other records indicate that she was probably born in Missouri. One census of the District of Cooweescooee taken in 1893 indicates that she was then only in her fifties, but that is probably wrong as other records put her in her sixties by then.) Fouts's father was apparently already dead, but his mother and aunt still lived. (For more on them, see below.) In the national censuses

of 1900 and 1910, Fouts stated that his parents were both born in Kansas, which is in keeping with their having been teens or in their twenties when he was born in 1862.

7. The name literally means "He throws something in this direction [toward the speaker]." Grumet, *Voices*, 198. This is how Fouts himself translated his name for Mark Harrington.

8. There exist excellent historical studies of this period. See Jean Soderlund, *Lenape Country: Delaware Valley Society before William Penn* (Philadelphia: University of Pennsylvania Press, 2015) and *Separate Paths: Lenapes and Colonists in West New Jersey* (New Brunswick, NJ: Rutgers University Press, 2022); as well as Amy Schutt, *Peoples of the River Valleys: The Odyssey of the Delaware Indians* (Philadelphia: University of Pennsylvania Press, 2007).

9. Today there are many active language revitalization movements leading to prolific new native-language writing as well as burgeoning Indigenous-focused interpretations of existing writings in English from the past century. Much rarer are books written by Indigenous authors who grew up in the years before their people had to deal with white people at all, and who spoke their own languages fluently before they began to learn English, but who nevertheless later published their own books. Examples include George Copway (*The Traditional History and Characteristic Sketches of the Ojibway Nation*, 1850), Sarah Winnemucca, *Life Among the Paiutes* (1883), and Charles Eastman (Dakota), *Indian Boyhood* (1902). Examples of authors whose formative years predated contact and who then dictated their autobiographies to white editors include Black Hawk (Sauk), Black Elk (Lakota), and Geronimo (Chiricahua Apache). For a study of the nineteenth-century Native literary moment, see Maureen Konkle, *Writing Indian Nations: Native Intellectuals and the Politics of Historiography, 1827–1863* (Chapel Hill: University of North Carolina Press, 2004).

10. For an introduction to the oldest native-language writings in the hemisphere, see Dennis Tedlock, *2000 Years of Mayan Literature* (Berkeley: University of California Press, 2010). For an introduction to early colonial writings in Nahuatl, many of which transcribe precolonial oral texts, see Camilla Townsend, *Annals of Native America: How the Nahuas of Colonial Mexico Kept Their History Alive* (New York: Oxford University Press, 2017).

11. For instance, careful research demonstrates that the Ramapo people are descended of fugitive or manumitted Africans who had once been enslaved by the Dutch, who then intermarried with various Native Americans and white settlers. See David Cohen, *The Ramapo Mountain People* (New Brunswick, NJ: Rutgers University Press, 1974). The "Nanticoke Lenni-Lenape" claim their descent from various unrelated individual New Jersey and Delaware citizens in the nineteenth century who

each believed they had at least one Indigenous forebear. (An applicant for membership must provide documentation of the four most recent generations, or until their family line connects with one of the surnames shared by one of the individuals in the 1800s who made the claim to having Indigenous ancestry. See their website: https://nlltribe.com/citizenship.) All of these people have interesting histories to share, but that is not the same as having a Lenape tribal identity.

12. The Bureau of Indian Affairs, whose governance is now largely in the hands of Native Americans, offers federal recognition to tribes with a record of having done this. The three federally recognized Lenape Tribes (the Delaware Tribe of Indians, the Delaware Nation, and the Stockbridge-Munsee Band of Mohican Indians; see below) have all passed resolutions that only those who participated in their communities' ongoing multicentury struggle to defend their tribal identity can now claim it. It behooves outsiders to read their statements in their own words. See the Delaware Tribe of Indians' Resolution 2015–55 ("To Oppose Fabricated Delaware Tribes, Groups and Indians") and Resolution 2021–11 ("To Combat Corporations Posing as Indigenous Nations"), accessible on the tribal website at https://delawaretribe.org/tribal-documents/.

13. Brice Obermeyer and John P. Bowes, "'The Lands of My Nation': Delaware Indians in Kansas, 1829–1869," *Great Plains Quarterly* 36, no. 1 (2016): 3. For the full, sweeping story, see C. A. Weslager, *The Delaware Indian Westward Migration* (Wallingford, PA: Middle Atlantic Press, 1978).

14. For a study of the very last years of the tribe's life in late eighteenth-century New Jersey, see Camilla Townsend, "'I Am Old and Weak . . . and You Are Young and Strong': The Intersecting Histories of Rutgers University and the Lenni Lenape," in *Scarlet and Black: Slavery and Dispossession in Rutgers History*, ed. Marisa Fuentes and Deborah Gray White (New Brunswick: Rutgers University Press, 2016), 6–42. For a study of later years, see David Silverman, *Red Brethren: The Brothertown and Stockbridge Indians and the Problem of Race in Early America* (Ithaca, NY: Cornell University Press, 2010).

15. Nicky Michael teaches Lenape language regularly at Bacone College in Oklahoma, both in person and online. The website of the Delaware Tribe of Indians hosts the Lenape Talking Dictionary, which keeps alive not only individual words but sentence structures as well.

16. Jane Merritt, *At the Crossroads: Indians and Empires on a Mid-Atlantic Frontier, 1700–1763* (Chapel Hill: University of North Carolina Press, 2003).

17. Weslager, *Delaware Indians*, 282–322.

18. Weslager, *Delaware Indians*, 331–337. For more on this period, see Greg Dowd, *A Spirited Resistance: The North American Indian Struggle for Unity, 1745–1815* (Baltimore: Johns Hopkins University Press, 1992).

19. For a discussion of the incident and its place in American history, see Peter Silver, *Our Savage Neighbors: How Indian Wars Transformed Early America* (New York: Norton, 2007).

20. For an entrée into the substantial literature, see John Sugden, *Tecumseh: A Life* (New York: Henry Holt, 1998).

21. John Johnston, Piqua, Ohio, to William Clark, Saint Louis, March 20, 1821, reprinted in Richard C. Adams, *A Delaware Indian Legend and the Story of Their Troubles* (Washington, DC, 1899), 41–42.

22. Weslager, *Delaware Indians*, 361.

23. Chief Anderson to William Clark, February 1824, in Weslager, *Delaware Indians*, 364.

24. Weslager, *Delaware Indians*, 364–370.

25. On the specific descriptions of the Kansas lifestyle, see Lewis Henry Morgan, *The Indian Journals, 1859–1862*, ed. Leslie White (New York: Dover, 1993), 55–66. For a full treatment of the Kansas years, including the complex relations between the dispersed subdivisions of the tribe, see Obermeyer and Bowes, "Lands of My Nation."

26. Weslager, *Delaware Indians*, 401.

27. B. F. Richardson to Commissioner of Indian Affairs, September 29, 1857, in Pratt Papers, roll 5.

28. Delaware Council to the President of the United States, n.d. 1858, in Pratt Papers, roll 5.

29. *Annual Report to the Commissioner of Indian Affairs* (Washington, DC, 1862), 23.

30. The complexity of such tensions, particularly as they unfolded in the early Oklahoma years, is explored in Brice Obermeyer, "Landscape, Identity, and Politics in an Oklahoma Indian Tribe," *Plains Anthropologist* 54 (2009): 181–199. The school was first a day school, then established as a boarding school. See 1864 correspondence in the Pratt Papers, roll 6. Lewis Henry Morgan described it in very positive terms in his *Indian Journals*.

31. See entry 110, 1858 Delaware Indians per capita pay, facsimile of original document in Bartlesville Public Library history collection, document 1960.6943; and entry 1101, Delaware Indian Diminished Reserve, July 4, 1866, Pratt Papers, roll 11, as well as ongoing listings for the interim period in the Pratt Papers, roll 6. In the Cranor notes, Too-loo-qua is called "Too-loo-qua-swannock," which might indicate that she was "white." Most likely, she was not white herself but the daughter of a captive taken in the late eighteenth-century wars in the Ohio Valley. Elkhair took pride in being a full blood, but in the 1910 census, he did say he had one white grandparent.

32. It is clear that Charles Elkhair did not know exactly how old he was, as he seems to have given a different estimate of his birth year each time he was asked. Listing all his guesses, the median turns out to be 1853. This is likely, as he could have been no older than fourteen in the fall of 1867 (as the Baptist teachers could not have believed he was about twelve had he been older than that).

33. "List of Delaware Indian Pupils in Attendance at Baptist Mission School, Kansas Territory, for the Six Months ending December 31, 1867," from the Pratt Papers, roll 6. It is the Delaware Indian Diminished Reserve listing from the summer of 1866 that mentions Too-loo-qua as recently dead, and in the complete tribal listing made by Pratt in February 1867, on the eve of departure, Too-loo-qua's name does not appear with her family members. Charles Elkhair referred to his father by the Christian name of "James" in his Dawes Roll card report (Cherokee Nation, Delaware Roll, 1904). The Cranor notes in the Bartlesville Public Library also refer to Elkhair's father as "James" and quote a local white doctor in saying that in acting as a healer, he sometimes lost patients.

34. Contract dated February 1, 1866, between N. Pratt, widow of Lucius Pratt, and U.S. Government, in Pratt Papers, roll 6.

35. On the school, see Weslager, *Delaware Indians*, 385–387. Delaware-language teaching materials were initiated by the Moravians in the late eighteenth and early nineteenth centuries and pursued by men of other faiths, including Pratt. Weslager said he saw archival evidence that Pratt printed some of these materials at a previous assignment at the Shawnee Mission, where he was in charge of a printing machine, but we have not seen it. A number of missionary-produced Delaware-language texts have been edited and reprinted by Raymond Whritenour. See, for example, *Denke's Lenape Word List of 1801* (Bethlehem, PA: Moravian Archives, 2015).

36. About a decade after their arrival in Oklahoma, a group of thirteen modernist men, including both William and Richard Adams (father and son), sat for a formal photograph to commemorate their having come together from Kansas to Indian Territory. Adams later published the photo in *A Delaware Indian Legend*. At the very back, the tallest one present is a young Julius Fouts, about eighteen or twenty years old. The legend specifically identifies him, and in addition the man resembles other known photos of Fouts.

37. Julius identifies his father as "Dave Fouts" in his Dawes Roll card report (Cherokee Nation, Delaware Roll, 1904).

38. John Benedict, ed., *Muskogee and Northeastern Oklahoma*, vol. 3 (Chicago: S. J. Clarke, 1922), 47–48. Oil had been found on the Fouts land, thus explaining his inclusion in this volume. The story of his childhood is borne out in some cryptic notes in the Bartlesville Public Library history collection, document 1960.6352.

39. This last possibility seems most likely, not only because of the surname, but also because Julius Fouts was later allowed to own his oil-bearing lands in fee simple, without government oversight, which was usually granted only to those who could prove themselves to be at least half white *and* who satisfied interlocutors at court that they were "competent" (generally by being light-skinned, educated in white schools, and with a knack for self-presentation as cosmopolitan). Mark Harrington in his notes said that Julius Fouts was also Julius Fox, as if he were really named in honor of an animal with whom he or his family had a relationship, but there is absolutely no other evidence of that being the case.

40. Entry 840, Delaware Indian Diminished Reserve, July 4, 1866, Pratt Papers roll 11; complete tribal listing of adults and minors February 1867, Pratt Papers roll 8. The latter list indicates that the family was headed by a presumed grandmother, Ne-la-che-now. Julius's young aunt, Ke-she-lung-o-no-shkwa, who would later adopt him, is listed as a minor, along with him. One of the other listed minors (probably Ah-pah-me-now-o-shkwa) must have been his young mother, as she was still alive at the time.

41. Weslager, *Delaware Indians*, 415–416. The Kirkwood was shortly to become famous, as it was where Andrew Johnson was staying when Lincoln was assassinated, and where he was therefore sworn in. For the denial of the Indians' initial request, see Commissioner of Indian Affairs to Indian Agent, March 8, 1862, Pratt Papers, roll 5. For a copy of the Missouri & Western Telegraph message on April 29, 1864, which suddenly ordered them to D.C., see Pratt Papers, roll 6. For the involvement of the railroads, see newspaper clippings from the summer of 1865, also preserved in Pratt Papers, roll 6. It is clear that the railroads were behind the visit to Washington.

42. An excellent summary of these events is provided in Brice Obermeyer, *Delaware Tribe in a Cherokee Nation* (Lincoln: University of Nebraska Press, 2009), 80–86.

43. John Pratt to the Commissioner of Indian Affairs, September 19, 1866, Pratt Papers, roll 6.

44. His father's family has only one child on the annuity listing made in June 1868, Pratt Papers, roll 8.

45. Obermeyer and Bowes, "Lands of My Nation," emphasize that this was the only way that the main body of the Delaware people could remain together as a tribe.

46. Obermeyer, *Delaware Tribe*.

47. Obermeyer, *Delaware Tribe*, esp. chap. 3. On Nannie Journeycake Pratt Bartles, 81 and 120. For more on Jacob Bartles and his marriage, see Margaret Withers Teague et al., *History of Washington County and Surrounding Area*, vol. 1 (Bartlesville, OK: Bartlesville Historical Commission, 1967).

48. U.S. Secretary of the Interior, "Allotment of Lands to the Delaware Indians" (Washington, DC: Report to the 58th Congress, 2nd Session, 1904), 160.

49. Census of the Cherokee Nation, 1880. Jesse had not been born yet. See his obituary, August 30, 1961, preserved in the Bartlesville Public Library history collection, document 1960.6313, for details about his life. (Charles Elkhair also had a daughter, Annie, born to him when he was very young by another woman whose name we cannot be certain of. See Probate of Charles Elkhair's estate, Washington County, State of Oklahoma, 1935.)

50. Census of the Cooweescooee District of the Cherokee Nation, 1890, 1893. She disappears from one census to the next. In an 1894 listing, her name is annotated, "Died." See "Payments of 1886, 1890 and 1894," included with Oklahoma and Indian Territory, Delaware Roll, 1904. Elkhair's first daughter (by another mother), Annie (see preceding note), is also included here.

51. Susan Half Moon's Delaware name appears in numerous documents, so she regularly used it. But the only place where the meaning is given is Mark Harrington, "A Preliminary Sketch of Lenape Culture," *American Anthropologist* 15, no. 2 (1913): 214.

52. In the U.S. Census of 1900 and again in 1910, she reported that her father was born "in Mexico." The second time, the census taker was confused when he learned this and scratched out "full blood" and put "½ Indian." He would not have been aware of the history of the splinter group. It is possible that she really meant that her father was a Mexican man. According to Lewis Henry Morgan (*Indian Journals*), there were some living near the Delaware in Kansas as merchant traders and artisans. On the Delaware passage to Spanish territory, see Weslager, *Delaware Indians*, 372–373. Unfortunately, little is known of their experiences.

53. See Rosa Elkhair Frenchman's obituaries, January 21, 1969, collected in the Bartlesville Public Library history collection as document 1960.6317. On the school, see K. Tsianina Lomawaima, *They Called It Prairie Light: The Story of Chilocco Indian School* (Lincoln: University of Nebraska, 1994). The book provides a study of student culture at the school beginning about 1920, a bit after the Elkhair girls' time there.

54. See Afterword, Interviews.

55. He was mentioned repeatedly in interviews conducted with elders in the 1970s by Native American artist Ruthe Blalock Jones. These have been printed in Grumet, *Voices*, 151–178. In addition, he was mentioned as having conducted funeral rites in Delaware and according to ancient tradition at the funerals of his friends. See, for instance, "Tribal Rites to Be Conducted This Morning for George Fall Leaf," September 12, 1933, Bartlesville newspaper, preserved in the Bartlesville Public Library history collection, document 1960.6332.

56. Kansas, County Marriage Records (1811–1911), Charley Elkhair and Susie Half Moon, Chautauqua County, June 29, 1903.

57. Interview with Elizabeth Longbone in Grumet, *Voices*, 163.

58. This much is very clear from the Ruby Cranor notes in the Bartlesville Public Library history collection. Further genealogical work could easily be done. In 1932, Frank Speck recorded in his field notebook that Charles Elkhair and his last wife were distant relatives: their mothers were cousins. American Philosophical Society, Frank Speck Papers, Series III Northeast, box 6, file 9c2d.

59. Benedict, *Muskogee and Northeastern Oklahoma*, 3:47–48.

60. For a sample of his signature on a legal document, see Oklahoma and Indian Territory Land Allotment Jackets for the Five Civilized Tribes, 1884–1934, Cherokee Land Office, Tahlequah, May 12, 1904, Ancestry.com. (He and George Bullette had each claimed a certain tract of three acres.) We learn from Benedict (above) that he went briefly to a "mission school in eastern Oklahoma." In the U.S. census of 1900 he said he could read and speak English, but not write very well. But then in 1910 and 1920, he allowed the census taker to check "no," he could not read.

61. Census of the Cooweescooee District of the Cherokee Nation, 1890.

62. Census of the Cooweescooee District of the Cherokee Nation, 1893.

63. Bartlesville Public Library history collection, document 1960.6133.

64. Interview with Fannie McCartlin in Grumet, *Voices*, 169. The child Fannie appears in their family, listed first as a daughter and then (accurately) as a niece, in the U.S. census of 1910 and 1920.

65. U.S. census 1910. Other legal documents show extensive improvements to their lands.

66. Elizabeth Longbone in Grumet, *Voices*, 165. What is remarkable is that four other interviewees also spoke of Minnie Fouts. Only Charley Elkhair was mentioned more.

67. Grumet, *Voices*, 162–166.

68. Obermeyer, *Delaware Tribe*, 129–136. See also Deborah Nichols, "Richard C. Adams: Representing the Delaware Indians," introduction to Richard C. Adams, *Legends of the Delaware Indians and Picture Writing*, ed. Deborah Nichols (1905; Syracuse, NY: Syracuse University Press, 1997). Nichols explains that the Bullettes were closely related to the Adams family.

69. U.S. Bureau of the Census, "Population of Oklahoma and Indian Territory," Bulletin 89 (Washington, DC: Government Printing Office, 1907), 24. On the total Delaware count in that year, see Weslager, *Delaware Indians*, 9.

70. It was also growing increasingly difficult to find any deer, whose meat formed a centerpiece of the ceremonies. (See chapter 2.) On the closing of the Big

House, see Obermeyer, *Delaware Tribe*, 94–95, as well as "Salvaging the Delaware Big House Ceremony: The History and Legacy of Frank Speck's Collaboration with the Oklahoma Delaware," *Histories of Anthropology Annual* 3 (2007): 188. What he says matches what Mark Harrington said he found the situation to be at the time of his first visit: see his "Preliminary Sketch," 235.

71. See especially Schutt, *Peoples of the River Valleys*.

72. See Morgan, *Indian Journals*.

73. On the friendship with the Adams family, see note 27. For a study of Richard Adams, see Deborah Nichols, "Richard C. Adams: Representing the Delaware Indians," introduction to Adams, *Legends of the Delaware Indians*.

74. Frank Speck, *A Study of the Delaware Indian Big House Ceremony* (Harrisburg: Pennsylvania Historical Commission, 1931), 43.

75. George Heye to George Gordon, December 19, 1910, Penn Museum Archive, George Heye Papers, box 1. "Due to his infirmity of speech, he is naturally very diffident, and the first month or two you may have difficulty in getting information out of him, or getting him to talk to you freely."

76. Marie Harrington, *On the Trail of Forgotten People: A Personal Account of the Life and Career of Mark Raymond Harrington* (Reno, NV: Great Basin Press, 1985), 11–21. Harrington's fourth and last wife wrote a brief biography of her husband after he died and self-published it. It is remarkably honest in some regards.

77. Many years later, the map of that village formed the core of a creative book Harrington wrote for young people, *Dickon among the Lenape* (New York: Holt, Rinehart & Winston, 1938).

78. Mark R. Harrington, "Primitive New Yorkers," *New York Press Sunday Magazine*, [date?] 1899, as cited in Marie Harrington, *On the Trail*, 22.

79. Quoted in Joy Porter, *To Be Indian: The Life of Iroquois-Seneca Arthur Caswell Parker* (Norman: University of Oklahoma Press, 2001), 50.

80. Harrington, *On the Trail*, 30, 36 and 42; Porter, *To Be Indian*, 53–54. It is striking that both biographies characterize the early years of the two men's friendship in similar terms.

81. Harrington, *On the Trail*, 44–45. One might rightly argue that in either case, Harrington was still working to separate Native Americans from their heirlooms. But at least in this case the materials were preserved to become part of what is now the largest Indigenous-run cultural organization in the world. For more on this complicated question, see Nathan Sowry, "Museums, Native American Representation, and the Public: The Role of Museum Anthropology in Public History, 1875–1925" (PhD diss., Department of History, American University, 2020).

82. Harrington, *On the Trail*, 48–50; Penn Museum Archives, George Heye Papers, box 2, Acquisition lists.

83. A 1910 clipping from an unidentified Shawnee, OK, newspaper, quoted in full in Harrington, *On the Trail*, 60–61.

84. Mark R. Harrington, "The Thunder Power of Rumbling Wings," in *American Indian Life*, ed. Elsie Clews Parsons (New York: Viking, 1925), 125.

85. George Gordon to M. R. Harrington, July 15, 1910, Penn Museum Archives, George Gordon Director's Office, 1910–1928, box 8.

86. Mark R. Harrington, *Religion and Ceremonies of the Lenape* (New York: Museum of the American Indian Smithsonian, 1921), preface. Marie Harrington claimed that he actually spoke Seneca and was therefore able to surprise local people on one of the Iroquois reservations, but almost certainly that story was exaggerated, either by her or by him, *On the Trail*, 47–48.

87. Harrington's notes are now housed at the Archive Center of the National Museum of the American Indian Smithsonian, in Suitland, Maryland. The materials pertaining to the Delaware are catalogued as MAI, Heye Foundation Records, boxes 233 through 237. Box 237, folder 11, contains his rough draft of the preface acknowledging the families with whom he worked, a version of which was later published in *Religions and Ceremonies*. He also mentions William Brown in that preface, although his notes refer to him only twice, as he was apparently the guide or intermediary.

88. See Regula Trenkwalder Schonenberger, *Lenape Women, Matriliny and the Colonial Encounter: Resistance and Erosion of Power (c. 1600–1876)* (New York: Peter Lang, 1991).

89. Julius Fouts to M. R. Harrington, March 20, 1909, Smithsonian MAI, Heye Foundation Records, box 237, file 4.

90. Memo from Harrington to George Gordon, undated but found in 1910 section. Harrington requested money for materials, interpreters, gifts for his sources, board, and lodging. Penn Museum Archives, George Gordon Director's Office, 1910–1928, box 8. Harrington continued to plead for a phonograph and eventually received one in 1912, but without the needed winding key.

91. Mr. R. Harrington to Julius Fouts, March 28, 1912, Penn Museum Archives, George Heye Papers, box 3, Harrington letterbook. The museum preserved carbon copies of all of Harrington's outgoing correspondence, but Harrington did not preserve the incoming letters.

92. Harrington to Fouts, June 14, 1912, Penn Museum Archives, George Heye Papers, box 3, Harrington letterbook.

93. Harrington to Gordon, January 2, 1913, Penn Museum Archives, George Gordon Director's Office, 1910–1928, box 8.

94. There were five exchanges between the two men on this topic (and others) in 1913. Penn Museum Archives, George Heye Papers, box 3, Harrington letterbook. He does not mention staying with the Fouts family, but then he does not mention

any housing arrangements, and he generally did in his correspondence with other Indians he visited. It is possible he was staying in the Dewey Hotel operated by Jacob Bartles and his wife, Nanny Journeycake. The interesting building still stands and is now a museum.

95. Harrington to Fouts, December 20, 1913, Penn Museum Archives, George Heye Papers, box 3, Harrington letterbook.

96. Telegram from Harrington to Gordon, July 21, 1914, Penn Museum Archives, Office of the Director Gordon, 1910–1928.

97. Harrington to Gordon, September 17, 1914, and final report on Harrington's employment, February 1915, both in Penn Museum Archives, George Gordon Director's Office, 1910–1928, box 8.

98. Constantine Rafinesque produced "Wallam-Olum: First and Second Parts of the Painted and Engraved Traditions of the Linnilinapi: Translated Word-for-Word by C.S. Rafinesque" (now in the University of Pennsylvania Rare Book Room) in 1832, saying that it was a copy of an original set of tablets that he had seen but could no longer produce, and wrote about it in *The American Nations; or Outlines of a National History of the Ancient and Modern Nations of North and South America* (Philadelphia, 1836), 1:8–9 and 122–124. He was doubted at the time, but years later Daniel Brinton of the University of Pennsylvania published it in its entirely and wrote an analysis in his book, *The Lenape and Their Legends* (Philadelphia: Historical Society of Pennsylvania, 1885). For years, anthropologists, including both Harrington and Frank Speck, were drawn to the tale.

99. David Oestreicher, "The Anatomy of the Walam Olum: The Dissection of a 19th-Century Anthropological Hoax" (PhD diss., Department of Anthropology, Rutgers University, 1995). See also Andrew Newman, "The Walam Olum: An Indigenous Apocrypha and Its Readers," *American Literary History* 22, no. 1 (2010): 26–56.

100. David Zeisberger, "History of Northern American Indians," trans. and ed. Archer Butler Hulbert and William Nathaniel Schwarze, in *Ohio Archaeological and Historical Quarterly* 19 (1910): 1–173, 114, 133, 145; John Heckewelder, *An Account of the History, Manners and Customs of the Indian Nations Who Once Inhabited Pennsylvania and the Neighboring States* (1819; repr., Philadelphia: Historical Society of Pennsylvania, 1876), chaps. 10 and 39. A copy of comparable tree carvings by Iroquoians and copied down by a French observer still survives. Readers can see it in Colin Calloway, ed., *The World Turned Upside Down: Indian Voices from Early America* (New York: Bedford/St. Martin's, 1994), 121.

101. Their denial appears several times in his notes, and Harrington acknowledged as much in "Preliminary Sketch," 234. Nevertheless, years later, he incorporated the Walam Olum into *Dickon among the Lenape*, 208–210.

102. Only the barest outline of the story appears in Virgil's *The Aeneid* (New York: New American Library,1961), 16-17. However, an extensive European folk tradition about the matter often embellished the story in its telling. On its popularity in the New World, see Andrew Newman, *On Records: Delaware Indians, Colonists, and the Media of History and Memory* (Lincoln: University of Nebraska Press, 2012).

103. The richest accounts come from Adriaen Van Der Donck in 1655 and appear well translated in Grumet, *Voices*, 23-28.

104. There are a number of closely related extant Cass-Trowbridge manuscripts. For a clear discussion of them, see Weslager, *Delaware Indian Westward Migration*, 160-161.

105. A helpful edition is Nichols, ed., *Legends of the Delaware Indians*.

106. Zeisberger, "History of Northern American Indians," 147.

107. Grumet, *Voices*. Fouts also provided a statement, extant in the National Museum of the American Indian (NMAI), which is not included in Grumet's book but appears in this one.

108. John Bierhorst, *Mythology of the Lenape: Guide and Texts* (Tucson: University of Arizona Press, 1995). Bierhorst included the text of a number of stories, focusing on those that had not appeared in print elsewhere. Because the book is difficult for a nonspecialist to follow, he also published *The White Deer and Other Stories Told by the Lenape* (New York: William Morrow, 1995). The latter is a charming book, emphasizing cultural continuity by including a variety of stories attributable to Delaware authors in different times and places.

109. Zeisberger, "History of Northern American Indians," 132.

110. We have no full, early version of the creation story from the Delaware. However, we find elements of it in numerous places: For the seventeenth century, we have Jasper Danckaerts, *Journals, 1679-80*, ed. B. B. James (New York: Scribner's, 1913), 77-78; Peter Lindeström, *Geographia Americae*, ed. Amandus Johnson (Philadelphia: Swedish Colonial Society, 1925), 208-209; and Van Der Donck in Grumet, *Voices*, 26-27. For the late eighteenth and early nineteenth centuries, we have Zeisberger, "History of Northern American Indians," 131-132, and Heckewelder, *Account of the History*, chaps. 34 and 40; and the Cass-Trowbridge Manuscripts in Weslager, *Delaware Indian Westward Migration*, 113, 170-171, 180-183. The reason that we can make good sense of the story from the fragments that we have is that the Haudenosaunee or Iroquois share a very similar creation story; this makes sense as the two groups were neighbors for centuries. Numerous Iroquoian versions were recorded over the years, including, in the nineteenth century, some rich oral texts in the original language. See, for instance, Seth Newhouse's relation in J. N. B. Hewitt, ed., "Iroquoian Cosmology," in *Twenty-First Annual Report*

of the Bureau of American Ethnology, 1899–1900 (Washington, DC: Government Printing Office, 1903), 255–295. See appendix A. This version is far more detailed than what we have given here, but we have included only aspects of the story that are documented in Lenape versions as given above.

111. Literally, "We are glad you [plural] came." In English we would say, "Welcome."

CHAPTER 1 — CREATION STORIES

1. There are few Native American stories that exist in only one tribe; most are shared to some extent. And the Great Plains Indians, probably because of their mobility, tell the widest array. See Stith Thompson, ed., *Tales of the North American Indians* (Cambridge, MA: Harvard University Press, 1929). (Readers will have to bear with his early twentieth-century views, but there are nevertheless important perspectives found here.) During the years in Kansas, the Delaware would most certainly have heard stories originally stemming from the Southwest.

2. An excellent introduction is Ake Hultkrantz, *Native Religions of North America* (New York: Harper & Row, 1987). This essential work is still in print.

3. Donald Fixico, *"That's What They Used to Say": Reflections on American Indian Oral Traditions* (Norman: University of Oklahoma Press, 2017), 47. (Fixico reminds us that he is also partly Sak, Fox, and Seminole.)

4. Smithsonian, National Museum of the American Indian (NMAI), Heye Foundation Records, box 237, file 9.

5. Jasper Danckaerts, *Journals, 1679–80*, ed. B. B. James (New York: Scribner's, 1913), 77–78; Peter Lindeström, *Geographia Americae*, ed. Amandus Johnson (Philadelphia: Swedish Colonial Society, 1925), 208–209; and Adrian Cornelius Van Der Donck, "Description of New Netherland, 1655," published *Voices from the Delaware Big House Ceremony*, ed. Robert Grumet (Norman: University of Oklahoma Press, 2001), 26–27.

6. J. N. B. Hewitt, ed., "Iroquoian Cosmology," in *Twenty-First Annual Report of the Bureau of American Ethnology, 1899–1900* (Washington, DC: Government Printing Office, 1903), 255–295.

7. The best tracing of its appearances is John Bierhorst, ed., *Mythology of the Lenape: Guide and Texts* (Tucson: University of Arizona Press, 1987), 28–31.

8. This means "Creator." More literally: "he who created us by his thought." See Charles Trowbridge, *Delaware Indian Language of 1824* (Merchantville, NJ: Evolution Publishing, 2011), 287. Harrington's notes indicate that this was inserted, apparently in response to a question from him. The narrator seems to have continued thinking about the matter, given what he says a few lines later.

9. This was Harrington's representation of *tachquoch*, land turtle, *Lenape-English Dicitonary*, p.136.

10. Remember that the word he used, *Lenape*, meant "people."

11. Smithsonian, NMAI, Heye Foundation Records, box 237, file 4.

12. Over long periods of time, a star's heliacal rising shifts. In ancient Greece, the appearance of the Pleiades signified the start of the war season.

13. In the version relayed to Charles Trowbridge in 1823, this was because of illness. (Reprinted in C. A. Weslager, *The Delaware Indians: A History* [New Brunswick, NJ: Rutgers University Press, 1972], 494.) When the Seven lived among humans with their parents, they could not stop vomiting. Had interest in illness perhaps receded by the early twentieth century, when fewer people were dying of disease?

14. Certain spots in the natural world were considered sacred and were often visited, almost like shrines in other societies. See Hultkrantz, *Native Religions*, 14.

15. Smithsonian, NMAI, Heye Foundation Records, box 234, file 4.

16. See Camilla Townsend, *Annals of Native America: How the Nahuas of Colonial Mexico Kept Their History Alive* (New York: Oxford University Press, 2017), 126, 172.

17. Trowbridge manuscript in Weslager, *Delaware Indians*, 494.

18. Townsend, *Annals of Native America*. See also Paul Zumthor, *Oral Poetry: An Introduction* (Minneapolis: University of Minnesota Press, 1990).

19. This was penciled in by Harrington as an addition, presumably in response to his question, "Where?"

20. Meaning "white wash." This was a thin paint made of calcium carbonate, ubiquitous in the Americas before and after conquest.

21. Smithsonian, NMAI, Heye Foundation Records, box 234, file 4.

22. David Zeisberger, *History of Northern American Indians* (1780; repr., Columbus: Ohio State Archaeological Society, 1920), 147.

23. Smithsonian, NMAI, Heye Foundation Records, box 234, file 4.

24. William Penn, *A Letter from William Penn Proprietary and Governour of Pennsylvania in America to the Committee of the Free Society of Traders* (London: Andrew Sowle, 1683).

25. Mark Harrington, "A Preliminary Sketch of Lenape Culture," *American Anthropologist* 15, no. 2 (1913): 226. Harrington included photographs of two beautiful woven bundles.

26. Meaning for ceremonial power.

27. Smithsonian, NMAI, Heye Foundation Records, box 237, file 4.

28. An animal spirit who comes in a vision to a youth and becomes that person's protector.

29. The Lenape had used East Coast mussel shells to make practical and spiritual objects for many centuries. See Herbert Kraft, *The Lenape-Delaware Indian Heritage: 10,000 BC—AD 2000* (Shamong, NJ: Lenape Books, 2001), 276–278.

CHAPTER 2 — BIG HOUSE STORIES

1. From the roots -*chink*- ("great" or "large") and *wikwam* or *wikawan* (house), attested in *Lenape-English Dictionary*, throughout.

2. A truly fine study of the Big House tradition is Robert Grumet, ed., *Voices from the Delaware Big House Ceremony* (Norman: University of Oklahoma Press, 2001). Grumet collected accounts of the ceremony from the seventeenth century through the 1920s.

3. There is disagreement about the symbolism of the colors, perhaps life and death, perhaps male and female. Other Indigenous groups, such as the Nahuas, use the phrase "the red and the black" to refer to ritually symbolic writings encompassing the meaning of life.

4. Smithsonian, National Museum of the American Indian (NMAI), Heye Foundation Records, box 234, file 2.

5. Elkhair's knowledge of the essence of the history is remarkable. Although there were no serious earthquakes in the late eighteenth century in the northeastern United States, it was nevertheless a period of catastrophe, and the people of that era were in fact gathering in villages containing bark wigwams.

6. Elkhair changes his mind here, determining that it was important to underscore that people volunteered to be brave and go to speak to the Misingw, rather than simply being chosen.

7. A dish made of corn meal. It was a central element of the food served at the Big House ceremony, which took place near harvest time, though it was not explicitly a harvest celebration.

8. This may be a misreading of the handwriting. Alternatively, it may have been the translator's attempt to express in English the idea that they depended on the image of the misingw in the Big House, both the masks and the figure wearing the fur outfit.

9. Elkhair means that a certain family was charged with keeping the misingw outfit.

10. Again Elkhair is seen changing his form of expression, moving from the past to the present tense: he is telling us that Misingw still drives people's horses home to them—after having first mischievously sent them off.

11. Here is a reference to the idea that the wearer of the symbolic misingw outfit is there not just to thrill the children but to remind everyone of the spiritual world's presence.

12. These three sentences offer strong evidence that Elkhair was speaking to Harrington through a translator, as he suddenly writes "we," as though he were transcribing the words of another Delaware person. The translator could have been a son or daughter or Julius Fouts.

13. Harrington was struggling to capture the word—both the pronunciation and the concept.

14. A comment that Julius Fouts makes in "Delaware Church" (this section) tells us that this is the way the people had been taught to speak—probably by missionary teachers—of the practice of sending young boys out into nature alone to seek their visions.

15. See above. Only boys were sent to seek visions.

16. As in "stout of heart," strong, brave.

17. Elkhair was probably talking about the actual Rocky Mountains, which the people would have known about because in their time in Kansas, some of the young men participated in wide-ranging buffalo hunts. The mountains were relatively near, but not close enough to see. Harrington seems to have asked him if he was referring to a land of the dead; Elkhair gave a categorical "no."

18. The keeper of the outfit.

19. Harrington had difficulty gathering much information about the doll dance, but he said that certain wooden figures or dolls were understood to possess life, in the sense of understanding what was said to them and protecting the owner. "Usually, but not always, representing the female figure, they were kept as a rule by women, and were given yearly feasts, at which outfits of new clothes were put on them." Mark R. Harrington, *Religion and Ceremonies of the Lenape* (New York: Museum of the American Indian, 1921), 45–46.

20. Again Harrington appears to have asked a question and received an explanation.

21. This is the only story in this volume that comes not from Harrington's papers but rather from the work of Frank Speck and James War Eagle Webber. (See below.)

22. The statement is still among Harrington's papers in the Smithsonian, NMAI, Heye Foundation Records, box 234, file 1. Both the published version and the manuscript statement appear in Grumet, *Voices*.

23. Frank Speck, ed., *A Study of the Delaware Indian Big House Ceremony* (Harrisburg: Pennsylvania Historical Commission, 1931), 117–127. The translation

given is stilted and romanticized. The linguist R. H. I. Goddard's improved version is reproduced in Grumet, *Voices*, 104–106.

24. Speck, *Study of the Delaware Indian*, 121.

25. Irene Anderson Tiger in Grumet, *Voices*, 176. ("A song I remember was Mr. Elkhair's!") Ollie Beaver Anderson remembered a version quite close to this text, although it mixed in the story Rock Shut-Up. (See "Humans Learning Lessons.") She thought a cloud had come to Elkhair in a vision. See Grumet, *Voices*, 152–153.

26. Meaning the northern horizon.

27. We should not give this word its modern meeting of "pathetic." At the time that James War Eagle and Frank Speck chose to use it, it meant vulnerable, worthy of sympathy.

28. Meaning this earthly place, the nonspiritual world.

29. This comes from Frank Speck's notes.

30. The chant is difficult to understand, even for fluent speakers of Lenape, as it represents a crystallized older form. It begins with words that mean something like "wind rushing by me" or "going by fanning the air," and the rest is even less clear. See Speck, *Study of the Delaware Indian*, 118–119. Goddard chose to omit this segment of the text, presumably because it was so opaque, and his goal was to increase legibility, not add to any sense of alienation.

31. Below, he explains that this grandfather is the Misingw. Others are Fire and Water.

32. Spiritually pure and clean, meaning wild animals of the woods, not domesticated barnyard animals.

33. This is the last chant mentioned in Speck's transcription of the recording of Webber. But it is probable that an eleventh and twelfth were intended.

34. This sections comes from miscellaneous notes in Smithsonian, NMAI, Heye Foundation Records, box 234, file 1.

35. Letter, April 28, 1805, in Lawrence Henry Gipson, ed., *The Moravian Indian Mission on White River* (Indianapolis: Indiana Historical Bureau, 1938), 531. There were many such comments about Beate.

36. This was slang for "get into trouble."

37. Smithsonian, NMAI, Heye Foundation Records, box 234, file 1.

38. Note that there had been one Delaware person to describe the ceremony previously: this was Richard Adams, during his trip to the nation's capital to pursue his people's lawsuit. (See the introduction.)

39. He means the very beginning of the process, the initial step that must be taken.

40. These were called the *askkashak* (singular *ashkash* or eventually *ashka*). Julius's wife Minnie was always an *ashkash*, and he often was too, hence his intimate knowledge of all the practical work that had to be done.

41. Note the central importance of the turtle's shell. Such a rattle may still be seen in the Woolaroc Museum and Wildlife Preserve in Bartlesville, Oklahoma. An example of the hide drum described below is to be found there as well.

42. It is obvious by the end of the paragraph that Julius Fouts does not really believe this was a form of abuse. However, he had been taught to refer to the custom that way by whatever white teachers he had had.

43. He meant that although only some were qualified to lead the prayers and singing, everyone was welcome to attend.

44. Now the women could sing and lead the prayers, too, even though they did not necessarily go out into nature to seek their visions when they were young. Minnie Fouts often sang and shared her vision. A friend later recalled that Rosa, Charley Elkhair's daughter, had done it once, too.

45. In earlier times, the Big House religion involved exchanges of meat. Recently, as venison had become scarcer, the people had turned to wampum, shell beads. The idea was that some people provided singing or leadership or labor, while others did the hunting or made or obtained the pretty beads, and then everyone exchanged their contributions. It served much the same purpose as mutual holiday gift giving in our own times, helping to knit a community together.

46. The Lenape word for Sumac.

CHAPTER 3 — CULTURE HEROES

1. For examples of multiple iterations of the same drama, see John Bierhorst, ed., *Mythology of the Lenape: Guide and Texts* (Tucson: University of Arizona Press, 1995).

2. Numerous scholars have noted the multiplicity of characters found among Indigenous culture heroes. Donald Fixico emphasizes that even for one story there may be multiple possible forms of presentation in *"That's What They Used to Say": Reflections on American Indian Oral Traditions* (Norman: University of Oklahoma Press, 2017), 25.

3. Smithsonian, National Museum of the American Indian (NMAI), Heye Foundation Records, box 237, file 4.

4. She is a water being, as in the Girl who Sounds the Thunders.

5. Meaning that she should not have gotten married.

6. "Naked Bear" was the translation given to Harrington. It is not found in any old Lenape word lists, but Bierhorst finds a similar character in Seneca (Haude-

nosaunee) lore: the *nyakwaeheh*. See his *Mythology of the Lenape*, 12. Jim Rementer recalls that Nora Thompson Dean knew the word (personal communication).

7. By now the exhausted writer is using ditto marks to express the lengthy name, somewhat evocative of the breathless repetition of the name as the narrator tells the story orally.

8. Smithsonian, NMAI, Heye Foundation Records, box 237, file 4.

9. Brice Obermeyer, *Delaware Tribe in a Cherokee Nation* (Lincoln: University of Nebraska Press, 2009), 151–155.

10. That version has been printed in Bierhorst, *Mythology of the Lenape*, 99–101. The original is in the Smithsonian, National Anthropological Archives, MS. 2776, folder 6.

11. Meaning she gave birth to the fish, as in "She had a baby."

12. At this point, we do not know what they mean. But it turns out they have recognized him as a spirit of the underwater world; to destroy him, they must destroy his lacustrine environment.

13. Elkhair is shortening the tale here. In the longer version he explains that the two turn into a raven and a pigeon, and the raven has to help the pigeon fly so high. When they get to the sun's home, they have to wait for him, for he is out—presumably busy shining down on the earth.

14. Again the tale has been shortened. In the longer version, the boys notice that the fish ignores a passing butterfly rather than lunging for him, so a butterfly becomes a useful form to take. Indeed, the whole last segment is much condensed, presumably because the amanuensis was growing tired.

15. Smithsonian, NMAI, Heye Foundation Records, box 232, file 4.

16. Trowbridge manuscript in C. A. Weslager, *The Delaware Indians: A History* (New Brunswick, NJ: Rutgers University Press, 1972), 476.

17. Richard Adams, *Legends of the Delaware Indians and Picture Writing*, ed. Deborah Nichols (1905; repr., Syracuse, NY: Syracuse University Press, 1997), 3–9. This was the first story Adams included, so it was important to him; and it is the more notable because many of the other stories he included are clearly Western stories in disguise.

18. This was Nora Thompson Dean. For a complete listing of the Wehixamukes stories, and particularly those coming after Elkhair's rendition, see Bierhorst, *Mythology of the Lenape*, 23.

CHAPTER 4 — HUMANS LEARNING LESSONS

1. Ake Hultkrantz, *Native Religions of North America* (New York: Harper & Row, 1987), 17.

2. Donald Fixico, *"That's What They Used to Say": Reflections on American Indian Oral Traditions* (Norman: University of Oklahoma Press, 2017), 124–127.

3. Smithsonian, National Museum of the American Indian (NMAI), Heye Foundation Records, box 234, file 4.

4. "Lost Boy and the Little People," in *Old Man Coyote*, ed. Frank Linderman (Lincoln: University of Nebraska Press, 1931), 35–49.

5. Recollections of Ollie Beaver Anderson in Robert Grumet, ed., *Voices from the Delaware Big House Ceremony* (Norman: University of Oklahoma Press, 2001), 152–153.

6. Pecans grow farther south than any of the territories that the Delaware had ever lived in. However, the Lenape word for nut meat in general, *pahkasun*, shares a root with numerous other Algonkian-language words. During the colonial era, phonemes resembling *pakan* were used throughout the Eastern Woodlands to speak of any nut and eventually were applied to what we call pecans when traders came across them in the South and West. The Delaware storytellers, in using the word here, likely did not realize it probably should be translated into English not as "pecan" but rather as "nut." See Jim Rementer's "Lenape Names for Fruit and Nuts Trees," http://delawaretribe.org.

7. At this point, the transcriber (Harrington) skips a space and begins to write in the same handwriting, but in larger characters, almost as though he were in a different mood. Though he has not run out of ink, he changes writing implement. One can only assume it is another day, or at least another session.

8. Harrington must have asked "Who?!" as material is added: "The bears called the boy 'aᶜsŭn kē poneᵗ', 'Rock-shut-up.' That was his name."

9. Jim Rementer notes the probability that Harrington was hearing a name with the term *ya-qua-ha* embedded, a ferocious mythic bear.

10. Smithsonian, NMAI, Heye Foundation Records, box 237, file 4.

11. Mark R. Harrington, "The Thunder Power of Rumbling Wings," in *American Indian Life*, ed. Elsie Clews Persons (New York: Viking, 1925), 107–126.

12. "He Who Hit it and Broke it." Personal Communication from Jim Rementer. He is certain, because he found the name in notes from a 1969 conversation with George Wilson. See Daniel Brinton, ed., *A Lenape-English Dictionary* (Philadelphia: Historical Society of Pennsylvania, 1888), 119, for related words.

13. Meaning the Heye Foundation.

14. Smithsonian, NMAI, Heye Foundation Records, box 234, file 4.

15. The same word appears in *Lenape-English Dictionary*, 88, with the same meaning. But with an additional suffix, the word becomes "to sing." It thus clearly conveyed the sense of the situation here, of a voice carrying, seeking others.

16. Meaning resilient, tough, having the wherewithal to handle an overwhelming situation.

CHAPTER 5 — TALKING TO THE DEAD

1. This is the Iroquoian version. For an explanation of their sharing the story with the Lenape, see the introduction. For an iteration of the story itself, see appendix A.

2. Ake Hultkrantz, *Native Religions of North America* (New York: Harper & Row, 1987), 33–34. We have extensive written texts on death in the form of bereavement songs coming to us from the Nahuas, and they too indicate that taking joy in life and appreciating what humans have on earth are spiritual acts. See Tara Malanga, "The Earth Is No One's Home: Nahua Perceptions of Illness, Death and Dying in the Early Colonial Period" (PhD diss., Department of History, Rutgers University, 2020).

3. "Tribal Rites to Be Conducted This Morning for George Fall Leaf," Bartlesville newspaper, September 12, 1933, preserved in the Bartlesville Public Library history collection, document 1960.6332.

4. Brice Obermeyer, "'We Call It Put Him Away': Contemporary Delaware Burial Practices and NAGPRA," *North American Archaeologist* 37, no. 2 (2016): 112–135.

5. David Zeisberger, *History of Northern American Indians* (1780; repr., Columbus: Ohio State Archaeological Society, 1920), 150.

6. This tradition, too, the Delaware share with many other Indigenous groups. Consider, for instance, the memories of Donald Fixico as shared in *"That's What They Used to Say": Reflections on American Indian Oral Traditions* (Norman: University of Oklahoma Press, 2017), 145–146.

7. Smithsonian, National Museum of the American Indian (NMAI), Heye Foundation Records, box 237, file 4.

8. The Trowbridge manuscript alludes to a story of a young woman who killed herself because her love for a man was thwarted (in C. A. Weslager, *The Delaware Indians: A History* [New Brunswick, NJ: Rutgers University Press, 1972], 497). However, we have no way of knowing if the hearer understood the story fully or not.

9. It is not clear what this note refers to. Harrington himself added a question mark. It is known, however, that the Lenape did originally line their burial pits with bark.

10. Smithsonian, NMAI, Heye Foundation Records, box 237, file 4.

11. Zeisberger, *History of Northern American Indians*, 119.

12. On the origin of this name in the Delaware community, see Weslager, *Delaware Indians*, 379. (Saghundai became Secondyan and then Secondine.)

13. Meaning experience a vision.

14. Smithsonian, NMAI, Heye Foundation Records, box 234, file 4.

15. Mark Harrington clearly wanted the elderly, highly respected, and male Charles Eklhair to be his major informant. In his published work, he mentioned him as his source often, as a way of underscoring his work's reliability. Women anthropologists would later change their field's understanding of who a reliable source could be.

16. Smithsonian, NMAI, Heye Foundation Records, box 234, file 5.

17. Anonymous, "Answers to the Questions Proposed [by Lewis Cass]" (1822), printed in C. A. Weslager, *The Delaware Indian Westward Migration* (Wallingford, PA: Middle Atlantic Press, 1978), 128.

18. Mark R. Harrington, *Religion and Ceremonies of the Lenape* (New York: Museum of the American Indian, 1921), 179.

19. The implication is that a wild creature should not be kept imprisoned as a pet.

20. The speaker was likely showing Harrington the otter hide.

21. They were selling it to Harrington, as he tells us in *Religion and Ceremonies*, 176.

CHAPTER 6 — THE COMING OF THE WHITES

1. Smithsonian, National Museum of the American Indian (NMAI), Heye Foundation Records, box 234, file 5.

2. In chronological order: David Zeisberger, *History of Northern American Indians* (1780; repr., Columbus: Ohio State Archaeological Society, 1920), 27–28; John Heckewelder, *An Account of the History, Manners and Customs of the Indian Nations Who Once Inhabited Pennsylvania and the Neighboring States* (1819; repr., Philadelphia: Historical Society of Pennsylvania, 1876), 71–75; response to Cass questionnaire in C. A. Weslager, *The Delaware Indian Westward Migration* (Wallingford, PA: Middle Atlantic Press, 1978), 165–167; Trowbridge manuscript, in C. A. Weslager, *The Delaware Indians: A History* (New Brunswick, NJ: Rutgers University Press, 1972), 475.

3. Donald Fixico has commented on the element of Indian humor that consists of recounting the travails of reservation Indians upon first moving to the city. *"That's What They Used to Say": Reflections on American Indian Oral Traditions* (Norman: University of Oklahoma Press, 2017), 153.

4. The term "Big Knives," *(a)choankshikan* in Delaware, appears in numerous sources, first of all in Zeisberger, *History of Northern American Indians*, 122.

5. It seems that Harrington most likely asked Fouts if he knew any stories about the arrival of the Dutch at Manhattan. He himself was familiar with the version recounted by Zeisberger.

6. Smithsonian, NMAI, Heye Foundation Records, box 234, file 5.

7. Jean Soderlund, *Lenape Country: Delaware Valley Society before William Penn* (Philadelphia: University of Pennsylvania Press, 2015), 23.

8. Smithsonian, NMAI, Heye Foundation Records, box 237, file 4.

9. Elkhair told the story again a few years later to Truman Michelson. There, he provided a few more details at each stage. In the end, he "pulled his punches" even more. He concluded, "The Indian does everything his brother white man tells him. So now the Delawares have come to be civilized at this day, and now they're the same as the white people." See John Bierhorst, ed., *Mythology of the Lenape: Guide and Texts* (Tucson: University of Arizona Press, 1995), 121. The original is in the Smithsonian, NMAI, National Anthropological Archives, MS 2776, folder 7.

10. The symbolism of a falling tree branch hitting someone and marking the beginning of a war is ancient and is found in other Indigenous lore, such as that of the Mexica, or Aztecs.

CHAPTER 7 — TALES OF ORDINARY LIFE

1. Smithsonian, National Museum of the American Indian (NMAI), Heye Foundation Records, box 233, file 12.

2. This was an old game, in which a pebble or bullet was placed underneath an upside-down moccasin, which was then shuffled with several other moccasins. The watchers had to discern which one harbored the hidden object. It is not known when the game became associated with funerals, but it had happened by the time the Delaware lived in Indiana. C. A. Weslager, *The Delaware Indians: A History* (New Brunswick, NJ: Rutgers University Press, 1972), 384.

3. This custom was followed until very recently. See Brice Obermeyer, "'We Call It Put Him Away': Contemporary Delaware Burial Practices and NAGPRA," *North American Archaeologist* 37, no. 2 (2016): 112–135.

4. Smithsonian, NMAI, Heye Foundation Records, box 233, file 12.

5. Lewis Cass collected such information in the early 1800s, and Lewis Henry Morgan's informants told him the same in the mid-1800s. See Weslager, *Delaware Indians*, 392, 480.

6. The same root appears in other Algonkian languages, often written in English as "sachem."

7. This was almost certainly Charley Elkhair's mother, who may have been the daughter of a captive (see the introduction) and therefore potentially clanless.

8. This was part of the Wolf clan (see list below).

9. "Like the ground worn out under a camp," Julius added.

10. Fouts seemed to say that the names "Easy Mad" and "Stepping Down" imply something humorous, but the joke is lost to us now.

11. Smithsonian, NMAI, Heye Foundation Records, box 234, file 4.

AFTERWORD

1. These stories exist in manuscript form at the National Anthropological Archive of the Smithsonian. Most are printed in John Bierhorst, ed., *Mythology of the Lenape: Guide and Texts* (Tucson: University of Arizona Press, 1995), 102–123. One is included in appendix C.

2. For a year-by-year breakdown of the oil discoveries, see Dan Boyd, "Oklahoma Oil: Past, Present and Future," *Oklahoma Geology Notes* 6, no. 23 (2002): 97–106. For oil on the Fouts farm, see John Benedict, *Muskogee and Northeastern Oklahoma*, vol. 3 (Chicago: S. J. Clarke, 1922), 47–48. Eastern Oklahoma's oil was originally found on the allotment of a Delaware child, Anna Anderson, but control of it was taken away from her and her full-blood parents and placed in the hands of Frank Bartles.

3. Only mixed-heritage people were legally allowed to own their allotments outright, in fee simple. See Brice Obermeyer, *Delaware Tribe in a Cherokee Nation* (Lincoln: University of Nebraska Press, 2009), 125. Julius Fouts was among these, apparently due to his paternal heritage. (See the introduction.) The Elkhairs, as pure bloods, did not have such control. On the other hand, they did both have tribal allotments. Charles and Susie held neighboring allotments, which was undoubtedly helpful. (See Oklahoma and Indian Territory Land Allotment Jackets for Five Civilized Tribes, 1834–1934, Cherokee Land Office, May 1904, Charles Elkhair.) Elkhair had also inherited land from a cousin on his mother's side who lived on an adjoining farm. (Oklahoma County Court, Nowata County, Probate Record, Charles Elkhair, 1935–1939.) There were oil drillings on the land, but the wells were plugged by the 1930s. The heirs petitioned to be allowed to sell that land to George Chappell for just under $1,500. Sallie's irritation with the questions she was asked was palpable: "What reason do you have for wanting to sell your interest in this land? Do you have a reason?" "Yes, Sir. I could use it for a lot of things. Building a house for one thing" (280).

4. Nicky Kay Michael, "Lenape Women in a Transitional Culture" (master's thesis, Oklahoma State University, 1999), 115–117.

5. Nora Thompson Dean with Jim Rementer, "Delaware Indian Religion," *Bulletin of the Archaeological Society of New Jersey* 50 (1996): 28.

6. Fred Washington to Frank Speck, undated, cited in Brice Obermeyer, "Salvaging the Delaware Big House Ceremony: The History and Legacy of Frank Speck's Collaboration with the Oklahoma Delaware," *Histories of Anthropology*

Annual 3 (2007): 190. A rich set of letters from Fred Washington to Frank Speck is preserved in the American Philosophical Society, Frank Speck Papers, Section III Northeast, box 6.

7. The collaboration between these two men is recounted in detail in Obermeyer, "Salvaging the Delaware Big House Ceremony." Today, some elements of the Big House are preserved at the Woolaroc Museum and some at the Phillbrook Museum, both in Oklahoma. War Eagle's fascinating letters to Speck are preserved at the American Philosophical Society, Frank Speck Papers, Section III Northeast, box 6.

8. Obermeyer, "Salvaging the Delaware Big House Ceremony."

9. Image of 1935 petition uploaded by a private citizen to Ancestry.com under the name "Charles Elkhair." For more on the Big House Committee's struggles for tribal sovereignty in the 1930s, see Obermeyer, *Delaware Tribe*, 133–138.

10. "Tribal Rites to be Conducted for George Falleaf," Bartlesville newspaper, September 12, 1933, History Collection, Bartlesville Public Library. Further evidence that the people were very aware of losing their last living links to the past is found in a letter from War Eagle to Speck, September 7, 1937, American Philosophical Society, Frank Speck Papers, Section III Northeast, box 6, file 9C2z.

11. War Eagle to Frank Speck, January 2, 1935, American Philosophical Society, Frank Speck Papers, Section III Northeast, box 6, file 9C2z.

12. These stories are preserved by the American Philosophical Society, Frank Speck Papers, Section III Northeast, box 6. They are summarized in Bierhorst, *Mythology of the Lenape*, 53–63. In 1944, War Eagle reported that he was in the hospital and was too ill to continue sending any more.

13. Fred Washington to Frank Speck, April 21, 1942, American Philosophical Society, Frank Speck Papers, Section III Northeast, box 6, file 9C2f. Many years later, Ollie Beaver remembered the event as taking place in 1944. "They had a fire in the middle. A lot of boys were gone to service, but we tried to have it the best we could." Interview with Ollie Beaver, 1972, printed in Robert Grumet, ed., *Voices from the Delaware Big House Ceremony* (Norman: University of Oklahoma Press, 2001).

14. The clearest listing of Jesse's and Sallie's children is to be found in the 1920 U.S. census. For a sense of their role in the community, see Jesse Elkhair's obituary, August 30, 1961, History Collection, 1960.6313.01, Bartlesville Public Library.

15. See comments in Grumet, *Voices*.

16. Readers can find the stories online at www.talk-lenape.org. In 1961, Jim Rementer, a true kindred spirit, read Fred Washington's letters in the American Philosophical Society and wrote to the man at the address he saw on the envelopes. Fred Washington answered him! Rementer eventually moved to Oklahoma,

working not only with Fred Washington but also with Nora Thompson Dean's father and then with Nora herself. He learned the Lenape language and has spent decades devoting himself to its preservation.

17. Michael, "Lenape Women in a Transitional Culture," esp. 3–5, 106, 117–125, 140–146.

18. Rosetta was almost certainly talking about her sister, Elgie, who was also a strong presence in their community for many years. They clearly had different views as to whether it was or was not right to tell stories that had been updated for the modern world.

19. Rosetta's great aunt, Rose Elkhair Frenchman, was said to have been the last Elkhair to have possessed one of the ceremonial dolls. She had given it away because she believed that in tending it wrongly, she had brought her family bad luck. Interview with Anna Anderson Davis (b. 1897) on August 5, 1968, printed in James Brown and Rita Kohn, eds., *Long Journey Home: Oral Histories of Contemporary Delaware Indians* (Bloomington: Indiana University Press, 2008).

20. The child probably died in the Spanish flu pandemic.

21. If there was such a recording, it does not seem to have survived.

22. Deganawidah-Quetzalcoatl University was founded in California by Native student activists. It was an accredited two-year college and lasted until 2005.

23. Her mother was Josie, and Josie's three sisters were Rosie, Kate and Cass. All will appear in the narrative.

24. A full interview with Michael Pace appears in Brown and Kohn, *Long Journey Home*, 252–260. The latter is a rich volume, containing interviews with many other living Delaware.

25. For an example of John Sumpter's work, see "The Story of the Worst Defeat the United States Ever Faced from Native Americans," *Invisible History of America*, June 22, 2022, https://invisiblehistory.blogspot.com.

26. For a study of the evolution from early Oklahoma Indian dance gatherings to the powwows of today, see Gloria A. Young, "The Intertribal Powwow in Oklahoma," in *Remaining Ourselves: Music and Tribal Memory*, ed. Dayna Bowker Lee (Oklahoma City: State Arts Council of Oklahoma, 1995). On the survival of Lenape social dances even after the sacred or ceremonial ones were "put away," see Jim Rementer and Doug Donnell, "Social Dances of the Northeastern Tribes," in the same volume.

27. Very similar versions were found in the first half of the twentieth century in both Bartlesville and Anadarko, though they had been separated for over a century. The latter's version survives in the original Lenape language. See Lillie Hoag Whitehorn with Jim Rementer, Bruce Pearson, and Nora Thompson Dean, "The Lenape Story of the Origin of the Woman Dance," in *When Dream Bear*

Sings: Native Literatures of the Southern Plains, ed. Gus Palmer (Lincoln: University of Nebraska Press, 2018), 29–40. The words are very beautiful.

APPENDIX A

1. We retain Hewitt's rendition of a word meaning "humanlike creature" out of a desire to be true to his text. We have edited his words only where his nineteenth-century English might impede modern people's understanding.

2. For those wishing to read the piece aloud: C-cedilla (ç) indicates our "s" sound. Extended X (X) indicates our "sh" sound. N-tilde (ñ) is pronounced as in Spanish. Accents on the vowels indicate their length. We have used lowercase, right-side-up E (e) to represent the schwa sound, rather than the phonetic symbol Hewitt used. The latter is the only amendment we made to Hewitt's notation.

3. Later the speaker clarified that this "in" indicates "it is said," conveying the possibility of doubt, since the storyteller is not speaking from their own experience.

APPENDIX B

1. This is not really how the Dutch officers dressed in 1609. It is, however, how British officers dressed in the eighteenth century, when the story was told to Heckewelder.

APPENDIX C

1. The files immediately before and immediately after are clearly labeled as the work of Charles Elkhair. This one is unlabeled but is likely to have come from the same informant. It is conceivable that Michelson collected the story in some other part of the country, but that is highly unlikely, as the text is in the southern or Unami dialect of Delaware spoken in Oklahoma.

Bibliography

ARCHIVAL COLLECTIONS

American Philosophical Society (Philadelphia, PA)
  Frank Speck Papers
Bartlesville Area History Museum (Bartlesville, OK)
  BAHM Digital Collection
Bartlesville Public Library (Bartlesville, OK)
  Local and Family History Room Collection
Delaware Tribe of Indians (Bartlesville, OK)
  Tribal Archive
Kansas Historical Society (Topeka, KS)
  John G. Pratt Papers (microfilm)
Penn Museum Archives (Philadelphia, PA)
  George Gordon Director's Office Correspondence
  George G. Heye Papers
Smithsonian Institution Archive Center (Suitland, MD)
  National Museum of the American Indian (NMAI), Heye Foundation Records
  National Museum of Natural History, National Anthropological Archives

GOVERNMENT DOCUMENTS

Commissioner of Indian Affairs, Annual Reports
Oklahoma and Indian Territory District Census Papers and Land Allotment
  Jackets
U.S. Bureau of the Census
U.S. Secretary of the Interior, Reports to Congress

PUBLISHED MATERIALS

Adams, Richard C. *A Delaware Indian Legend and the Story of Their Troubles.* Washington, DC, 1899.

———. *Legends of the Delaware Indians and Picture Writing.* Edited by Deborah Nichols. 1905. Reprint, Syracuse, NY: Syracuse University Press, 1997.

Benedict, John, ed. *Muskogee and Northeastern Oklahoma.* Vol. 3. Chicago: S. J. Clarke, 1922.

Bierhorst, John, ed. *Mythology of the Lenape: Guide and Texts.* Tucson: University of Arizona Press, 1995.

———. *The White Deer and Other Stories Told by the Lenape.* New York: William Morrow, 1995.

Boyd, Dan. "Oklahoma Oil: Past, Present and Future." *Oklahoma Geology Notes* 6, no. 23 (2002): 97–106.

Brinton, Daniel, ed. *A Lenape-English Dictionary.* Philadelphia: Historical Society of Pennsylvania, 1888.

———. *The Lenape and Their Legends.* Philadelphia: Historical Society of Pennsylvania, 1885.

Brown, James, and Rita Kohn, eds. *Long Journey Home: Oral Histories of Contemporary Delaware Indians.* Bloomington: Indiana University Press, 2008.

Calloway, Colin, ed. *The World Turned Upside Down: Indian Voices from Early America.* New York: Bedford/St. Martin's, 1994.

Child, Brenda. "The Boarding School as Metaphor." *Journal of American Indian Education* 57, no. 1 (2018): 37–57.

Cohen, David. *The Ramapo Mountain People.* New Brunswick, NJ: Rutgers University Press, 1974.

Cranor, Ruby. *Kik Thu We Nund: The Delaware Chief William Anderson and His Descendants.* Bartlesville, OK: self-published, n.d.

———. *Talking Tombstones: Graves of Washington County.* Bartlesville, OK, 1973.

Danckaerts, Jasper. *Journals, 1679–80.* Edited by B. B. James. New York: Scribner's, 1913.

Dean, John, and Randall Dean, eds. *Journal of Thomas Dean, 1817.* Indianapolis: Indiana Historical Society, 1918.

Dean, Nora Thompson, with Jim Rementer. "Delaware Indian Religion." *Bulletin of the Archaeological Society of New Jersey* 50 (1996): 14–28.

———. *Lenape Language Lessons.* 2nd ed. CD. Delaware Tribe of Indians, 2015.

Dencke, Christian Frederick. *The Three Epistles of the Apostle John: Delaware Language.* New York: American Bible Society, 1818.

Dowd, Greg. *A Spirited Resistance: The North American Indian Struggle for Unity, 1745–1815*. Baltimore: Johns Hopkins University Press, 1992.

Fixico, Donald. *"That's What They Used to Say": Reflections on American Indian Oral Traditions*. Norman: University of Oklahoma Press, 2017.

Flemming, George. *Brotherton: New Jersey's First and Only Indian Reservation*. Medford, NJ: Plexus, 2005.

Fur, Gunlog. *A Nation of Women: Gender and Colonial Encounters among the Delaware Indians*. Philadelphia: University of Pennsylvania Press, 2009.

Gehring, Charles, and Robert Grumet. "Observations of the Indians from Jasper Danckaert's Journal, 1679–1680." *William & Mary Quarterly* 44 (1987): 104–120.

Gipson, Lawrence Henry, ed. *The Moravian Indian Mission on White River*. Indianapolis: Indiana Historical Bureau, 1938.

Goddard, Ives. "Three Nineteenth-Century Munsee Texts: Archaisms, Dialect Variation, and Problems of Textual Criticism." In *New Voices for Old Words: Algonquian Oral Literatures*, edited by David J. Costa, 198–314. Lincoln: University of Nebraska Press, 2015.

Grumet, Robert. *The Munsee Indians: A History*. Norman: University of Oklahoma Press, 2009.

———, ed. *Voices from the Delaware Big House Ceremony*. Norman: University of Oklahoma Press, 2001.

Harrington, Marie. *On the Trail of Forgotten People: A Personal Account of the Life and Career of Mark Raymond Harrington*. Reno, NV: Great Basin Press, 1985.

Harrington, Mark R. *Dickon among the Lenape*. New York: Holt, Rinehart & Winston, 1938.

———. "A Preliminary Sketch of Lenape Culture." *American Anthropologist* 15, no. 2 (1913): 208–235.

———. *Religion and Ceremonies of the Lenape*. New York: Museum of the American Indian, 1921.

———. "Some Customs of the Delaware Indians." *Museum Journal University of Pennsylvania* 1, no. 3 (1910): 52–60.

———. "The Thunder Power of Rumbling Wings." In *American Indian Life*, edited by Elsie Clews Parsons, 107–126. New York: Viking, 1925.

Heckewelder, John. *An Account of the History, Manners and Customs of the Indian Nations Who Once Inhabited Pennsylvania and the Neighboring States*. 1819. Reprint, Philadelphia: Historical Society of Pennsylvania, 1876.

Hewitt, J. N. D., ed. "Iroquoian Cosmology." In *Twenty-First Annual Report of the Bureau of American Ethnology, 1899–1900*, 255–295. Washington, DC: Government Printing Office, 1903.

Hultkrantz, Ake. *Native Religions of North America*. New York: Harper & Row, 1987.

Johnson, Jeremy. "The Hands of My Grandmothers." Philadelphia Museum of Art, July 4, 2022. https://blogspot.philamuseum.org.

Kimmerer, Robin Wall. *Braiding Sweetgrass: Indigenous Wisdom, Scientific Knowledge, and the Teachings of Plants*. Minneapolis, MN: Milkweed Editions, 2013.

Konkle, Maureen. *Writing Indian Nations: Native Intellectuals and the Politics of Historiography, 1827–1863*. Chapel Hill: University of North Carolina Press, 2004.

Kraft, Herbert. *The Lenape: Archaeology, History and Ethnography*. Newark: New Jersey Historical Society, 1986.

———. *The Lenape-Delaware Indian Heritage: 10,000 BC—AD 2000*. Shamong, NJ: Lenape Books, 2001.

Linderman, Frank, ed. *Old Man Coyote (Crow)*. Lincoln: University of Nebraska Press, 1931.

Lindeström, Peter. *Geographia Americae*. Edited by Amandus Johnson. Philadelphia: Swedish Colonial Society, 1925.

Lomawaima, K. Tsianina. *They Called It Prairie Light: The Story of Chilocco Indian School*. Lincoln: University of Nebraska Press, 1994.

Luckenbach, Abraham. *Forty-Six Scripture Narratives from the Old Testament . . . for the Use of Delaware Indian Youth*. New York: Daniel Fanshaw, 1838.

Malanga, Tara. "The Earth Is No One's Home: Nahua Perceptions of Illness, Death and Dying in the Early Colonial Period." PhD dissertation, Department of History, Rutgers University, 2020.

Merritt, Jane. *At the Crossroads: Indians and Empires on a Mid-Atlantic Frontier, 1700–1763*. Chapel Hill: University of North Carolina Press, 2003.

Michael, Nicky Kay. "Lenape Women in a Transitional Culture." Master's thesis, Oklahoma State University, 1999.

Morgan, Lewis Henry. *The Indian Journals, 1859–1862*. Edited by Leslie White. New York: Dover, 1993.

Newman, Andrew. *On Records: Delaware Indians, Colonists, and the Media of History and Memory*. Lincoln: University of Nebraska Press, 2012.

———. "The Walam Olum: An Indigenous Apocrypha and Its Readers." *American Literary History* 22, no. 1 (2010): 26–56.

Obermeyer, Brice. *Delaware Tribe in a Cherokee Nation*. Lincoln: University of Nebraska Press, 2009.

———. "Landscape, Identity, and Politics in an Oklahoma Indian Tribe." *Plains Anthropologist* 54 (2009): 181–199.

———. "Salvaging the Delaware Big House Ceremony: The History and Legacy of Frank Speck's Collaboration with the Oklahoma Delaware." *Histories of Anthropology Annual* 3 (2007): 184–198.

———. "'We Call It Put Him Away': Contemporary Delaware Burial Practices and NAGPRA." *North American Archaeologist* 37, no. 2 (2016): 112–135.

Obermeyer, Brice, and John P. Bowes. "'The Lands of My Nation': Delaware Indians in Kansas, 1829–1869." *Great Plains Quarterly* 36, no. 1 (2016): 1–30.

Oestreicher, David. "The Anatomy of the Walam Olum: The Dissection of a 19th-Century Anthropological Hoax." PhD dissertation, Department of Anthropology, Rutgers University, 1995.

Olmstead, Earl. *David Zeisberger: A Life among the Indians.* Kent, OH: Kent State University Press, 1997.

Penn, William. *A Letter from William Penn Proprietary and Governour of Pennsylvania in America to the Committee of the Free Society of Traders.* London: Andrew Sowle, 1683.

Perry, Linette, with Manny Skolnick. *Keeper of the Delaware Dolls.* Lincoln: University of Nebraska Press, 1999.

Porter, Joy. *To Be Indian: The Life of Iroquois-Seneca Arthur Caswell Parker.* Norman: University of Oklahoma Press, 2001.

Rementer, Jim. *Conversational Lenape: Mini-Dictionary.* Bartlesville, OK: Delaware Tribe of Indians, 1999.

———. "Delaware Indian Humor." *Bulletin of the Archaeological Society of New Jersey* 47 (1992): 69–75.

Rementer, Jim, and Doug Donnell. "Social Dances of the Northeastern Indian Tribes." In *Remaining Ourselves: Music and Tribal Memory*, edited by Dayna Bowker Lee, 37–41. Oklahoma City: State Arts Council of Oklahoma, 1995.

Schonenberger, Regula Trenkwalder. *Lenape Women, Matriliny and the Colonial Encounter: Resistance and Erosion of Power (c. 1600–1876).* New York: Peter Lang, 1991.

Schutt, Amy. *Peoples of the River Valleys: The Odyssey of the Delaware Indians.* Philadelphia: University of Pennsylvania Press, 2007.

Silver, Peter. *Our Savage Neighbors: How Indian Wars Transformed Early America.* New York: Norton, 2007.

Silverman, David. *Red Brethren: The Brothertown and Stockbridge Indians and the Problem of Race in Early America.* Ithaca, NY: Cornell University Press, 2010.

Soderlund, Jean. *Lenape Country: Delaware Valley Society before William Penn.* Philadelphia: University of Pennsylvania Press, 2015,

———. *Separate Paths: Lenapes and Colonists in West New Jersey.* New Brunswick, NJ: Rutgers University Press, 2022.

Sowry, Nathan. "Museums, Native American Representation, and the Public: The Role of Museum Anthropology in Public History, 1875–1925." PhD dissertation, Department of History, American University, 2020.

Speck, Frank. *A Study of the Delaware Indian Big House Ceremony.* Harrisburg: Pennsylvania Historical Commission, 1931.

Spence, Lewis. *Myths and Legends: The North American Indians.* Boston: David Nickerson, 1914.

Sugden, John. *Tecumseh: A Life.* New York: Henry Holt, 1998.

Sumpter, John. "The Story of the Worst Defeat the United States Ever Faced from Native Americans." *Invisible History of America*, June 22, 2022. https:// invisiblehistory.blogspot.com.

Teague, Margaret Withers, et al. *History of Washington County and Surrounding Area.* Bartlesville, OK: Bartlesville Historical Commission, 1967. Reproduced by the Staff of the Bartlesville Area History Museum, 2020.

Tedlock, Dennis. *2000 Years of Mayan Literature.* Berkeley: University of California Press, 2010.

Thompson, Charles N. *Sons of the Wilderness: John and William Conner.* Indianapolis: Indiana Historical Society, 1937.

Thompson, Stith, ed. *Tales of the North American Indians.* Cambridge, MA: Harvard University Press, 1929.

Townsend, Camilla. *Annals of Native America: How the Nahuas of Colonial Mexico Kept Their History Alive.* New York: Oxford University Press, 2017.

———. "'I Am Old and Weak . . . and You Are Young and Strong': The Intersecting Histories of Rutgers University and the Lenni Lenape." In *Scarlet and Black: Slavery and Dispossession in Rutgers History*, edited by Marisa Fuentes and Deborah Gray White, 6–42. New Brunswick, NJ: Rutgers University Press, 2016.

———. *Pocahontas and the Powhatan Dilemma.* New York: Hill & Wang, 2004.

Trachtenberg, Alan. *Shades of Hiawatha: Staging Indians, Making Americans, 1880–1930.* New York: Hill & Wang, 2004.

Trowbridge, C. C. *Delaware Indian Language of 1824.* Edited by James Rementer. Merchantville, NJ: Evolution, 2011.

Virgil. *The Aeneid.* New York: New American Library, 1961.

Weslager, C. A. *The Delaware Indians: A History.* New Brunswick, NJ: Rutgers University Press, 1972.

———. *The Delaware Indian Westward Migration.* Wallingford, PA: Middle Atlantic Press, 1978.

Whitehorn, Lillie Hoag, with Jim Rementer, Bruce Pearson, and Nora Thompson Dean. "The Lenape Story of the Origin of the Woman Dance." In *When*

Dream Bear Sings: Native Literatures of the Southern Plains, edited by Gus Palmer, 29–40. Lincoln: University of Nebraska Press, 2018.

Whritenour, Raymond, ed. *Denke's Lenape Word List of 1801*. Bethlehem, PA: Moravian Archives, 2015.

Young, Gloria. "The Intertribal Powwow in Oklahoma." In *Remaining Ourselves: Music and Tribal Memory*, edited by Dayna Bowker Lee, 18–23. Oklahoma City: State Arts Council of Oklahoma, 1995.

Zeisberger, David. *A Grammar of the Language of the Lenni Lenape or Delaware Indians*. Edited by Peter Du Ponceau. Philadelphia: American Philosophical Society, 1816.

———. *History of Northern American Indians*. 1780. Reprint, Columbus: Ohio State Archaeological Society, 1920.

Zumthor, Paul. *Oral Poetry: An Introduction*. Minneapolis: University of Minnesota Press, 1990.

Index

About the Authors

CAMILLA TOWNSEND is Board of Governors Distinguished Professor of History at Rutgers University–New Brunswick in New Jersey. She has published widely on Indigenous history and language in the Americas. Her books include *Pocahontas and the Powhatan Dilemma*, and most recently, *Fifth Sun: A New History of the Aztecs*, which won the 2020 Cundill Prize in History.

NICKY KAY MICHAEL has a BA in American studies from Stanford and a PhD in history from the University of Oklahoma. She has taught Native American studies for many years and is currently the interim president of Bacone College in Muskogee, Oklahoma, where she is also the executive director of Indigenous studies and curriculum. She is serving a seven-year term on the Delaware tribal council.

A Note on the Cover Art

Delaware Misingw Dancer (1967) by Ruthe Blalock Jones (Chun-Lun-Dit).

Artist Ruthe Blalock Jones (b. 1939) is the daughter of the late Lucy Blalock, the last fully fluent speaker of the Unami dialect of the Lenape language. Both the Misingw and the Misingw dancer figured in stories told by Charles Elkhair when Lucy was a girl. (The painting appears here courtesy of the artist and the National Museum of the American Indian, Smithsonian.)